ALSO BY CHRIS ROBERSON

Novels of the Celestial Empire
The Dragon's Nine Sons
Iron Jaw and Hummingbird

Novels
Voices of Thunder
Cybermancy Incorporated
Any Time At All
Here, There & Everywhere
Paragaea: A Planetary Romance
The Voyage of Night Shining White
X-Men: The Return
Set the Seas on Fire
End of the Century

Series
Shark Boy and Lava Girl Adventures:
Book 1
Shark Boy and Lava Girl Adventures:
Book 2

THREE UNBROKEN

A novel of the Celestial Empire

CHRIS ROBERSON

SOLARIS

First published 2009 by Solaris
an imprint of BL Publishing
Games Workshop Ltd
Willow Road
Nottingham
NG7 2WS
UK

www.solarisbooks.com

ISBN-13: 978-1-84416-707-4
ISBN-10: 1-84416-707-0

A CIP catalogue record for this book is available from the
British Library.

Designed & typeset by BL Publishing
Printed and bound in the UK

HEXAGRAM 1
PURE YANG
BELOW HEAVEN ABOVE HEAVEN

The action of Heaven is strong and dynamic. In the same manner, the noble man never ceases to strengthen himself.

"Soldiers, airmen, and sailors of the Middle Kingdom, your emperor greets you."

The skies over Fire Star were crowded, new constellations being formed and reformed by the running lights of nearly five thousand vacuum-craft of various sizes and types. From the flagship of the Interplanetary Fleet was broadcast the words of the emperor himself, recorded months before in secret at the heart of the Forbidden City. Carried here to the red planet, the valedictory address was played back over the airwaves, broadcast in coded transmissions to the ships in orbit, and to those waiting on the red sands below.

"You are about to embark upon the great crusade, toward which we have striven these long years. The eyes of two worlds are upon you. The hopes and prayers of virtuous people everywhere march at your sides. In the days and months to come, you will bring about the destruction of the Mexic war machine, the elimination of their blood-hungry tyranny over the colonies of Fire Star, and security for ourselves here on Earth."

In hidden airfields on the red planet's surface, the twelve thousand atmospheric craft of the Interplanetary Fleet Air Corps were fueled and ready—heavy and light bombers, rotary-winged fighters, and troop transports.

"Your task will not be an easy one. Your enemy is well trained, well equipped, and battle hardened. He will fight savagely, for the glory of his brutal gods."

The Bordered Yellow and Plain White Banners had already been in theater for some time, each with troop strength of nearly two hundred thousand men. They had been joined by the Plain Yellow and Bordered Blue Banners, bringing the total number of bannermen on Fire Star to three-quarters of a million. Factoring in the First and Third Armies of the Green Standard, together representing one and a half million men, there was a total of well over two million troops altogether.

"But this is the year Water-Monkey! Much has happened since those dark hours of Metal-Monkey, twelve years ago, when the Mexic Dominion unleashed their cruel fury upon our subjects on Fire Star. The militaries of the Dragon Throne have inflicted upon the Mexica great defeats, in open battle, man-to-man. Our air offensive has seriously reduced their strength in the air and their capacity to wage war on the ground. Our resources have given us an overwhelming superiority in weapons and munitions of war, and placed at our disposal great reserves of trained fighting men. The tide has turned! The noble and virtuous men of the world are marching together to victory!"

From their secure facilities deep within Zhurong, the fortified moonbase of the Middle Kingdom forces, the tacticians and strategists of the Dragon Throne consulted the plans one final time, insuring that all of the elements were in place.

"Your emperor has full confidence in your courage and devotion to duty and skill in battle. We will accept nothing less than full victory!"

As thousands upon thousands of chronometers chimed the appointed hour, the forces were given the final order to attack.

"Good fortune! And may heaven smile upon this great and noble undertaking."

Operation Great Holdings had begun.

≡≡ HEXAGRAM 2
PURE YIN
BELOW EARTH ABOVE EARTH

Here is the basic disposition of Earth. In the same manner, the noble man with his generous virtue carries everything.

By the time Operation Great Holdings was underway, in the fifty-second year of the Taikong emperor, the war between the Middle Kingdom and the Mexic Dominion for possession of the red planet Fire Star had raged for over twelve years.

It had been twenty-eight years since the Treasure Fleet of the Dragon Throne had reached Fire Star, ten vessels of ceramic and steel powered by nuclear furnaces, which carried the men and women of the Middle Kingdom to a new world. But when the Treasure Fleet arrived on the red planet, they found that subjects of the Mexic Dominion had beaten them there, a team of researchers exploring the red planet's surface from the safety of their stepped-pyramid habitats. The men of the Treasure Fleet had made short work of the Mexic researchers, and then laid uncontested claim to the world they called Fire Star.

It had been one hundred and twenty-two years since the Mexica drove the Middle Kingdom out of their isthmus, establishing the new Mexic Dominion. In the long years between that day and the hour in which the Mexica attacked the Middle Kingdom colonists on Fire Star, there had been no armed conflict between the two great powers, only an uninterrupted cold war, employing proxies to fight in their stead.

It had been one hundred and forty-seven years since the end of the First Mexic War, when the forces of the Dragon Throne had defeated the armies of the Mexic's Great Speaker and brought the Mexica to heel. For twenty-five years the Mexic isthmus would be ruled by the emperor's hand-picked governor-general, and for the first and last time the banner of the Dragon Throne would fly over every nation on the Earth.

It had been almost four hundred years since the Manchu emperors of the newly-established Clear Dynasty had begun to expand their influence through conquest as well as trade, on land and on sea. Constructing navies that dwarfed even the innumerous ships of the Treasure Fleets, they initiated a campaign of conquest in Hind, Arabia, and

Africa, before beginning to extend their reach even into parts of Europa.

It had been almost six hundred years since the Treasure Fleet of the Dragon Throne had circumnavigated the African Cape of Storms and reached the ocean the Europans called the Atlantic. In the months and years that followed, the Treasure Fleet had opened trade routes by sea with the Europans, beginning with Espana and Italia, then Britain, France, and Deutschland.

It had been more than four thousand years since the Yellow Emperor, Huangdi, had invented the calendar, taught men how to keep track of the seasons, and instituted the Middle Kingdom.

But for those who fought on Fire Star, either on the ground or in the skies or in the heavens above, history was far from the most pressing concern. The men and women of the Middle Kingdom's military—the Eight Banners, the Green Standard Army, and the Interplanetary Fleet—were more concerned with the taking of a hill or farm, or the destruction of a Mexic convoy or crawler, or the establishment of one beachhead or another. History was something for scholars to remember; all that mattered to the soldiers, airmen, and sailors of the Dragon Throne was the duty they carried, and the red earth beneath their feet.

HEXAGRAM 3
BIRTH THROES
BELOW THUNDER ABOVE WATER

Clouds and Thunder. In the same way, the noble man weaves the fabric of government.

Outside, dark clouds roiled through the skies over Bhopal, and pealing thunder rattled the window panes, counterpoint to the shrieking cries of Arati Amonkar's nephew, now only moments old. Grey and pink and squirming, he'd slid out from Arati's sister already protesting, as though eager to be thrust back inside. His newborn cry, with a strange gurgling undercurrent as descant, was piercing and high.

"Ah, how handsome," Arati's mother said, the newly minted grandmother clapping her hands with glee. And then, before anyone'd had a chance to respond, she turned to Arati and said, "Now, second daughter, when will *you* be marrying and giving me a grandchild of your own, mmm?"

That was the moment, though Arati didn't consciously realize it at the time. It was in that instant, in which her mouth hung open as her brain struggled in vain to frame some response, Arati knew she would fly.

She didn't know where she would go, at first, or how she would get there, but the answer came soon enough. Arati's sister was not yet out of bed, just learning the trick of nursing her young son, friends and family still enjoying the betel packs distributed in celebration of the birth, when Arati announced her intentions to her parents, gathered in the house's main room.

"The navy?" Arati's father, eyes widened, showing white all around the pupils, repeated the word as though it were some vile curse.

"The Interplanetary Fleet Air Corps," Arati corrected, with mounting impatience. "I want to be a pilot."

Arati's mother just shook her head, back and forth, back and forth, repeating the words, "Oh, no, oh, no, oh, no," over and over again like a mantra.

"No," Father said with a note of finality, slapping his knee with an open palm like it was drum. "It is not fitting. I will not allow it. Tradition prohibits."

"*Tradition?*" Arati's face contorted as if the word tasted sour in her mouth. "What tradition is that, Father?" She pointed to her mother, dressed in *sadi* and *coli*, her face, neck, and arms bare. "The one that says Mother has to remain covered by a *mola*, her face hidden in public." Arati snapped her fingers, throwing her head back with a humorless bark of laughter. "Oh, that's right, I forgot. Some traditions are *meant* to be abandoned." She paused, and narrowed her eyes. "Or do you mean for Mother to go back into seclusion?"

Father shook his head, scowling darkly. "Of course not. Don't be ridiculous. Some tradition it is right to leave behind, but we cannot abandon *all* that makes us what we are."

Arati nodded. "Right! And what are we, Father?" She didn't wait for him to answer. "Have we forgotten the proud tradition of the Maratha caste? Is *that* something to be left behind, or something to be cherished?"

"Well, I—"

Arati interrupted him before he could continue. "How long since a member of the Dharmaraj clan observed the traditional role of the Maratha caste and entered military service willingly?" She drew herself up straighter, with pride. "Maybe there are some traditions that we should reinstate, after all."

Mother left off her mantra, and reaching out trembling hands toward her said, "But daughter... Will you not marry?"

Arati reached up and touched her neck, hesitating. Then she nodded. "I will, but not in any way that would please you, I think. I won't wear the *mangalsutra*, but will put around my neck a string of seven cowries, and become a bride of the sword-father."

Father's eyes widened even further, which Arati hadn't thought possible, and Mother looked as though she might faint. The practice of dedicating children to the gods had been abolished decades ago, deemed immoral, and the image of the urchin child forced to dance and sing for her divine "husband" while spreading her legs for any who visited the temple was one relegated to lurid historical dramas. But Arati thought that something sublime might be rescued from those abandoned practices, while leaving the less reputable aspects behind. She would become a Murli, devadasi to Khandoba, the divine sword-father, Siva incarnate and guardian of the country. Like Khandoba, she would drive away the evil that causes illness, dedicating her life to his service.

Or the emperor's service, she supposed, but it was all one to her. What was important was that she serve something larger than herself, larger than the immediate concerns of her family and friends, that she not lose herself and her dreams in the minute concerns of the everyday. What was important to Arati was that she fly.

Her parents, it was clear, did not agree.

"No," Father said, crossing his arms over his chest. "I will not allow it. I *forbid* it."

Arati's mouth broke into a sad little smile. "But Father, I'm a grown woman, and can make my own decisions." She shrugged, a gesture of helplessness at odds with her resolute decision. "Besides, it's too late. I've already enlisted, and will be leaving in the morning for basic training."

Father seemed frozen, mouth hanging partially open, a defeated expression on his face. Mother left off her mantra, stood, and straightened her *sadi* around her.

"No," Mother said, with a final shake of her head. "You'll stay here and marry and give us armloads of grandchildren, that's all there is to it." When Arati opened her mouth to explain that, no, she wouldn't be doing any of those things, her mother wouldn't hear it. She held up her hand, and refused to meet Arati's eyes. "Now stop all this nonsense and come help me in the kitchen. We have your nephew's jatakarma to prepare."

Mother left the room, with Father still frozen as a statue on his seat. Arati sat for a moment, feeling the weight of her decision settle around her shoulders, then she stood and crossed the floor to stand before her father.

"Goodbye, Father." She leaned down, and kissed him on his cheek, the stubble of his afternoon beard rasping her lips. "A girl couldn't have asked for better parents."

And with that she left the room, to finish packing her things.

The next day, by the time of her nephew's jatakarma ceremony, as her sister's husband ritualistically touched and smelled his new son, uttering benedictory mantras into his tiny ears, whispering wishes that his son might be endowed with long life and intelligence and happiness, Arati was already on her way. The cloud-flyer shuttle had lifted off from the Bhopal airstrip just after dawn, bound for the headquarters of the Interplanetary Fleet in Guangdong where she would begin her training.

Arati's chest tightened, and she felt a stab of pain deep within, a sorrow made manifest. There was some part of her pained at the thought of leaving family and friends behind, abandoning everything in life she knew and loved. But a larger part knew that it was necessary and that the twinges she felt were merely the pangs of a new life being born.

The skies over Bhopal had been clear on takeoff, but as the shuttle arced over Bengali Bay, toward Annam and the Middle Kingdom beyond, the skies darkened with smothering clouds, lit from within by flashes of lightning. The shuttle pierced the clouds, and continued until it burst into the daylight beyond, with clear blue skies above and storm clouds roiling beneath. Somewhere, Arati knew, thunder pealed, but she was flying too fast and too high to hear it.

HEXAGRAM 4
JUVENILE IGNORANCE
BELOW WATER ABOVE MOUNTAIN

Below the Mountain emerges the Spring. In the same way, the noble man makes his actions resolute and nourishes his virtue.

The local offices of the Imperial Bureau of Evaluation were housed in a towering structure in the city of Brazos, the largest building Micah Carter had ever seen. He was sure that the principal offices in Northern Capital, on the far side of the world in the Middle Kingdom, were larger and grander still, but he knew now that he would never see them.

All candidates who sought to serve the imperial bureaucracy in the southwestern Commonwealth of Vinland came here to the capital of the state of Tejas to take their examinations. Those who passed the *xiucai*-level exams, becoming "flourishing talents," could be assured of posts in the bureaucracy somewhere in the neighboring regions, perhaps as far afield as Kentuck or Tennessee. Those who went on to pass the *juren*-level exams, becoming "elevated persons," might even find posts across the continent in Khalifa, or across the sea in Britain, France, or Deutschland, perhaps even as far as Rossiya or Arabia. And those lucky few who passed the *jinshi*-level exams would journey to the Middle Kingdom itself, to Northern Capital, seat of imperial power, to be presented to the emperor himself, honored by a personal audience before the Dragon Throne—personal, at least, not considering the hundreds of other "presented scholars" who would be standing at his side in the ceremony.

Micah would never stand before the Dragon Throne, never journey to Britain or Rossiya, would likely never even get as far as Kentuck or Tennessee. He had failed his *xiucai*-level examination for the third and last time, and would not be given another chance.

Micah would never be going anywhere, that much was clear. His only option was to return to Duncan in northern Tejas, there to live with his parents and work on the neighbor's farm, driving the tractor just like he had done every summer since he was a boy. It was like some ironic punishment for the sins of his forefathers, being forced to work land that had once belonged to his family, never allowed to roam.

The Carters had always been farmers, back since this land had been an independent state, however briefly, before it had joined the Commonwealth of Vinland. They had always owned the land they worked, up until the time of Micah's grandfather, for whose sins Micah was sure he was now paying. The elder Carter had been a man of large dreams and larger ambitions, and had sunk everything he had into one failed money-making scheme after another, until finally the family lands had to be sold in lots to pay off his mounting debts. For as long as Micah could remember, his life had been shadowed by the steel skeleton of a building that hulked on the edge of the small plot of remaining family land, all that remained of his grandfather's dream, left incomplete when the money ran out. That steel structure had been a constant reminder of what came of those who let dreams blind them to reality.

Micah's father had been raised to help his father run the family business, and when the farm had been broken up and sold off, he'd instead found work as a teacher, putting his ability to read and speak fluent English and Official Speech to work, and instructed the children of Duncan in language, literature, and history. Micah's mother was a Duncan, one of those who gave the township its name, and had been another teacher at the school, instructing the local children in math and accounts. Not a few wags said that if the elder Carter'd had his future daughter-in-law looking after his affairs, he'd never have been forced to sell off lands that had been in the Carter family since white men had first come to this part of the world.

Micah, first born of three children, had not taken after either of his parents. He could speak perfect English and Official Speech alike, but had no talent for reading, the very letters of the words seeming to dance and jitter on the page when he tried to read them. Still, he'd wanted nothing more than to leave Duncan, and get away from the shadow of the steel structure that he always saw not as a skeleton, but as a cage. The township of Duncan was too small a world for him, and Micah was sure that his best chance of escape lay in seeking a post in the imperial bureaucracy. But those posts required imperial examinations, held regularly in the state capital.

He'd studied until it felt that his brain would explode, and his eyes run like jelly from their sockets. But the letters refused to stay still on the page, and in the end he'd been forced to enlist the aid of his sisters. They would read to him aloud from the Four Books, and from the Five Classics, and the Canon of Filial Piety. And though he could read no better than the youngest student in his father's class, Micah had an amazing gift for recall, and could memorize anything he heard spoken and recite it back flawlessly. When he felt that he couldn't possibly fit any more knowledge into his head, he'd made the journey south to Brazos, his heart in his throat.

But while he could practically recite the texts of the source materials in their entirety, the examination itself was in written form, the candidate required to attempt three questions on the Four

Books and four on any of the Five Classics, framing his answers in the standard eight-legged form. And though his brain was filled to bursting with the information it needed, Micah was hard pressed to parse out the characters of the questions themselves, much less frame his responses in anything like legible script.

And so, despite all that he had learned, even after repeated attempts Micah had still failed to pass even the lowest level of examination. An ignorant child would have fared as well, if not better, he was sure.

Insult compounded injury this last spring when the steel structure was broken up and donated as scrap to the state, sent to be melted down and used in the construction of new warships at the orbital shipyards beyond Diamond Summit, at the top of the Bridge of Heaven. The unfinished building which Micah's fancy had made a cage was being sent off to war, to see a new world out in the black void of the heavens, while Micah was being left behind to till another family's fields.

In front of the tower which housed the Bureau of Evaluation was a long reflecting pool, its waters sparkling as bright and blue as sapphires. When Micah climbed down the front steps for the third and last time, breathless as a climber descending a mountain, he scarcely noticed the man in the plain suit of green who stood behind the low table, at the pool's edge. So when the man called to him, Micah started, caught unawares.

"How did you fare, friend?" The man's voice rang as bright as a bell in the still morning air. "Do I see a life of service in the imperial bureaucracy before you?"

Micah scowled, and shook his head. "Not hardly," he said, sullenly. "Three failures and there won't be a fourth."

The man took on a sympathetic expression, lips pursed. "And that's a shame, friend. You look like a man with something to offer. With quite a lot to offer, in fact."

Biting his lip, Micah managed a nod. His eyes stung, and he realized for the first time how close to crying he was. Then he noticed the neatly arranged stacks of brochures on the table behind which the man stood.

"Of course," the man continued, "you should remember that there are other ways to serve the emperor, and those who may be looking for what you have to offer."

Micah rubbed his nose with the back of his hand, arching an eyebrow. "What?"

"Tell me, friend," the man said, coming around the table and taking Micah by the elbow, "have you ever considered the Green Standard Army?"

≡≡
≡ ≡
≡≡
≡ ≡
≡ ≡
≡≡

HEXAGRAM 5
WAITING
BELOW HEAVEN ABOVE WATER

Clouds rise up to Heaven. In the same way, the noble man takes this opportunity to enjoy himself in drinking and eating.

Niohuru Tie laid back in his upholstered chair, hands restless on the armrests, and watched clouds of steam and smoke from the water pipes rising languidly up to the rafters, which were painted to resemble a star-filled night sky. All through the teahouse the other sons and daughters of the Great Houses jostled and laughed, trying to agree on what their next amusement might be.

A girl Tie had known since early childhood, youngest daughter of a cadet branch of Suwan Guwalgiya, was all for visiting one of the private dinner theaters south of Zhengyang Gate. "Come along, you lazy slugs," she said, prodding the arm of the boy sitting next to Tie and glaring in his direction. "It will be *fun*."

Tie knew what she really wanted. Her tastes were somewhat... exotic, and based on his long experience with her, Tie knew that as soon as they had shadowed the front door of some private theater, she would be agitating to go instead through Qianmen Gate, to the quarter of dancing and prostitution. "*It's only a little way further*," she would say, as she had countless times before. Tie wondered what her father would say, himself a court official of the first rank, second class, if he knew the use to which his young daughter put her daily allotment of silver taels.

"It *won't* be fun," said the boy sitting across from Tie, a son of the Hoifa clan who seemed to wear a perpetual pout of annoyance. "It will be *boring*. Let's go racing instead, yes?" He looked to the others for support, eagerly.

If he was waiting for Tie to chime in, he'd be waiting a long time. They'd spent so many evenings racing three-wheeled speeders all over Northern Capital that Tie was sure he could navigate the route with his eyes closed. From the city's center north to the Great Bell Temple, then west to the Fishing Terrace, then finally ending up at Sandy Mouth in the Outer City. The loser would stand the others to their next round at some tavern or teahouse, complaining all the while that they'd been cheated by some tactic employed by another, with the winner boasting of their driving prowess until everyone shouted them down. Then they'd be back to the same spot in which they found themselves now, bored and trying to work out what to do next. Sitting around, waiting for something exciting to happen.

"I know!" A daughter of the Magiya clan clapped her hands, excitedly. "Let's go tip an elephant!"

The others groaned.

"Not that again," said a Nara girl with a moue of distaste. "Last time we went over there I had the smell of dung in my nostrils for *days*."

Tie couldn't help but sneer, though the Nara failed to notice. He glanced around at the other girls, all of them wearing the high, rigid Manchurian hairstyles favored by the fashionable women of the city this season. He wondered if any of them knew that the lacquering agent which held their coiffures aloft was derived from dung collected from the elephant grounds inside the Xuanusu Gate.

"I'm with Hoifa," another boy chimed in. "Let's go racing."

The Suwan Guwalgiya girl rolled her eyes. "Not *that* again…"

A serving girl went by with a plate of dumplings, and the boy sitting beside Tie, middle son of a Sumuru family, speared a couple of them on the end of a chopstick. Chomping one between his teeth, he extended the chopstick to Tie, offering him the other.

"Eighteen-hells!" Tie shouted, jumping up, sending his chair toppling backward. "Have none of you any *shame*?"

All of the others stopped talking at once, turning to look at him, blank-faced.

The Sumuru boy looked from Tie to the chopstick in his hands and back, confused. "But it was just a dumpling, Niohuru..."

"It's not about the dumpling, idiot!" Tie snarled.

"Then what *is* it about, Niohuru?" Nara asked, her eyebrow arched.

"Have any of you looked around, lately?"

The others looked at him, confused.

Tie gritted his teeth, and pointed a finger at a pair of old men seated at the far side of the teahouse, passing the nozzle of a water pipe back and forth. The exchange was made somewhat difficult due to the fact that one of the two was missing both hands, his arms instead ending in crude prosthetic claws, while the other was missing one leg beneath the knee. Both men had a haunted look, and had kept to themselves all evening.

"What about them?" the Hoifa boy asked. "They're not bothering us."

"But they *should* bother you," Tie snapped. "The very fact of them should bother you!"

Tie knew he would be better off addressing a collection of statues, but he couldn't help himself. For weeks the thought had been plaguing him, and he now simply had to give this thought voice.

"When we race through the city, or amble over to the theaters and taverns, do you happen to notice the countless veterans crowding the narrow streets? Or the poor legless wretches, blind or deaf or worse, busking for a few copper coins? Well, do you?!"

The others exchanged bewildered looks and shrugs. "Well, certainly," a girl said, "but..."

She trailed off, as the rest of the sentence didn't need uttering.

"But what is it to us?" Tie finished for her, mockingly.

The girl didn't speak, but nodded.

If the others had failed to notice, Tie most definitely had not. Most were not as fortunate as the two veterans sitting across the teahouse, who obviously had returned home to families or fortunes enough to keep them clothed, housed, and fed. Those in the city streets were not so fortunate. Tie had seen them, the walking wounded of the Second Mexic War. The street performers beating Manchu eight-cornered drums and singing the victory songs of bygone heroes. The men and women on crutches and carts, begging for alms, rattling a coin or two in a clay bowl to attract attention. Or those who simply lounged in the public places, lacking the will and means to go anywhere or do anything else, simply sitting and waiting, but for what Tie didn't know. For death to take them? For the war to finally end and their brothers-in-arms still on the red planet to be sent home? Or for those children of privilege who raced past them without a second glance to finally stop, and notice, and think?

There were few children more privileged than Niohuru Tie, and it shamed him that it had taken so long to realize what was wrong in his world.

"It is *everything* to us," Tie said, his jaw set.

Sons of the Niohuru family had been ranking members of the imperial court since the days of Nurgaci, before the Manchu came down from the north to establish the Clear Dynasty. Daughters of the Niohuru had married into the imperial Aisin Gioro clan ever since, becoming the mothers of emperors and empresses, as well as occasionally empresses in their own right. But like many wealthy families with ties to the court, those rare nobles who inherited their titles and estates rather than earning them through examination and service, the Niohuru in recent generations had become too comfortable and complacent, resting on ties of blood, marriage, and money.

"We waste our lives in gentle pursuits," Tie went on, "letting others suffer and die for our freedoms." He nodded toward the two wounded veterans at the chamber's far side, who as yet had taken no notice of their discussion.

Tie fancied that he was a man out of time, an atavistic throwback to his honored ancestor Niohuru Eidu, who served as councilor to the great Nurgaci, founder of the Manchu state and father of the Eight Banners. Niohuru Eidu had won glory and honor with the strength of his sword, the keenness of his wits, and the sureness of his seat on horseback, earning a hereditary title enjoyed by his descendants for generations. But those days were long gone, and now the sons of Niohuru, like the sons of the other noble Manchu and Han families, avoided military service if they could, and in those rare cases in which they could *not* avoid it altogether, used their families' influence to secure positions in the rear echelon, far from the dangers of the front lines.

"You may turn your nose up at 'gentle pursuits,' Niohuru," the Hoifa boy said, with a sly grin, "but if you ask me they are the *reason* for living, not its waste."

Tie shook his head, angrily. "We squander the legacy handed down to us by our honored forbears."

The Suwan Guwalgiya girl turned her head away, holding her hand up in a gesture that communicated boredom and dismissal.

"Then what do *you* intend to do about it?" said Sumuru, munching contentedly on his second dumpling.

Tie drew himself up even straighter.

"I will serve my emperor," he said proudly. "Tomorrow morning I'll be enlisting in the Eight Banners."

"You?" the Nara girl said, disbelievingly. "A *bannerman*?"

Tie held his chin up, refusing to be baited. "The name of Niohuru was once well-known in the Bordered Yellow Banner. It will be again."

The others exchanged uneasy glances, not sure whether Tie was joking, or to laugh if he was.

"In a few months' time," he said, raising his voice, "I'll be on the red planet Fire Star, helping to rout the Mexica, while you'll all still be here trying to decide whether to go racing or get drunk."

Tie strode away from the circle of chairs, heading toward the door.

"Farewell," he called back over his shoulder. He couldn't help but smile, seeing the confused looks on their faces. He had days of glory before him, while they had nothing at all.

On his way to the exit, still puffed up with pride, he passed the table where the pair of veterans sat smoking, and for the first time caught their eyes. He wasn't sure if they had heard him, and he thought to say something comradely to them before he left.

As he opened his mouth to speak, though, he noticed again the haunted look in their eyes. Close up, he saw now that they weren't old men at all, but perhaps only a few years his senior. A few years older, and a lifetime more worn.

No words came. Finding nothing suitable at all in his mind to say, he turned and walked from the tea-house, out into the night, clinging to the strength of his convictions.

HEXAGRAM 6
CONTENTION
BELOW WATER ABOVE HEAVEN

Heaven and water operate in contrary ways. In the same way, the noble man in conduction business carefully plans how such things begin.

By the time man began to move out into the stars, establishing outposts on the moon and colonies on the red planet fourth from the sun, there were two major powers on the Earth, the Middle Kingdom and the Mexica Dominion. The two powers, never allies, had been frequent enemies, the only peace obtained between them in recent history being the brief span in which one assayed the role of conqueror and the other as conquered. Despite interactions stretching back over nearly a dozen generations, the two nations still did not understand one another, in any profound sense, as the

31

beliefs and desires that motivated them were so different, so contrary even at the most fundamental level, that it was as difficult as a fish attempting to understand the world of a bird, or a bird to grasp the life beneath the waves. However much they might be exposed to one another, fish and fowl cannot share common ground as the very domains they call home, air and water, are so distinct in essential character. So it was with the Mexica and the Middle Kingdom.

The first contact between the Dragon Throne and the Mexica came during the last days of the Bright Dynasty, when the Shunzhi Emperor sent a Treasure Fleet across the broad ocean.

The fleet came ashore on the north continent, on the rocks and shoals where the Islamic colony of Khalifa would later be founded. And on the southern continent, where the coastal deserts and sentry mountains hid the abundant forests of Fusang. And on the isthmus that connected the two, where lived the people who called themselves the Mexica.

From his capital city of Place of the Stone Cactus, the Great Speaker of the Mexica ruled an empire that rivaled that of the Bright Dynasty itself, extending thousands of leagues to the north and the south, and reaching to the east and west until it reached the waters of two oceans.

In the days of the Clear Dynasty, when the Manchu rode down from the north and established the Aisin Gioro clan as the new imperial line, the armies of the Dragon Throne pacified the southern continent of Fusang. Some time before, the Treasure Fleets had transported followers of Mohammed to the newly christened land of Khalifa, establishing a khalifate in honor of the Muslim admiral of the first Treasure Fleet to circumnavigate the Earth's oceans. And already in those early days contact was established with the Briton colonies on the northern continent's eastern shores, who would one day form the Commonwealth of Vinland, and later still, bend their knees to the Dragon Throne.

Plans were drawn up to mount an invasion of the Mexic Empire, and to establish dominion over the entirety of the western hemisphere, but the intelligencers of the Eastern Depot had determined that the Mexica were fierce warriors, and that the Mexic isthmus would not be a prize easily won. In the end, plans to invade the Mexic Empire were shelved, and the decision was made instead to establish loose trading ties with the fierce nation.

It was not until the days of the Guangxu emperor, that the decision was made to normalize relations. A formal embassy was to be established, and diplomatic channels opened. To that point, there had been no formal representative from the Dragon Throne to the Great Speaker of the Mexica since the last days of the Bright Dynasty.

An envoy was dispatched, with full authority to speak for the Dragon Throne, and after a long sea voyage and a somewhat arduous overland passage, the Middle Kingdom envoy was received by the Great Speaker in the Place of the Stone Cactus. In the reception ceremony that followed, the envoy was asked to indicate which of his subordinates was most beloved to him. It was explained to the envoy that the Great Speaker wished to bestow special favor on the indicated individual, a token of goodwill. The envoy graciously singled out his nephew, the son of his sister, an attaché with the embassy.

The following day, a celebration was planned in honor of the Middle Kingdom envoy, and the nephew was invited to arrive in advance of the others. When the envoy arrived at the feast, he was greeted by the high priest of the Mexica, the man called Snake Woman, who wore the flayed skin of the envoy's nephew as a suit of clothes.

To the Mexica, to be sacrificed to the glory of the Flayed Lord, Xipe Totec, was a great honor, the rite signifying the fact that the arrival of spring means that the Earth must coat herself with a new skin of vegetation and thereby be reborn.

The Middle Kingdom envoy did not see the honor in the butchery of his sister's son.

The envoy ordered his guards to kill the priest on the spot, but his subordinates dissuaded him, pointing out the inadvisability of angering their hosts while still within the heart of their great empire, surrounded by fierce warriors on all sides. Instead, the envoy snatched his nephew's flayed skin back from the priest, to return it home for burial, and along with the surviving members of his company, left the Place of the Stone Cactus immediately.

The Great Speaker, outraged, ordered all Middle Kingdom subjects expelled from any Mexic Empire lands or satellite nations, whether envoys or traders, scholars or ship captains. The first war with the Mexica had begun.

The First Mexic War, as it was later known, was to last some six years, from Earth-Pig, the twenty-fourth year of the Guangxu Emperor's reign, to Wood-Snake, the thirtieth. It was fought on land, by the Eight Banners and Green Standard troops of the Middle Kingdom and by the Jaguar Knights of the Mexica, and in the skies, by the aces of the Imperial Navy of the Air and by the fierce flying warriors of the Eagle Knights.

In the end, the Middle Kingdom was victorious, but at considerable cost, the best of an entire generation lost in the trenches of Tejas, or the no-man's land that stretched between Khalifa in the north and Mexica in the south. Still, however costly, it remained a victory, and when the Middle Kingdom governor-general took authority over the Mexic isthmus, the last power to oppose the emperor's will had fallen. For a generation, the banner of the Dragon Throne flew over the nation of the Mexica, and for that brief span the emperor of the Middle Kingdom ruled the entire world, either by direct authority or through subservient monarchs and potentates who governed in his name.

After twenty-five years, the Mexica drove the Middle Kingdom out of the Mexic isthmus in a bloody revolt, and founded the new Mexic

Dominion. More than a century of cold war followed, as the two powers raced each other to develop the technology necessary to conquer the heavens, and then raced to be the first to reach orbit, the moon, and the planets beyond.

In the year Metal-Monkey, the fortieth year of the Taikong Emperor, the Mexic Dominion attacked Middle Kingdom colonists on Fire Star, a bloody reprisal for the deaths of Mexic scientists who had been found on the red planet's surface by the first Middle Kingdom forces to arrive. Whatever the reasons, though, whatever the provocations, one thing was certain.

The Second Mexic War had begun.

HEXAGRAM 7
THE ARMY
BELOW WATER ABOVE EARTH

The Earth holds water within itself. In the same way, the noble man cherishes the common folk and so brings increase to the masses.

Though his parents had named him Micah Carter, when he left home he was forever after Carter Micah, abandoning like all other Vinlanders and Europans who traveled abroad the tradition of placing the family name *after* the personal name, instead of before. After reaching the training camp of the Green Standard Army on Taiwan Island, however, he seldom heard either of his names, irrespective of order.

In the camp, he was only and always "Tejas."

There was never any confusion, though. Carter always knew when someone was addressing him. It might be...

"Damn your eyes, Tejas, what in the *rutting* hell kind of throw was *that* supposed to be?"

...or it could be...

"Tejas, you have got to be the *stupidest* pile of dung I've *ever* seen."

...or even...

"Only oxen and inverts come out of Tejas, boy, so which one are you?"

...but Carter always knew they were talking to him.

Still, he didn't feel singled out for the privilege. All of the other men in the unit received the same treatment.

The Arabian with the large ears was called, imaginatively, "Ears." The tall Rossiyan with the speech-impediment was called "Spitter." The African with the pox-scars dotting his cheeks and forehead was called "Moonface." And so on, and so on.

They had come from all corners of the Earth, from all of the nations who pledged allegiance to the Dragon Throne. They were the sons of clerks and school teachers, of miners and farmers, of bureaucrats and beggars. Nearly all of them spoke Official Speech, along with their native dialects and tongues, but some of them had accents so thick that their words were all but unintelligible, and may as well have been some foreign language. In the cloud-flyer that had brought Carter across the wide sea to Taiwan Island had been men from all over Vinland, from Khalifa in the west, and from Fusang in the south, and despite the widely varying shades of their skin and the Babel of languages they spoke, all of the men shared something in common: they had all grown up in the shadow of the Mexic Dominion, which squatted in the midst of their three nations like a canker.

Carter had been raised in a township surrounded by nothing but land in every direction. The largest body of water he'd ever seen was barely a pond, a widening of Ten-League Creek just outside of Duncan proper. When the cloud-flyer passed over the ocean, an endless plain of white-flecked blue that stretched to the horizon in every direction, Carter had been struck dumb. He'd never known that the Earth could contain so much water.

Now, he was on an island surrounded on all sides by sea, and it seemed to him sometimes as if he would never leave, the rest of his life spent on this hard and unforgiving ground. Of course, in those dark moments he rarely considered that the rest of his life would be too long a span, so he hardly worried about being bored.

"Come on, you worms, my *grandmother* can run faster than that!"

Outside the grounds of the Green Standard training camp was a mountain, and though it was not the tallest on Taiwan Island, it was far from the smallest, and so Carter was sure that whoever had named it "Peaceful Hill" had been employing irony, or perhaps had just been a master of understatement. Every day since they had first arrived in the camp, and been given their uniforms, their kits, and their colorful new sobriquets, they had been forced to run from the gate of the camp to the top of Peaceful Hill and down again, without pausing for rest or water.

Carter had no fear of war, since he was reasonably sure that the daily run was going to kill him.

Just when he reached the point when he thought he might be able to survive the run, his muscles built and toned to the point where they could take the strain and continue to place one foot in front of the other, and his lungs able to draw another breath without breaking into dry, rasping coughs, the rules were changed, and instead of running in a light cotton shirt and shorts they were required to make the circuit in full combat fatigues and boots, with a full pack strapped on their backs.

Some of the other recruits grumbled that they'd hardly be required to run in fatigues and full pack on Fire Star, considering the red planet's thin atmosphere would require a surface suit and the low gravity would make a full pack no kind of burden. But when the drill instructor heard their grumblings, those recruits were invited to make a second daily run, this time instead wearing one of the surface suits that the camp had on hand for demonstrations. And though the surface suits were well-designed for use on the red planet, they were somewhat less well-suited for Earth's heavier gravity and thicker atmosphere. Those that managed to make it up the hill and back seldom grumbled again.

"Tell me, recruit, are you trying to hit him or seduce him? I can't tell."

If the drill instructor with his colorful nicknames was a hard taskmaster, compared to their combat instructor he was as soft and gentle as a nursemaid.

"It is given to me to instruct you in the arts martial, but it makes no difference to me if all of your bones are broken to dust in the process. Better not to send a man into combat than send one ill-prepared to fight."

Master Singh had been a member of the Akali Sena, the elite battalion of Sikh warrior-saints from the nation of Hind who were more commonly known as the Immortals. Singh had served in the early days of the Second Mexic War with distinction, fighting in close-quarters with the Mexica on the surface of Fire Star, until a Mexic fire-lance doused him with burning liquid magnesium, which seeped into the rents cut into the fabric of his surface suit by a Jaguar Knight's obsidian-edged club. The Jaguar Knight had fallen before Singh's saber, as did the other Mexica who had wielded the fire-lance, but by the time Singh was able to seek medical attention the fast-burning magnesium had done its work on his flesh and bone. Hidden beneath the starched fabric of his green shirt and pants was a ruined landscape of burned flesh, but even if Singh kept his burns and scars concealed, he could not hide the stump of his left arm, extending less than a hand's-breadth from his shoulder. Singh had received an imperial commendation for gallantry in combat, helping to secure victory that day while a torrent of liquid magnesium burned through the skin and bone of his arm.

With his commendation and his wounds, Singh could have also taken a pension and retired, returning home to Lahore to live out his days in comfort with his wife and children. But Singh had felt that he still had service he could perform, and secured a post as combat instructor on Taiwan Island.

Like countless recruits before him, Carter had come to wish that Singh had taken the retirement instead.

"May almighty God and the memory of all the gurus give me strength, but I cannot imagine what that was meant to be. Did you intend to block the blow, recruit, or invite him to dance?"

And at night, when the day's drills were done, and their meager meals consumed and cleared away, the men were sent back to their barracks to clean floors and walls until they were spotless, to launder their fatigues and polish their shoes with boot-black. Then, when the camp's drummer beat out the All Quiet, they used what little strength was left them to crawl onto their cots and drift into dreamless sleep. In only a few hours, long before the sun rose, they'd be rousted from their beds by the thunder beat of All Wake, and it would feel as though their heads had just hit the cots only moments before.

Carter did not recall the last time his muscles didn't ache, the last time he wasn't covered in bruises, the last time he felt rested. Suddenly, a life of riding tractors on the neighbor's farm didn't seem so bad, after all.

What worried him, though, was the nagging thought that this might be the *easy* part.

≡≡

HEXAGRAM 8
CLOSENESS
BELOW EARTH ABOVE WATER

There is Water on the Earth. In the same way, the former kings established the myriad states and treated the feudal lords with cordiality.

Niohuru Tie still dreamt of glory, but his first days as a bannerman were hardly getting off to a glorious start. It had been only a handful of days since he'd marched into the recruiting offices of the Eight Banners in Northern Capital, signed his name, and entered the emperor's service. He'd been instructed to make his farewells to family and friends and report to the transport depot the following morning.

The ride down to Hangzhou by rail had taken the better part of a day, and Niohuru had taken the opportunity to settle his thoughts. His parents and brothers had been little more impressed by his decision to enlist than his tearaway friends had been, which shouldn't have come as a surprise, he now realized. But still he couldn't help but feel a disappointed resentment that his own father, an officer of the court, hadn't been able to muster something like pride for his son.

Instead, the old man had taken hold of Niohuru's shoulders, looked into his eyes, and in a strangely quiet voice, said simply, "Try not to get killed, my son."

Niohuru had puzzled over it during the jostling ride down from Northern Capital. Everyone agreed that the Mexic Dominion was a blight, and that the atrocities committed by its troops on the innocent colonists of Fire Star were an abomination. Niohuru had heard his own parents express precisely those sentiments for years, ever since the Mexic invasion when he'd been just a boy. But when the question arose as to what would be done about it, it seemed too often the answer was that the sons of some other family would be sent to make the Mexica answer for their crimes. Never did his parents consider that one of *their* sons might need to make any sacrifice.

By the time the train had reached its destination, Niohuru was cramped from the close quarters of the compartment, somewhat drowsy with the late afternoon heat, but no nearer an answer.

Along with the few hundred men who'd ridden in the train from the north, the depot was filled with hundreds more, even thousands, who had come from other parts of the countryside. From the south came men from Guangdong, Fukian, and Guangxi, from the west, men of Sichuan, Yunnan, and Gansu. And not just men of the Middle Kingdom, either, but those who had journeyed by boat to the port of Hangzhou from Choson, Nippon, Annam, and even farther afield. There even bobbed in the crowd a few pale white faces, from Rossiya, perhaps, or even further west in Europa, or else from Vinland across the sea. Niohuru was surprised. While fairly common in the ranks of the Green Standard Army and on the ships of the Interplanetary Fleet, it was his understanding that natives of Europan nations and of Vinland were somewhat rare in the Eight Banners.

The depot was a mass of confusion, with countless men jostling this way and that, following the direction of the stern-faced bannermen who'd been waiting to receive them. The bannermen, all wearing the dark-colored fatigues of the Eight Banners combat dress, with carbines slung on their shoulders and sabers at their hips, shouted for the men of one classification to go this way, the men of another to go that. It reminded Niohuru nothing so much as cattle being herded through pens. He remembered what often became of cattle when they reached their destination, and tried not to dwell on any possible parallels.

As the light faded in the sky, the day slowly creeping onto night, they were ushered in their hundreds the short distance from the depot to the walls of the Hangzhou Garrison, facing out onto West Lake. Their shoes squelched in the mud underfoot where the ground wasn't paved, and splashed in puddles where it was, while the slate gray skies overhead threatened even more rain. Finally, they reached the garrison, and the drill field near the Qiangtang Gate. Their bannermen escorts managed to get them into some sort of ragged order, and then they were called to attention. The ranks were packed in so tightly together that Niohuru could scarcely draw a breath, the men on either side pressing in as closely as did the men in front and behind.

The man standing atop the garrison wall passed his gaze over them as a child might survey an assortment of unwanted toys. He was dressed in the same dark fatigues as their bannermen escorts, but even at a considerable distance Niohuru could see something different about the way this man carried himself, something that set him apart from the others.

"Eight Banners Recruit Intake present and accounted for, General-in-Chief!" barked one of the escorts in a voice that echoed off the garrison walls like a gunshot. He snapped off a salute, standing to rigid attention.

The man atop the wall returned with a lazy salute of his own, and Niohuru thought he had recognized what it was that set this man apart from the others. It was a haughty quality, perhaps, but not an undeserved one. This was a leader of men, who knew his place and expected others to know theirs. When he spoke, his voice rang even louder than the escorts had done, booming like a cannon.

"Men! I am General-in-Chief Hao, commander of Hangzhou Garrison, and from this day forward your lives are not your own."

Niohuru had expected a stirring call to action, a valediction. The commander's words were that, if only in part.

"The proudest day of your lives was the day you decided to enroll in the Eight Banners. That decision set you apart from the sons and younger brothers, those who quail at home, afraid to take up the yoke of imperial service. But know this. Though there is no finer creature in all the world than a bannerman, your hearts, your bodies, your very lives are no longer yours to own. Each man enrolled under the Eight Banners should consider himself a slave. A highly trained, highly valued slave, but a slave nonetheless. He is never free, and he is never rich, and never will be either. The emperor is his master and benefactor, and a slave does not serve his master for money, or for glory, but because his master wishes it."

Many around Niohuru began to shift uneasily, appearing perhaps to question their decision to serve.

"There is no greater civilizing force in all the world than the Eight Banners of the Dragon Throne. When the great Manchu leader Nurgaci founded the Banners, it was with the intent of uniting the various people under one rule. In the year the corrupt Bright Dynasty finally fell, giving way for the Clear Dynasty, it was the bannermen who helped liberate this very city of Hangzhou, and in that same year that the Hangzhou Garrison was established. By that time, the Eight Banners had already led the way to victory over the Chahar Mongols, and over the kingdom of Choson. In time, the emperor would dispatch the Eight Banners to help pacify New Dominions in new lands, west across the great lands, and east across the seas. And in all that time, the Eight Banners have fulfilled their purpose, uniting the people under one rule. Eight Banners, one world, one emperor."

From his studies of history, Niohuru knew it was hardly as simple as that. Having begun as eight Manchu banners, more were added in later years, until there were at one point some two dozen in all. His boy tutor, an old Nipponese bannermen named Etsuko, had told him that, by the time of the Xian-feng Emperor, the Banners had become a confusing mess, ill-organized and inefficient. The Tongzhi Emperor had changed all that, reorganizing the militaries along more rational lines, making the Banners once more eight in number, each of them a force large enough to subdue and secure an entire region on its own. His successor, the Guangxu emperor, had put this newly restructured Eight Banners to good use, leading it to victory over the Mexica in the First Mexic War, over a century and a half before. For a brief time, just as General-in-Chief

Hao had said, it was one world under the Dragon Throne, united by the Eight Banners.

But within a generation, the Mexica had expelled the forces of the Middle Kingdom in a bloody uprising, establishing the Mexic Dominion, and beginning the long cold war that led, finally, to the present troubles.

"Once united under one rule," Hao went on, voice booming, "the nations of the world will be united again. This time, though, our battlefield is not the streets of Hangzhou, or the plains of Vinland, or the mountains and forests of Fusang. Now the field of battle is to be found on the red sands of Fire Star. And it will be you, proud bannermen and new-made slaves of the emperor, who will help achieve that victory."

Niohuru felt a swell of pride, the sting of his parents' lack of enthusiasm beginning to fade. Still, he couldn't help but recall the muttered conversations he'd overheard on the troop train from Northern Capital, other recruits discussing rumors they'd encountered, wondering if they were true. Rumors that some within the Eight Banners argued that the leaders of the emperor's militaries in the Second Mexic War were still fighting old conflicts, trying to wage war on a new world with tactics better suited to another.

Standing in the muddy drill field of Qiangtang Gate, packed close with thousands of bannermen recruits, Niohuru felt sure that those voices of dissent were wrong. The Eight Banners were guided by centuries of tradition, and by the tactics handed down by brave men who had conquered the world in the Dragon Throne's name. What chance was there that those traditions and tactics would not win the day again?

≡

HEXAGRAM 9
LESSER DOMESTICATION
BELOW HEAVEN ABOVE WIND

Wind moves through the Heavens. In the same way, the noble man cultivates his civil virtues.

When she mustered with the others on the tarmac, the man in the uniform of an Interplanetary Fleet captain looked her up and down, nodding appreciatively. "Not bad, Flight Cadet Amonkar. Lose a kilo or two and you'll mass out just fine."

As if in counterpoint, a roar crescendoed overhead before fading away again, as a two-man flyer buzzed over the flight school, its contrail a stark white banner against the bright blue sky that almost immediately began to fuzz at the edges as it spread. Amonkar fancied that the breeze kissing her cheek was the wind of the flyer's passing, and resisted the impulse to smile.

Back home in Bhopal, Arati Amonkar's mother had always fussed over her during mealtimes, pestering her to eat more, to take second helpings. Amonkar's older sister was tall, with wide hips and breasts that swelled under the silk of her coli, and for as long as Amonkar could remember their mother had gone on about how men always looked for such things in potential brides, indicators of fertility.

Amonkar, though, had always known that a few extra *samosas* or another bowl of rice was never going to give her a figure like her sister's.

She'd always been smaller than the other children of her age, but even so it had seemed as if she'd stopped growing early, while the other girls in her class continued to gain a centimeter or two in height. But if she was short, she wasn't exactly slender, more like compact. She'd never presented a particularly feminine profile in *sadi* and *coli*, and now that she wore the unisex light-colored tunic and pants of an Interplanetary Fleet duty uniform, with her black hair shorn close to the scalp, she might have passed at a distance for a boy just entering pubescence.

Amonkar saw it as a sign that she'd made the right decision to discover herself in the one place where her stature and shape were assets and not liabilities.

"Half-rations for you, Flight Cadet Bu," the captain said to the Han woman standing beside her, shaking his head. "You'll need to slim down if you want to make the cut."

The woman stood only a few centimeters taller than Amonkar, but the swell of her breasts pressed against the fabric of her duty tunic. Amonkar's mother would have been suitably impressed, as would supposedly the potential bachelors of Hind, but apparently the Interplanetary Fleet was less so. The attributes that made for a good wife and mother in the eyes of Hindi tradition did a potential pilot no favors.

The captain continued down the reviewing line, inspecting the men and women of the flight cadet company. The visual inspection was more a formality than anything else, of course, since later in the day they'd have their daily weigh-in and height check, after their physical exercises and before heading inside for their course work.

When Amonkar had been asked to step onto the scale when first visiting the recruiting office in Bhopal, she'd been confused, to say the least. As he'd checked her weight and height, clearly impressed, the recruiter had explained.

Though the gravitational attraction of the red planet Fire Star was only a third that of Earth's, its atmosphere was far thinner. As a result, any aircraft, whether fixed-wing bombers or rotary-wing fighters, had to offset the lack of lift in the thin medium by keeping its mass as low as possible. In the early days of the Interplanetary Fleet on the red planet, pilots had been selected first by their aptitudes and capacities with regards to flight skills—hand-eye coordination, depth perception and visual acuity, spatial relations and mathematical skill—and then narrowed down to those who either already were or could quickly become light enough in mass. The diminishing pools of potential pilots from such a process of selection meant that the Fleet was constantly short-handed, and always in need of qualified pilots.

Within a few years of the onset of the Second Mexic War, imperial decree changed Interplanetary Fleet recruitment policies, and in particular the pilot selection process. Now, rather than choosing those with the necessary skills and aptitudes and then winnowing down to those who fit the physical requirements, the Fleet would instead recruit those who had the necessary physical characteristics, and then train them to develop the requisite skills and aptitudes as needed.

When Amonkar entered the Bhopal recruitment offices of the Interplanetary Fleet, she was given sight and hearing tests, a battery of examinations designed to gauge her basic intelligence, and then asked to stand on a scale. And that was the extent of it. She had walked in the door wanting to become a pilot, and expecting that she would have to endure a long term of basic training before being allowed to take tests to determine her fitness for that duty. Instead, when she walked out the door she carried in her hand orders to report to the flight school in Guangdong immediately to begin training and evaluation.

The Interplanetary Fleet was the only branch of the imperial military that inducted women in any significant numbers, with the Eight Banners and the Green Standard Army employing women only in support and rear echelon capacities. What surprised Amonkar, on reaching the flight school, was how *many* women she found there. A moment's reflection explained it. With the principal requirements for a flight cadet being their weight and height, women would actually have a statistical advantage over men, and thus be disproportionately represented in any class of flight cadets.

Everyone in the flight cadet company, men and women, were comparatively short in stature, and most of them relatively slender. Even the heavier of them were only a few kilos overweight, and heaviest would have looked slender when compared to most people in normal society. But Amonkar had quickly learned that flight school was anything but normal society, and on arriving all of them were informed of the weight goals they would have to meet before moving to the next stages of flight training.

Another flyer roared past overhead, echoed by grumbling in Amonkar's stomach. She allowed herself a slight smile, the captain's attention on another cadet in the line. Only a few more missed meals and continued high marks in the simulator, she knew she would be up there herself, not just feeling the wind, but *making* it.

HEXAGRAM 10
TREADING
BELOW LAKE ABOVE HEAVEN

Above is Heaven, and below is Lake. In the same way, the noble man makes distinction between the high and the low and so defines how the common folk shall set their goal.

Carter Micah was treading water, his carbine in a waterproof bag slung across his back, with four men on either side. In the heavy dawn mists that clung like a blanket to the surface of Green Jade Summit Lake, Carter could scarcely see the others, much less the opposite shore. But overhead he could see the last stars twinkling as the sky gradually lightened, the rising sun still hidden by clouds to the east.

Most of Blue Team was "dead," tagged with paint cartridges during the first two days of the maneuver and removed from the field by referees. Only Carter's squad was still in play, twelve men altogether. If they were captured or hit, the maneuvers would be at an end, and Red Team would have won the mock combat exercises.

Carter wasn't prepared to let that happen.

They had spotted Red Team's bivouac, late the day before as the sunlight faded in the west, on the opposite shore of the lake. Using a remote-viewing mirror and keeping concealed behind the tree line, Carter had been able to confirm that the enemy had their flag under guard. The Red Team had faired somewhat better in the first days of the ninety-six-hour field exercises, taking comparatively fewer "casualties," and nearly a full platoon was in evidence, more than two dozen men, with the red armbands around their biceps visible even from that distance.

Carter hadn't asked to be tapped as squad leader, when the team started out on the six-hour hike from Peaceful Hill, but he figured that so long as he followed orders and kept his head down, he'd at least have a good chance of not embarrassing himself. Now, he was somehow in charge of all that remained of Blue Team, and their only chance of victory.

In the dying light of day, they'd assessed the enemy's strength and position. Red Team appeared to have set up a picket to guard the approaches, with men positioned to the east and the west along the shoreline, and in a long arc to the north watching the mountainside. The few men not on post had sacked out on the ground near the tree from which the red banner hung, their weapons close at hand.

Somewhere in the woods hidden referees watched, noting each team's progress. Carter half-hoped that they'd be mauled by the black bears who made this forest their home. Maybe then they'd all just be able to go home, and neither side the winners or losers. But that wasn't likely to happen.

If neither team captured the other's flag, then the team with the most "kills" would be declared the victors, and Red Team was certain to win. Blue Team's only real chance at victory lay in capturing the red banner.

The squad had gathered in the woods on the lake's southern edge, hidden from view, around the blue banner tied to a lower branch of a towering Nipponese maple.

"There are fewer men on the eastern approach," said Ears, his voice hushed and rasping. "We should circle the lake and attack from that direction."

"No," said Moonface, shaking his head. "Didn't you see the field of interlocking fire they've set up? Even if there are fewer men, they're better positioned. The wiser choice is from the west."

"We should circle and come down from the north," said Spitter, saliva flecking the corners of his mouth as he lisped. "We can use the trees for cover and pick them off." He slapped the trunk of the Nipponese maple.

The others debated, as though they were led by consensus, more of them agreeing with Spitter than with either of the other two, finding the notion of something to hide behind while attacking an attractive one.

But they were not led by consensus, Carter knew. The decision was his.

"No," he said, shaking his head with a note of finality. "They've had too much time to get entrenched on all three sides. And even if we *did* manage to pick off the men in front, they've got more in reserve to send up from the rear. If… *if* we had enough men, we could come at them from two fronts, try to divide their attentions and their reserves, but we don't have that luxury." He gestured at the bare dozen of them seated around the blue banner.

"Then what do you suggest?" asked Spitter with condescension.

Carter and the Rossiyan had never got on, not since the young Tejan had managed to throw the Rossiyan three falls out of four in hand-to-hand combat. Carter hadn't put any stock in the matter, but the lisping Rossiyan seemed to take his martial prowess very, *very* seriously, and never forgave Carter for the perceived slight.

That was alright with Carter, though. He didn't much like *him*, either.

"I'm not suggesting anything," Carter said, his jaw set. "I'm in command of the squad, so anything I've got to say is more along the lines of an *order*."

He paused for a moment to let that sink in. "And it's that we should attack them from the south, instead, where there's a gap in their defenses."

The others exchanged looks, their expressions clearly baffled even in the gloaming.

"Across the lake," Carter clarified.

In the grey twilight, their opinions were plainly visible.

"Look," he said, drawing with his finger in the dirt at their feet. "They're treating the water like it's a brick wall. They've got their forces spread out in a wide arc from the east to the west, but they've hardly got anybody facing the lakeside at all."

Moonface shook his head. "Why should they? Do you have any idea how cold that lake is, this time of year?"

"No, do you?"

Moonface nodded, slowly. "It's *cold*."

"And deep, too, as the joke goes," Carter replied. A couple of the others who'd heard the joke of the two men urinating off a bridge chuckled. "But it's the only way I see this working. Now, we've got our rain gear, and should be able to rig up watertight bags. The way I figure, we leave a small detachment here to guard the banner, and the rest of us go swimming."

Ears whistled, low. "It is going to be *cold*, my friend."

Carter nodded. "I figure it will, at that. But if we win these exercises we get a two-day furlough in the town, and I don't know about you fellows, but I can think of a few ways I'd like to get warm down there."

Smiles and nods rippled around the circle. There were still some dissenters, clearly, but they knew better than to challenge the chain of command.

"Alright, then, any questions?" Hearing none, Carter clapped his hands lightly together, and rose to his feet. "In that case, let's get started. We're wasting darkness."

It had taken much of the night to get their gear together and ready for the water crossing. By the time they were done, they'd converted nine of their rain panchos into waterproof bags, and in each secured a string of smoke-bombs, rolls of paint cartridges, and their carbines. Carter selected three of the squad to stay behind and guard the blue banner, choosing those who'd scored highest in marksmanship on the Known-Distance Range the week before. Moonface, who had no desire to go swimming, objected that he'd have done better on the range, but that he'd been distracted when zeroing his rifle by Spitter's farting next to him. The Rossiyan, in response, lifted one leg and let off a peal of flatulence, and Carter figured that was as good an answer to him as any. Carter might not have liked Spitter all that much, but he had to hand it to him: the Rossiyan *did* know how to fart. It was likely all of the beets he ate.

Then they were down to the water's edge, across the green grass which led almost to the waterline, moving doubled low to the ground. The moon shone overhead, so that out in the open the world was painted in a monochromatic gray, more twilit than dark, but Carter could only hope that the Red Team's attentions were elsewhere. The nine of them slid into the crystal-clear waters as quietly as they were able, and then keeping all but their heads submerged, with only their noses, eyes, ears, and hair visible, they began to dog-paddle their way across to the north shore.

They were more than halfway across the lake when the sun began to pink the sky to the east. Carter hadn't counted on the dawn mists, but as the rays of the rising sun warmed the air above the water, they created a fog that hugged the lake's surface like a veil. Obscured by the mist, they had less chance of being spotted, and so they had simply to avoid being heard. Considering that the ducks who made the lake their home in spring had already migrated long before, if Carter and the others could keep from splashing, and assuming that the grass carp who swam beneath them didn't begin to raise a ruckus, which hardly seemed likely, they just might be able to pull this off.

Then, of course, they'd reached the lake's north shore, and everything that *could* have gone wrong, did.

They'd crouched in the shallows at the water's edge, as planned, opening their waterproof bags and slipping out their carbines and cartridges and belts of smoke-grenades. Rising up out of the mists like specters, they appeared not to have been spotted yet by any of Red Team.

Then came the thundering sound of flatulence to Carter's left.

The Red Team was immediately on the alert, heads snapping around and men jumping to their feet, reaching for their paint-loaded carbines.

"Damn it, Spitter!" Carter heard one of the others curse.

Carter saw no reason to delay. Their only chance now lay in fast action.

Lobbing a smoke grenade overhand, he raised his carbine to his shoulder and began firing, sending paint-cartridges whizzing through the air, and shouted, "Charge!"

The Blue Team had the element of surprise, but only barely, and the Red Team was quickly getting their bearings. As it was, Ears and Moonface both went down before they'd taken three steps from the water's edge, both of them incarnadine with red paint splatters up and down their chests. Spitter made it a bit further up the shore, until his chest was painted a red to match the embarrassed blush on his cheeks.

Carter was halfway to the tree from which the red banner hung, sure that he would be caught by enemy fire any moment, when all of the rules suddenly changed.

"Bear!" shouted one of the Red Team members, running from the tree line as though his hair was on fire and bees infested his ears. "Bear!!"

The creature lumbered out of the woods, rearing up on his hind legs, a bright blue splotch of paint staining one side of his head. He was not much taller than any of the men present, but outweighed the heaviest of them, and besides, none of the men had paws ending in wicked claws, or a snout full of viciously-sharp teeth. Apparently an errant shot from one of the Blue Team carbines had pegged one of the bears native to these woods, who'd been walking through the forest, minding his morning business. Enraged, and likely half-blinded by paint, he had bellowed in anger and roared into the bivouac.

The Red Team was immediately thrown into chaos, like school-children running from a skunk.

Carter, for his part, was already resigned to "die", having run headlong into enemy fire, and it didn't even occur to him for the moment to be afraid of this new threat. He was focused on one thing, and that only: the red banner, and the victory it represented.

While the others ran in all directions, both the Red Team and the scattered remains of his Blue Team squad, Carter simply snatched the red banner down from the tree, spun on his heel, and pounded back toward the water's edge. Carbine and smoke-bombs he discarded on the soft grasses, and with the red flag clenched in his hand he dove back into the waters, beating for the other side.

He was halfway across before he stopped to realize that while the red paint cartridges of the enemy could do little worse than sting and bruise and cost him a weekend's furlough, the claws and teeth of the bear were likely to have done considerably more damage.

When he climbed out on the south shore, half-frozen and exhausted, he was met by a pair of referees and the three surviving members of Blue Team.

"Congratulations, recruit," one of the referees said, checking off a box on a clipboard. "Blue Team is victorious."

HEXAGRAM 11
PEACE
BELOW HEAVEN ABOVE EARTH

Heaven and Earth perfectly interact. In the same way, the ruler, by his tailoring, fulfills the Dao of Heaven and Earth and assists Heaven and Earth to stay on the right course; in so doing, he assists the people on all sides.

Niohuru Tie stood at the panoramic window, looking up at the cloud-striped curve of the Earth above him. For the hundredth time, his fingers traced the image of the sea-horse embroidered on the chest of his long dark surcoat, insignia of a ninth-rank military officer. He had only received his Eight Banners dress uniform two days before, and though it was tailored to his exact measurements, fitting him like a glove, he was still having difficulty growing accustomed to it. Perhaps it was not the weight of the surcoat that was on his mind, but the weight of responsibility and duty that it represented. No longer a cadet, he was now a full-fledged bannerman, slave to the emperor.

The orbital city of Diamond Summit rotated to provide the semblance of gravity, its axis the tether of the Bridge of Heaven, stretching down to Gold Mountain in Fragrant Harbor, far below. Rotating at right-angles to the orbital elevator, Diamond Summit's orientation to the Earth was forever unchanged, and so while the stars slid by the wide window, in their slow and stately dance, the Earth slowly turned overhead. Looking up Niohuru could see the coastline of Annam, and beyond that the Bengali Bay and the arc of Hind. If he stood here long enough, he knew, he would see the eastern shore of the Middle Kingdom and the mountains of Nippon far beyond, or perhaps the unbroken arc of the broad ocean, blue as sapphires.

Every element of the scene—stars, Earth, tether, and station—moved in perfect unity, as though following the precise choreography of some celestial dance.

When the page called his name, Niohuru destroyed the perfect image by stumbling over his own feet as he turned, only narrowly avoiding sprawling face first onto the tiled floor.

The page gave him a sympathetic smile. "I take it you've been up *there*, Bannerman Niohuru?" The page pointed down between his feet, an incongruous gesture, but one Niohuru immediately understood.

He nodded, righting himself.

"I find it helps closing my eyes when looking away from the window," the page said, stepping over to the door and holding it open for him. "I reorient quicker that way."

Niohuru took a deep breath through his nostrils before it occurred to him to nod. "My thanks," he said absently, "I'll remember that."

The page shrugged, unconcerned whether Niohuru remembered or not. "Bannerman Magiya will see you now."

When civilians or those serving in other military branches spoke to or of a member of the Eight Banners, it was customary to address them simply as "bannerman." Within the Banners themselves, though, ranks and titles were typically employed, as a sign of respect. So while the civilian page, an imperial servant of Diamond Summit, might refer to the man within simply as a bannerman, Niohuru addressed him with considerably more formality.

"Colonel Magiya," he said, bowing low as he stood at the threshold. "This one, Niohuru Tie, presents himself for inspection."

"Come in," the man within said. "At your ease, Private Niohuru."

Niohuru rose and entered the room. The man behind the aluminum desk was dressed in the long surcoat of the Eight Banners dress uniform, but unlike Niohuru's, his was emblazoned with a tiger rampant, insignia of a fourth-rank military officer.

When he still served in active combat, Colonel Magiya had been in command of an entire brigade, a strength of four battalions, more than four thousand men in all. Now, he supervised recruits to the Eight Banners in microgravity combat maneuvers, the final stages of bannerman training.

"Have a seat, private," Magiya said, indicating the chair opposite his. "You'll forgive me not rising, I trust."

Niohuru nodded eagerly, and slid gracelessly into the chair. Since arriving at Diamond Summit, he'd held Magiya in something approaching awe. The colonel was a scion of one of the Great Houses, a Manchu like himself, but more than that he was a hero of the Second Mexic War, his story repeated time and again in the news of the day, about how he valiantly led his men personally in a charge against the enemy on the high plains of Fire Star, until a mortar shell shattered his left leg beneath the hip. With only one leg, the other ending a few centimeters from the hip joint, Magiya had evident trouble maneuvering when under gravity, whether on the Earth's surface or simulated by rotation as on Diamond Summit. But in microgravity, such as in the training facilities out near the shipyards at the far end of the orbital tether, he moved as well or better than any man, making him perfectly suited to his present training post.

"You received the highest marks in microgravity combat I've seen in my tenure here, Niohuru," Magiya said. "Or should I instead call you 'Iron Wolf'?"

Niohuru smiled sheepishly, suddenly self-conscious. The other recruits had given him the nickname after he'd bested them all in practice bouts, derived from the meaning of his personal name in Official Speech and of his family name in Manchu.

"I just did my best, colonel."

"Yes, of course." Magiya nodded, thoughtfully. "We could use more men whose best reaches the level of yours, I should think." He spread his hands on the table's brushed surface. "I've spoken with the garrison commander about your performance, and General-in-Chief Hao reports that you've acquitted yourself with similar high marks in your other objectives, as well. You may be pleased to know that he has recommended you for a prized posting."

"Sir?"

"You'll be joining the First Raider Company, Third Battalion of the Bordered Yellow Banner's Ninth Brigade." He paused, and a wistful look stole over his face. "My old brigade, as it happens." He shook his head, as if knocking loose memories. "You're to report to Captain Hughes Falco on Zhurong in Fire Star orbit in six months' time."

Niohuru resisted the temptation to grin, but just barely. He inclined his head in a bow. "I am honored by this posting. I hope that I will win glory for the emperor and for the Eight Banners. I am only thankful that I'm alive and of an age at a time when men are called to prove their worth on the field of battle."

The corners of Magiya's mouth turned down in a frown. He let out a sigh and, with a grunt of exertion, pushed off his seat. His weight on his single leg, holding onto the desk's edge for balance, he hopped on one foot around the corner of the desk to stand before Niohuru.

"Tell me, private," Magiya said, his voice quiet and without a trace of bitterness, "does *this* look like glory to you?" He pointed to the stump of his missing leg.

Niohuru wasn't sure how to respond. He shook his head. "No... that is, I didn't..."

The colonel held up a hand, silencing him.

"Listen to me, Niohuru. I don't expect you to understand this now, but perhaps you'll remember it, and recall my words at a time more suited to understanding. I know that, like me, you have heard the voices of those who decry this war, who claim that we are engaged in nothing but the pursuit of vengeance, and the emperor would be better served to withdraw and leave the red planet to the enemy. They claim that soldiers care for nothing but blood and glory." He paused. "You *have* heard such voices, yes?"

Niohuru remembered the drunken talk of the other young tearaways in the teahouses and theaters, and nodded, lips pressed together.

"And I don't doubt that you've heard the proud old songs, or seen the dramas about the glorious victories, and of the heroes who win them in the emperor's name." The colonel didn't wait for him to respond, but continued. "Here is what I want you to remember. Those who sing war's praises are no less wrong than those who condemn it as sheer brutality. War is neither glorious nor blood-hungry, but is instead an unfortunate necessity. No man should march into battle reveling in the thought of combat, but neither should he shiver and quail like the craven who hides behind cover."

The colonel stopped, and fixed Niohuru with a close look.

"Tell me, private, what is the purpose of war?"

Niohuru straightened in his seat, proudly. "We wage war to defeat our enemies, to guarantee the will of the emperor, and to protect the people." The answer was straight out of the bannerman's training manual, which every recruit recited until he had fairly memorized it by heart.

Magiya shook his head, sadly. "No, I'm afraid that isn't it. Those are uses to which war is put, and the excuses offered for its existence, but none of them are the true purpose of war."

Niohuru was confused. "Then what *is* war's purpose, colonel?"

Keeping hold of the desk with one hand, Magiya leaned over, balanced on one foot, and brought his face near to Niohuru's.

"War," the colonel said, his expression grave, "is the coin in which men pay for peace." He straightened. "Peace, Private Niohuru. Not blood, and certainly not glory. We fight for *peace*."

HEXAGRAM 12
OBSTRUCTION
BELOW EARTH ABOVE HEAVEN

Heaven and Earth do not interact. In the same way, the noble man holds back the practice of his virtue and thus avoids disaster. He must not allow himself to be honored with rank and salary.

Amonkar had completed weeks upon weeks of training in the simulator, and logged nearly a hundred hours in the air with instructors, first in a single-engine flyer and then in the larger twin-engine and four-engine light bombers. After qualifying for solo flight, she and the rest of the graduating class had waited impatiently while the instructors reviewed their flight scores and aptitude tests, until finally the crew assignments were posted on the wall outside the main building.

A week later, she and the rest of the crew of the light bomber *Fair Winds for Escort* were completing one final training flight before the plane was dismantled and sent up the Bridge of Heaven to the cargo ships waiting in orbit above.

In the early years of the Second Mexic War, Amonkar had learned, crews were trained on terrestrial aircraft, then sent to Fire Star where low-gravity, low-atmospheric-pressure craft were waiting for them, already sent from the shipyards above Diamond Summit and constructed *in situ* on the red planet. The masters of the Interplanetary Fleet Air Corps had learned that even though the demands of flying a plane on Earth differed considerably from those involved in flying on Fire Star, there was a measurable advantage to a crew becoming acclimated to the eccentricities of their aircraft before being thrust into combat. The compromise that was reached, then, was to construct the craft on Earth, modified somewhat to fly in the heavier gravity and thicker atmosphere, and then after the crew had been allowed to familiarize themselves with their particular craft, the plane would be dismantled, sent in pieces to Fire Star, and then assembled there, the modifications removed so that it was now perfectly suited for its new environment. The attendant increase in cost of materials and manpower, to say nothing of the time and expense involved in lifting the dismantled craft from the Earth's surface to orbit on the Bridge of Heaven elevator, was deemed well worth the benefits of crews fully accustomed to their craft before flying into enemy fire.

Fair Winds for Escort was a Deliverer class light bomber, and Amonkar Arati was proud to serve as her co-pilot. Like so many of those in the flight training school, Amonkar had long dreamt of flying, and though she was still somewhat uncertain about the combat encounters that awaited on the red planet, the war was at least allowing her to fulfill those childhood dreams.

As a girl, Amonkar's favorite stories had been drawn from the Hindi national epics of the Ramayana and the Mahabharata, and she'd obsessed over those scenes involving the vimanas, flying chariots of gods and heroes. Later, in school, her favorite subject had been the study of history, at least on those days in which they discussed the Imperial Navy of the Air in the days of the First Mexic War, precursor to the modern Interplanetary Fleet Air Corps. She'd thrilled to accounts of ace squadrons like the Flying Immortals, the Spirits of the Upper Air, and the Golden Dragons, brave aeronauts who piloted their craft in dogfights against the lumbering but still-deadly airships of the Mexic Dominion's elite Eagle Knights.

From their discussions over meals, and late nights in the barracks, Amonkar knew that Navigator Geng, a Han woman about her own age, had also wanted to be a pilot since early childhood, but in the late stages of their training, Geng had failed a depth perception test, and so instead was tapped for the navigator's position. It was not flying, not as she'd always dreamed of doing, but it would be the closest that she would be allowed to get.

Pilot Bosch, a slender, pale-skinned young man from Deutschland, had wanted to be a fighter pilot, Amonkar had learned, jockeying one of the rotary-winged Dragonflies, or the larger Hornets with their hulls painted stark yellow and black. But when Bosch had completed his flight training, qualifying for solo flight, there had been more need in the Air Corps for skilled bomber pilots than fighters, and so he had been denied his first choice. Though he had yet to speak of it openly, Bosch's sour expression made plain that he was still far from pleased by the turn of events.

The other crewmen, so far as Amonkar knew, had never harbored any particular desire to fly, but had been drawn from the ranks of the Interplanetary Fleet's newest recruits, each selected first for their height and weight, and then for their skills and aptitudes. Tail Gunner Xiao, a Han from the Middle Kingdom, was nearly ten years Amonkar's senior, but was so diminutive that he might have passed for a teenage boy. Nose Gunner Siagyo spoke Official Speech with a Nipponese accent, dainty and slight as a flower, but with a wicked sense of humor and an infectious laugh. Bombardier Mehdi was from Persia, so thin he was almost skeletal, his features gaunt behind his prominent nose, but he was good natured and kind, Amonkar had found, with an easy smile and expressive hands.

The interior of a Deliverer like *Fair Winds for Escort* was not pressurized, to cut down on the additional mass that pressure-seals and airlocks would require, and to prevent the possibility of decompression at higher altitudes. As a result, the crew was forced to wear constrictive flight suits, in design much like the surface suits worn by troops on the ground, but less extensively armored. And unlike the armored surface suits of ground troops, the flight suits had helmets which featured much larger faceplates, broad expanses of transparent material, nearly unbreakable, that allowed a full one hundred-eight degrees of visibility. Although the flight suits were bulky and uncomfortable, the crew were grateful to have them since, even on Earth, at the high altitudes their flight plans required, temperatures dropped so far below water's freezing point that if any of the crew were to touch exposed surfaces inside the craft with their bare hands the skin would have frozen to the metal.

To enter the plane, the bombardier, navigator, and nose gunner had to squat down and edge under the nose of the craft, sidling up to their stations through the nose wheel well of the plane. The bombardier hunched over the bombsight and controls, while the navigator sat forward of the bombardier on a retractable stool, her maps and instruments spread over a folding shelf, her eyes at a level with the pilots feet in the cockpit, ahead of and above her. The nose gunner, for her part, crabbed down into her turret, strapped into her seat and able to rotate a full three hundred-sixty degrees along one axis, and over one hundred-eighty degrees along the other.

The rest of the crew, the pilot, co-pilot, and tail-gunner, entered the plane by crawling up through the open bomb bay doors. There was no corridor to move from the nose of the plane to the rear, only a catwalk as narrow as a man's shoulder, running over the bomb bay doors. The crewmen climbed up onto the catwalk, the pilot and co-pilot moving forward to the cockpit, the tail gunner aft to his turret. They had to take care not to fall off the catwalk, since the bay doors themselves, thin aluminum designed to roll up like window-blinds instead of opening on a hinge, only had a weight capacity of approximately fifty kilograms under Earth's gravity, and anyone who fell from the catwalk onto them was likely to continue falling into the open air beyond.

Amonkar sat on the right side of the cockpit, her seat unpadded and fixed into position, the bulky restraining straps over her shoulders, waist, and thighs. Pilot Bosch sat on the left side. In front of each of them was a yoke, either one of which could control the plane in flight, with an array of instruments, dials, and switches on the instrumentation panels before them. At the center of the panel was a gyro that showed the craft's attitude, fore and aft as well as port and starboard. To the left was an altimeter, which used atmospheric pressure to gauge altitude, and to the right an airspeed gauge, which used impact pressure to measure velocity. When they reached Fire Star, all of the instruments would be recalibrated for the red planet's atmosphere, but for this final training exercise, they had been set for use on Earth.

The crew would be using all of the instruments in this exercise, that was certain. The final stages of their training called for night flying in formation, using instrumentation only.

Instrument flying by night, their instructors had said, was the best test of a pilot's abilities. The inner ear, the trainees were told, provided the human body's primary sense of balance, acting in concert with sight, but when flying blind without any visual reference points the inner ear could be mislead. In instrument flying, then, one was required to learn how to ignore the senses and trust only the instruments.

To make things even more difficult, they would be flying in formation, just as if they were on a bombing run on Fire Star, with an entire squadron of light bombers flying in close quarters.

Their instructors had warned them about formation flying, drilling into them again and again the mistakes that rookie pilots made. Too often, they were told, beginning pilots had a tendency to over-control the craft, fighting to hold position with bursts of power. Then, when the craft would slip ahead of position, threatening to collide with the craft in the lead, the pilot yanked rearward on the throttle, pulling the craft out of alignment. Or they would try to hold lateral position using only the rudders, causing the plane to wallow back and forth through the air like the waddle of an overfed duck.

Throughout the early stages of the flight, Amonkar noted with approval, Pilot Bosch neatly avoided any of these rookie mistakes. She hadn't gotten the chance to get to know Bosch well, these last weeks, and before they were assigned to crew *Fair Winds for Escort* together she doubted they'd spoken more than a handful of words to one another. As it was, it was clear that they weren't likely to be friends, not like Amonkar and Geng were quickly becoming, but at least it appeared that their working relationship would be a smooth one. Still, Amonkar could see that Bosch still resented being denied his chance to pilot one of the rotary-winged fighters, and that he viewed the demands of piloting a light bomber as being beneath his level of skill.

They were flying by night over the coastal plains of Guangdong, the skies beyond moonless and dark. It was almost as if they were flying through an empty void, the only illumination the faint running lights of the craft on either side and in front of them. There were more than a half-dozen light bombers in the formation, a diamond-shaped wedge, with *Fair Winds for Escort* taking the rear position.

They hit a rough patch of air, the plane juddering in turbulence. Over their helmet radios, she could hear Bosch cursing beneath his breath. Then he seemed to relax. "Ah," he said, more to himself than to anyone else, "there he is."

Amonkar glanced ahead, and saw a bright light ahead of them. She reasoned that Bosch had been disoriented by the turbulence, and now had sighted the running lights of the plane in front of them.

"Co-pilot, how long till we reach our destination?"

Amonkar leaned down, calling between her feet to the space below. "Navigator Geng, how do you read our position?"

Geng consulted her maps, the curve of her helmet just visible through the space between Amonkar's feet. "Another hour, looks like, if course and speed hold. What's our current velocity, Arati?"

Amonkar straightened, glancing casually at the airspeed indicator.

She fought the urge to panic.

"Pilot Bosch," she said as quickly and calmly as possible. "We're flying *far* above the craft's top speed."

"What?!" Bosch said, perturbed, as though she had disrupted his thinking.

The two of them glanced ahead through the windshield at the bright light ahead, moving rapidly toward them. Then they both looked to the gyro, and the rapidly spinning altimeter, and immediately understood what had happened.

The light they were chasing wasn't the plane ahead of them in formation. It was a roadside lamp on the ground.

They were plunging toward the ground, banked over to one side.

But even if they didn't hit the ground, at their current speed, all it would take was another rough patch of air and the plane would break up, not designed for the stresses of such high velocity.

All of this passed between them, unspoken, in an instant, a matter of split seconds from the time that Amonkar first noticed their velocity. Any action they took would need to be immediate and decisive, or all onboard were going to die.

Pilot Bosch, to his credit, didn't waste time in self-recrimination or worry, but immediately moved into action. Unfortunately, his was the exact *wrong* action to take. Watching him, Amonkar could see that he intended to pull back hard on the stick. Unless she stopped him, pulling back hard on the yoke with the plane still banked to one side would put them into a descending spiral, one they wouldn't have time to pull out of.

Amonkar saw there was no time to explain, only time to stop him sending them all to their deaths. She grabbed her own stick, punching the toggle that switched full control to the co-pilot's station. She immediately reduced power, and rolled the plane to level off their trim. The second the gauges and gyro showed a level trim, *then* she yanked back on the stick, pulling them out of the dive.

"What in the eighteen-hells are you *doing* up there?" Geng shouted over her helmet radio.

Amonkar didn't answer, but turned to look at Bosch. The stricken expression on his face made plain that he'd realized the error of his approach, and knew just how close they'd all come to disaster. His mouth hung slightly open, eyes wide as saucers, but he remained silent, unspeaking.

He didn't say another word during the entire flight back to base.

The next day, Bosch was gone, scrubbed out and sent off to crew a vacuum craft of the Interplanetary Fleet, stripped of the ability to fly.

Amonkar found herself bumped to pilot, with another trainee being pulled up from the ranks to serve as *Fair Wind for Escort*'s co-pilot.

In addition to the elevation in position, Amonkar was offered a commendation for her quick thinking at the stick, which had saved the lives of six crew members, to say nothing of the man-hours and materials that had gone into the construction of the plane itself.

Amonkar declined the commendation, with all apologies, saying that the fault had been hers almost as much as it had been Bosch's, since she should have realized the error right away, and not so late that there was scarcely any chance to address it. Rectifying the error was simply a question of doing her duty, and addressing the earlier oversight.

It would not be the last time that Amonkar would deny honors which others felt were her due. But it would be the first and only time she would do so as a trainee. She, the rest of the crew, and *Fair Winds for Escort* itself, were all on their way to Fire Star.

HEXAGRAM 13
FELLOWSHIP
BELOW FIRE ABOVE HEAVEN

This combination of Heaven and Fire. In the same way, the noble man associates with his own kind and makes clear distinctions among things.

Hundreds of thousands of men and women, in hundreds of vacuum-craft, made their way across the black void of space, bound for Fire Star. The journey would take some six months all told, with unrelenting combat waiting for them at their destination.

Guardsman Carter and the rest of Fourth Company, Eleventh Armored Infantry Battalion, were billeted in the belly of an immense troop carrier of ceramic and steel. Once the ship was underway, leaving Earth behind, it had been made to rotate, spinning on a tether opposite a massive counterweight, the rotations imparting something like gravity to the ship's interior. The speed of the rotation meant that the force pulling their feet to the deck was roughly one-third that of Earth's gravity, identical with the gravitational attraction of the red planet Fire Star, so that when they arrived they would be well acclimated to its feel.

Long hours were spent every day in combat exercises, hand-to-hand bouts, and weapons training. But even the taskmasters of the Green Standard Army could not drill the men twenty-four hours a day—or rather all ten watches of the shipboard day—and so there were always spans of time when the men were left to their own devices, to eat, to seek recreation, and to relax, as best as they were able.

Like most in his recruit class, Carter had been assigned to the Fourth Company, an infantry unit supported by mechanized crawler-tanks. Carter found himself part of First Squad, Second Platoon, under the direct command of Corporal Eng, a broad-shouldered, round-faced Han who had already seen combat on Fire Star, before returning to Earth to help train up a new combat unit. Eng was frequently seen in the barracks assigned to the Second Platoon's First Squad, getting to know the men now under his command, learning their strengths, their weaknesses. From time to time the men also saw Captain Quan, leader of Fourth Company, but while Eng was personable, at least attempting to assay the role of the regular man with his smiles and hand clasps, while still maintaining a dignity befitting his authority, Quan was distant, aloof. It was almost as if Quan was uncertain of his own position, afraid that if he were to show any perceived sign of weakness, of being anything but the stone-faced leader of men, that he would find his position taken from him.

Still, there were some who saw in Quan's distance some kind of steely resolve, an awareness of forces moving at a level that the common foot soldier wouldn't understand.

Carter thought that men of that sort were just hungry for a father to whom they could look up, and that they would welcome any stern hand, whether it was worthy or not.

There was something almost comforting about being surrounded by so many familiar faces. The troop carrier carried thousands of men, and even a few women, both infantry of the Green Standard as well as sailors and airmen of the Interplanetary Fleet. Still, it occurred to Carter that it might have been preferable not to have been quite *so* familiar with the faces most immediately around him. He had taken some pride in the discovery that he was to lead a fire team of four men in the First-Second—First Squad of the Second Platoon—but that pride had been considerably leavened by the fact that the other three men were Spitter, Ears, and Moonface.

Ears was a right enough fellow, Carter decided, and Moonface had his good qualities, but Spitter? Aside from the man's seemingly boundless flatulence, it seemed that he was a positive glutton for punishment. It seemed that there was no circumstance that the Rossiyan would not turn to his own disadvantage.

Such as the incident with the airmen.

Pilot Amonkar felt edgy, confined as they were within the steel hull of the troop carrier. Having spent the last months flying, part of every day in the air, to be cooped up inside the vacuum-craft for so many weeks was to her like a cage to a bird, and she wanted nothing but to fly free. But they had no choice but to wait until they reached Fire Star, where they would be able to board the reassembled *Fair Winds for Escort* and take to the skies. What matter that the skies were pink over red sands, instead of blue over green forests and gray rock? They were skies, and flying was all that mattered.

Most days onboard the carrier were spent reviewing mission plans and hypothetical scenarios with the other flight crews of the Sixth Squadron, a group made up of twenty light bombers and a dozen rotary-winged fighter escorts. Like Amonkar, none of those onboard the trooper carrier, with the possible exception of Squadron Commander Khai, had any inkling what their mission on Fire Star would entail, but it was rumored that they were to take part in a major new offensive. And even Khai, if he knew anything of the mission, would still have been ignorant about most details, and either way Khai wasn't talking.

When at their liberty, not in mission reviews or in practice sessions with her crew in the flight simulators installed in the carrier's lower decks, Amonkar had found boon companions in her navigator and new co-pilot. With Bosch washed out, and Amonkar elevated to the position of pilot, another trainee had been brought up to round out the crew of *Fair Winds for Escort*. Co-pilot Seathl was an Athabascan woman from the nation of Khalifa, two years Amonkar's senior, one year older than Navigator Geng. When the three of them got together, away from the strictures of duty and training, it was almost as if Amonkar was once more a girl in Bhopal, getting together with her school friends, staying up half the night, laughing and talking about their hopes and dreams. But unlike those days in Bhopal, the hopes and dreams which the three crewmates stayed up late nights discussing did not involve boys, or fashion, or their aspirations for careers or lives beyond their parents' homes, but instead were about flying, about their plane, about their hopes that they would survive the war unscathed, and their dreams that they would one day be able to return home, to fly for the pure joy of it, and not into the gauntlet of enemy fire.

Mealtimes, the crew of *Fair Winds for Escort* ate together in the immense mess hall on the carrier's largest deck, along with hundreds of others of the ship's passengers, sailors, airmen, and soldiers.

It was in the mess, after the midday meal on a day when the Fire Star was still a journey of long weeks away, that Amonkar and the others came in contact with the soldiers.

Having trained for most of the previous year at the Interplanetary Fleet's air school in Guangdong, the airmen had, as a group, had little contact with outsiders for some time, dealing only with other members of the Air Corps, all of whom existed in the same chain of command, whether above them, on the same rungs of the ladder, or below. The troop carrier was the first time they had been forced to mix with others since first joining the Air Corps, but even here the different groups tended to keep to themselves, airmen to airmen, soldiers to soldiers. They had even had only limited encounters with the crew of the troop carrier itself, for all that they were their brothers- and sisters-in-arms in the Interplanetary Fleet.

Having completed their meal, Amonkar excused herself from the rest of the crew, and then she, Seathl, and Geng made their way back to their barracks to share a pot of hot green tea and while away the time in idle conversation.

Before they were able to leave the mess hall, though, they found their way blocked by the towering figure of a man in the fatigues of a Green Standard guardsman. His neck was as thick as his head was wide, making it appear that both were a single bullet-shaped growth jutting up from his wide shoulders. The backs of the man's broad hands were covered in coarse black hairs, as was his neck all the way around from front to back. He loomed over the three diminutive women, and if Amonkar had carried Geng on her shoulders the navigator might easily have been able to look him in the eyes.

"Our pardon, guardsman," Amonkar said, somewhat confused, dipping her head in an abbreviated bow, the respect one paid an equal, "but you appear to be blocking our way. May we pass?"

"I don't know," the man said, his deep voice laced with the accent of Rossiya. He scratched his stubbled chin, eyeing Seathl hungrily. "I think perhaps we should all stay a little longer, eh? Get to know each other better?" He lisped when he spoke, badly, flecks of saliva gathering at the corners of his wide mouth.

Amonkar decided that the time for etiquette had likely passed. "Come on," she said to the others, and shouldered her way past the towering Rossiyan.

"Wait a moment," the guardsman said, grabbing Seathl's arm as she passed, his thick fingers wrapped tightly around her bicep. "I think we can be friends, eh?"

Amonkar whirled, unsure how to respond but knowing that she had to do *something*. Seathl was under her command, after all.

She wasn't sure of the guardsman's rank, him wearing no identifiable insignia, and besides, chain of command between the different militaries was a problematic issue, at best. Even if she outranked him, it was clear that a simple verbal order would prove insufficient.

"Arati?" Geng said from Amonkar's side, sounding uncertain.

"Don't worry," she said with a confidence she didn't feel, stepping forward. "I'll take care of this."

As it happened, she needn't have bothered.

One moment the lisping Rossiyan was standing before them, towering over Seathl, her arm in a one-handed vice grip. The next moment, another guardsman grabbed his shoulder and spun him around.

"Damn it, Spitter," the man said, sounding like a character from a Vinlander gunslinger drama. He was considerably shorter than the Rossiyan, his fair hair close cropped, his eyes narrowed. "What the devil are you playing at?"

"None of your concern, Tejas," the Rossiyan said dismissively, scarcely even deigning to notice the other man, whose hand he shrugged off. He turned back to Seathl, puckering his lips. "Come on, now, pretty, just give us a little kiss, eh?"

Again the Vinlander guardsman grabbed his shoulder and spun him around, but this time when the Rossiyan turned in annoyance, the fair-haired man didn't waste time talking, but balled his fist and swung.

Even though the Rossiyan outweighed him by kilos, easily standing taller than him by more than twenty centimeters, the Vinlander clearly knew how to deliver a punch. The Rossiyan went down, laid out on the deck-plates with a moan.

The Vinlander guardsman turned to Amonkar, but before he was able to speak, the Rossiyan reached over and clawed at his leg, shouting obscenities.

"Excuse me," the Vinlander said, all courtesy, before spinning around and delivering a thudding kick to the Rossiyan's abdomen, knocking the breath from him, as well as any remaining fight. In an aside, he said, "Damn it, Spitter, don't you know when to stay down?"

The Vinlander glanced over at Seathl, who was more baffled than alarmed by the exchange. "Are you alright, ma'am?"

Seathl nodded, followed by a shrug.

The Vinlander turned to Amonkar, having seen her ranking insignia on her tunic's collar. "My apologies for my... well, for *him*." He jerked his head toward the Rossiyan on the floor, now holding his abdomen and moaning in pain. "We think he must have been raised by cattle, since he's only half as mannered as an ox, but smells twice as bad."

Amonkar smiled, and gave the Vinlander a slight nod. She motioned Seathl to her side. "You have my thanks, Guardsman...?" She let the name hang, like a question.

"Carter," the Vinlander said, snapping off a jaunty salute. "Carter Micah."

Amonkar nodded, and gave an absent-minded salute of her own. "Pilot Amonkar Arati." She glanced down at the guardsman sprawled on the floor. "Next time, if you can keep your 'him' from bothering innocent airmen in the first place, I'll be even more grateful."

Guardsman Carter smiled, sheepishly. Then, as if in response, the Rossiyan on the deck let out a thunderous peal of flatulence.

"Come on," Seathl said, grabbing Amonkar's arm, steering her and Geng away. "He smelled bad enough on the *outside*, I have no desire to discover the scent of his rotting innards."

As they were turning the corner out of the mess hall, Amonkar glanced back, and saw the Vinlander crouched down, bawling out the Rossiyan on the deck. For a moment, perhaps, she felt like a girl in Bhopal again, and for a fleeting instant, wondered if tonight they might not discuss boys instead of flying, just this once.

HEXAGRAM 14
GREAT HOLDINGS
BELOW HEAVEN ABOVE FIRE

Fire on top of Heaven. In the same way, the noble man suppresses evil and promulgates good, for he obeys the will of Heaven and so brings out the beauty inherent in life.

Regardless of whether the Middle Kingdom won or lost, Operation Great Holdings was to be a pivotal moment in the course of the Second Mexic War.

The war had by that point dragged on for twelve terrestrial years. On the red planet, whose journey around the sun was considerably longer, it had instead been seven Fire Star years. By either count, it had been a long and bloody undertaking, with considerable cost in material and lives on both sides.

Until recently, the war had seemed to have reached a kind of vicious stalemate, with each side able to inflect considerable harm on the other, but never enough to win a decisive victory. Each side, Mexic and Middle Kingdom, controlled large parts of the red planet's surface, and with reinforcements and supplies arriving from Earth on a regular basis, it was conceivable that the two enemies were so well entrenched that the war could carry on indefinitely. In the end, victory might fall to that side which outlasted the other, not by strength of numbers or numerical supremacy or superior weapons, but simply by dogged persistence, and through the willingness to sacrifice seemingly countless young lives in the planet's conquest.

In the year Water-Monkey, fifty-second year of the Taikong emperor and fifteenth Fire Star year, the opportunity for decisive victory was suddenly within the grasp of the Dragon Throne.

Earlier in the year, a secret mission, a combined effort of the Eight Banners, the Green Standard, and the Interplanetary Fleet, had succeeded in temporarily cutting off Mexic supply lines, albeit at considerable cost. Now, until the Mexic Dominion succeeded in reopening those lines, the Mexic forces on the surface and in orbit above Fire Star could not be easily resupplied, and were forced to cope with their existing, and dwindling, supplies of food, ammunitions, and armor.

Limited as their resources were, the Mexic forces were well-entrenched, holed up in former Middle Kingdom colonial settlements across the northern lowlands and down into the southern highlands on the planet's western hemisphere. Some of these settlements were pressurized domes on the surface, relatively vulnerable and difficult to defend, but some were well-defended and easily fortified, deep within mountains or in underground caverns, safe from orbital bombardment. Even if the Middle Kingdom decided it was worth the loss of the settlement structures themselves to retake the planet, no amount of bombing would reach the Mexic forces hidden beneath dozens of meters of rock and sand.

It was only a matter of time before the Mexic Dominion managed to re-establish supply routes. In the brief window after the old supply lines had been cut off, there was the opportunity to scour the Mexic off the red planet once and for all. If the Middle Kingdom was able to harry the Mexica from their strongholds, in a coordinated ground and air assault, and then overwhelm them with superior numbers and firepower, then the Dragon Throne stood a chance of cleansing Fire Star of the Mexica before reinforcements and supplies reached them from Earth.

And that coordinated ground and air assault was the operation codenamed Great Holdings.

HEXAGRAM 15
MODESTY
BELOW MOUNTAIN ABOVE EARTH

In the middle of the Earth, there is a mountain. In the same way, the noble man lessens what is too much and increases what is too little; he weighs the amounts of things and makes their distribution even.

Fair Winds for Escort rounded the bulk of Bao Shan like a satellite orbiting a world. The tallest mountain in the solar system, its twenty-four-kilometer-high peak dominated much of this part of the western hemisphere, visible for thousands of kilometers in every direction. Even the base up from which it rose was more than five-hundred kilometers in diameter, a massive shelf rimmed by a cliff some six kilometers high.

But measured alongside the scope and scale of what they were about to attempt, even the titanic mountain seemed to diminish in comparison.

From the cockpit of the light bomber, Pilot Amonkar could see practically the full range of territory involved in Operation Great Holdings, the landscape seen at so high a vantage that it resembled a raised-relief map of itself. As they completed their orbit of the mountain to the north, Bao Shan gradually waned in the port-side windows, and the lowlands of the Tamkung Plain spread out before them. With the early morning sun at their back, Amonkar could see the stark shadow of the great mountain as it speared across the wide plains, and there in the shade of Bao Shan lay their objective.

Orbital surveillance had determined that the lion's share of the Mexic ground forces on the red planet were concentrated on the Tamkung Plain, between Bao Shan in the east and the mountains of the Three Purities range in the west, with their strongholds being deep within the largest of the craters spreading northwards from the twelfth parallel of north latitude.

"Tail Gunner Xiao," Amonkar called her helmet mic, keeping one hand on the yoke and the other on the throttle controls. "How's our position?"

After a moment the answer came, buzzing in the speakers behind Amonkar's ears. "Looks good, pilot. I can see both craft on our flanks, and no one beyond looks out of alignment."

Amonkar nodded, more to herself than anyone else. Still, she couldn't help feeling anxious. *Fair Winds for Escort* flew at the vanguard of the squadron, out in front, and Amonkar itched to confirm the positions of the other bombers in the squadron. Unfortunately, though, the interference they were broadcasting downward to jam Mexic radio transmissions was playing havoc with their ability to communicate with one another as well, so she had to rely on her own crew to give visual feedback. She was just thankful for the hardlines that connected her to the members of the crew, or she'd likely be getting nothing but static in her own craft as well.

"I can see the lead Hornet, Arati," Co-pilot Seathl said, having loosened the straps holding her to her seat, and leaning forward to look backward through the starboard viewports as far as she was able. "The wedge looks tight from here, no gaps."

The squadron of light bombers was escorted by a flight of the black-and-yellow painted rotary-winged fighters. In the event that the Mexica were able to get any of their own planes off the ground during the bombing run, Amonkar was grateful that they'd have more than just her own craft's two gunners to keep the enemy off their tail. Flying at the vanguard she was in less immediate danger from enemy planes than the bomber bringing up the rear, but even so…

Of course, flying in the vanguard meant *Fair Winds for Escort* was at a greater risk from enemy flak once the Mexic got their anti-aircraft guns primed and firing, but Amonkar tried not to think about that at the moment.

"Co-pilot," she said, keeping her attention split between the instrumentation and the landscape below, "confirm course and speed."

Seathl leaned down between her seat, calling over the ship's hardline for Navigator Geng. When the navigator answered, the co-pilot relayed the response, even though Amonkar had already heard it herself over her helmet's speakers. Still, there were protocols to observe, and the co-pilot being the conduit for communication between pilot and navigator was one of them. Given the immediacy of fire-control, though, the pilot was able to address the bombardier and the two gunners directly whenever she liked.

"Bombardier Mehdi, are we set for the first run?"

"Ready and waiting, Pilot," came the voice over Amonkar's helmet-speakers. "We're ready to start the rain as soon as the target's in my bombsight."

"Good," Amonkar said. "Try to stay awake down there until we do, you hear me?"

"Amonkar," came the Persian's response, "I wouldn't miss this for the *world*."

They'd set off in the still dark hours of the morning from a hidden airfield east of Bao Shan, but it wasn't as if any of them had any sleep the night before, anyway, being too keyed up for the run. Still, Amonkar didn't envy the ground troops, who had been sent out *en masse* in ground transports the night before last, to hide in waiting under camouflage all the previous day, waiting for the order to strike. Thousands upon thousands of troops, Eight

Banners marines and Green Standard guardsmen, supported by heavy artillery, mechanized units, and a well-supplied rear guard, all waiting for the order to attack. And as soon as the bomber wing completed their first pass, softening up the Mexic line, that order would immediately follow.

The eastern extremity of the Mexic-held lands were a network of farms, ore processing facilities, habitats, and airfields, beginning a few dozen kilometers from the western rim of Bao Shan's base.

"Coming up on target," Navigator Geng reported over the hardline.

"We've got incoming!" shouted Nose Gunner Siagyo.

An instant later gray clouds erupted on all sides, and a sound like a light hail hammered into the plane's outer hull.

"They've spotted us," Amonkar said, tightening her grip on the stick. The plan had called for the Mexic anti-aircraft guns not to be employed until after they'd completed their first wave of bombings. But the Mexica appeared to be more alert and ready at this hour than the Middle Kingdom strategists had assumed, if the squadron was taking flak before it even overflew the target.

"Coming up," Geng repeated in clipped tones.

"Bombardier, prepare to drop," Amonkar said. The bomb-bay doors had been rolled up *en route* from the airfield, and the first of the heavy bombs lowered into position. Any moment now...

"First bomb is away!" Mehdi called out.

Amonkar felt like cheering. Instead, she said, "Don't stop now, bombardier, we've got a bellyful of the things."

"Bomb is away," came Mehdi's response.

An anti-aircraft burst erupted only a few dozen meters ahead of them, so that when *Fair Winds for Escort* flew through, the nose was pelted with shrapnel from the expanding sphere of the blast, their vision momentarily blurred by the gray smoke. Amonkar gritted her teeth, expecting the worst, but the reinforced glass of the viewports only pitted, and didn't crack and shatter.

"That first shot hit dead on target," called Tail Gunner Xiao from the rear. "Nice work, Mehdi."

"It is to the credit of the bomb-sight's artificers," the bombardier replied in all modesty. "All I do is pull the lever."

"Stow that, Bombardier," Amonkar called. "There's many in the corps who've got just as many fingers as you but couldn't pull that lever at the right time if their own lives depended on it."

Another shell burst just to starboard, and *Fair Winds for Escort* rocked to port with the shock-wave, even through the thin atmosphere.

"Now cut the chatter and concentrate on the job at hand," Amonkar added through gritted teeth. "We're far from done here, people."

▦

Hexagram 16
Contentment
Below Earth Above Thunder

Thunder bursts forth, and the Earth shakes. In the same way, the former kings made music in order to ennoble the virtuous and in its splendor offered it up to the Supreme Deity so that they might be deemed worthy of the deceased ancestors.

Carter Micah and the rest of his fire team had been given a seemingly simple task. They were quickly learning that, in combat, what seemed simple rarely was.

They'd deployed that morning with first light, packed tightly into their armored surface suits, and though the sun hadn't yet reached its zenith, it had already seemed like days. Having drilled for months on the troop carrier at an equivalent gravity to Fire Star's lesser pull, Carter and the others were well accustomed to the feeling of weighing less than a third of their Earth-normal weight, but what they were having trouble getting used to was the thin atmosphere. Even bound in the tight fabric of their surface suits, their muscles produced more force than was necessary to push their limbs through the thin air, and when gesturing all of them had been employing broad, overly exaggerated motions. And they'd been motioning a great deal, considering the difficulty in communicating verbally. The air surrounding them was too thin a medium for sound to travel effectively, so they'd have used their helmet radios if they could, but the interference being broadcast all over the lowlands by the Middle Kingdom planes overhead, intended to jam Mexic communications during the big push, had the side effect of impeding Middle Kingdom traffic as well. The only way to get a radio signal through was in close quarters on line of sight, and even then the signal to noise ratio was extremely low, their voices heavily peppered with static.

So when Corporal Eng had given the fire team their orders, just a short while ago, Carter had for a brief moment been sure he'd been talking to someone else.

"I want *you*," Eng had said, repeating himself and poking with a gloved finger at the hardshell carapace that covered Carter's chest, "to take *your* fire team, and take *that* building."

They were on the edge of a farming complex, domed greenhouses that stood twice as high as a man, linked by a network of low waist-high tubes. In the near distance, overlooking the complex, was an unpressurized storage structure, a sort of silo about twice as high as the surrounding domes, little more than a cylinder with a doorway at ground level and openings a few meters off the ground where oversized crawlers could load and unload supplies.

"Do you understand, guardsman?" Eng said with mounting annoyance, giving Carter's chest another poke.

"Yessir," Carter said, his voice squeaking. He nodded, the motion all but obscured by the heavy helmet encasing his head. Then, more loudly, he repeated, "Yessir!"

"Then do it!" the corporal said, and stalked off down the line to give another team their marching orders.

In their final briefings two days before, waiting in the hidden barracks on the other side of Bao Shan, they'd been told to expect the worst. They would be taking part in one side of a two-pronged attack into the Mexic strongholds to the west, starting with the settlements and farms on the eastern edge of the Mexic holdings.

So far, though, they'd encountered no resistance whatsoever.

It wouldn't last.

Theirs, at least, wasn't the first team to take fire. As they advanced through the maze of tunnels and domes to the silo, shouting voices crackled over their helmet radios.

"Contact! Incoming fire!"

Carter wasn't sure who was shouting, but his first thought was that it was one of his own. He spun around, looking behind to where Spitter, Moonface, and Ears followed. They all looked as startled and confused as he was.

"You guys alright?" he said over the helmet radio, getting only a burst of static in reply.

Instead, he pointed to them, and then stuck up a thumb, an affirmative gesture employed as a question. The others exchanged glances, and then gave exaggerated nods.

Whoever was taking fire was someone else, further up the line. Carter tightened his grip on his carbine, and then motioned the team forward, moving hunched to the ground, presenting as low a profile as possible.

They were a few meters behind one of the waist-high tunnels, with the silo only a dozen or so meters beyond, when the red dust at Carter's feet suddenly erupted into little clouds. It took him a split second to realize what was happening.

"Contact!" Carter shouted into his helmet mic, and then dove forward toward the tunnel, hoping against hope that the shots were coming from ahead. If the shooter—or shooters, he realized—were in front of them, the tunnel might provide some cover. If the shots were coming from the left or right, though, they'd still be out in the open.

The other three slammed into the red dirt on either side of him, as the ground behind them was raked by fire. In the low gravity the dust plumes sent up by the impact rose higher and drifted longer than they'd have done on Earth, obscuring their view in a haze of pink.

Through the thin air, they could scarcely hear the shots being fired, but given the angle of impact of the shots peppering the ground a few meters behind them, Carter knew that they had to be coming from the other side of the tunnel. And more than that, the shooter had to be firing from an elevated position. The most likely scenario put the shooter in the silo ahead of them, firing from one of the overhead loading bays.

There was either one shooter with a fair amount of ammunition, or more than one, Carter couldn't tell.

"What...we... to do...Tejas?" crackled Ears' voice over the radio. Something about their position, maybe their proximity to the tunnel, was worsening the effects of the interference. Maybe the materials used to construct the tunnel, whatever it was—whether ceramic or steel or something else, Carter couldn't say—was reflecting the jamming broadcast back at them from above. Either way, talking was going to be difficult.

Carter wasn't sure what to answer, even if he could. He could try angling his carbine's barrel up over the top of the tunnel, firing rounds blindly at the silo, but in that position it would be difficult to entrench against the weapon's recoil, and the first time he fired the kick would likely be sufficient to send him flying back at least a few meters, into the shooter's line of fire. And besides, firing single shots blindly wasn't likely to do much good. There was always the heavy automatic rifle that Spitter carried, which could spray belt-fed shots against the silo, but its recoil was even worse. As for the sniper rifle Ears carried or the recoilless grenade launcher over Moonface's shoulder, neither of them seemed more likely to do the team much good.

Carter was still considering their options when a body thudded onto the ground next to him, followed by a half-dozen more on the other side. At first glance Carter took them simply for other guardsmen, having moved laterally up the line, moving from the cover of one of the nearby domes. On closer inspection, though, Carter could see the character painted on the man's surface suit, indicating the rank of lieutenant. Then the helmet turned to face him, expression angry, and Carter recognized the leader of Second Platoon, Lieutenant Seong.

The lieutenant's mouth was moving, but all Carter got over the radio was static. With a look of annoyance, Seong balled both his hands into fists and touched them together, knuckle to knuckle. It took Carter a moment to remember the signal to bring their faceplates together.

He leaned forward, feeling uncomfortably like a boy going in to kiss a girl, and when the faceplate of his helmet came into contact with that of the lieutenant's, he could hear Seong's words buzzing through.

"Happy, are you, guardsman?" Seong's lip curled. "Content with your little spot of red dirt here?"

"Um, nosir," Carter answered, uncertainly.

"Then just what in the eighteen-hells are you doing? Weren't you ordered to take that structure?"

Carter nodded, for an instant pulling his faceplate away from Seong's. As he leaned back forward, he caught the tail-end of the lieutenant's next statement.

"...the rutting hell aren't you taking it, then?"

Carter shrugged, a simple-minded gesture he immediately regretted. "There are Mexica inside, sir," he said quickly. "We're taking fire."

The lieutenant opened his mouth to speak, then clearly thought better of it. He closed his mouth and sighed, all without breaking contact with Carter's helmet. "Okay, guardsman, here's what I want you to do. On my signal, you and your team start shooting at those loading bays, and don't stop until you hear from me. Got it?"

Carter nodded as the lieutenant broke off to turn back to his men. Then Carter turned to relay the orders to the others, one by one, faceplate to faceplate. Then all four guardsman waited for the lieutenant's signal, unsure what he was going to do next.

The lieutenant turned back to them, a grenade held in either hand. He leaned forward and tapped his helmet's faceplate against Carter's. "Now I'm going to show you how to take an enemy-held structure. Watch closely!"

Seong gestured to his men, and then flashed the signal to Carter's team. As the four guardsman lifted up onto their knees, bracing as best they could with their feet dug into the dirt and firing over the top of the tunnel at the silo, the lieutenant and the six men with him leapt to their feet and, without warning, vaulted over the top of the tunnel, beating their heels toward the silo.

Carter and the others kept up their fire as best they could from their awkward positions, splattering slugs against the outer wall of the silo, perhaps even sending a few in through the partially open loading bay doors, through which the shooters had undoubtedly been firing.

Seong's men fired at the building as they ran, with the fire team's shots whizzing over their heads. Seong didn't fire at all, with a live grenade in either hand, but ran right up to the partially open ground-level door of the silo, kicked it open, then threw both grenades inside, overhand. Then he and his six men flattened against the walls on either side.

White smoke puffed out through the doors, and the ground beneath Carter vibrated, as though shaken by distant thunder. He could feel the vibrations in his chest, like standing too near a loudspeaker playing bass-filled music.

While Carter's team watched, Seong and his men burst through the door and into the silo as soon as the grenades had blasted, the lieutenant with a drawn saber in one hand and a pistol in the other, his men following close behind.

Within a matter of moments it was all over, and Lieutenant Seong was striding casually back to where Carter's team was hunkered down. The lieutenant had holstered his pistol, but still held his saber's hilt in his fist.

Standing, the interference wasn't as bad, and words made it unscathed through the static.

"You were watching that, guardsman?" Seong asked, eyes narrowed. "You know now what to do?"

Carter glanced at the others. "Y-yessir."

Seong gave an abbreviated nod, then slammed his saber back into its sheath at his side. "Good," he said, his tone flat and even. "I won't be there to do it for you a second time."

HEXAGRAM 17
FOLLOWING
BELOW THUNDER ABOVE LAKE

Within the Lake, there is Thunder. In the same way, the noble man when faced with evenings goes in to rest and leisure.

Niohuru Tie shuffled his feet restlessly, staring at the featureless walls of the corridor, hands gripped on the stock of the semi-automatic slung over his shoulder. For the hundredth time he checked the safety, worrying over the possibility of an errant shot. Firing a weapon onboard the Zhurong moon-base, inadvertently or not, anywhere outside a designated firing range was grounds for disciplinary action, up to and including court martial, if not worse. Satisfied that the rifle wouldn't discharge if he were jostled, he let his hand slip to his side, feeling for the hilt of the saber that hung at his hip, as though it might have somehow vanished in the few moments since last he checked it.

Like all the bannermen gathered in the corridor, Niohuru was dressed in an armored surface suit, carrying all of his weapons and supplies with him. But for the faceplate visor lifted up, the cool breeze wafting against his bare cheeks, he could have been ready to step at any moment onto the surface of Fire Star. Except, of course, it wasn't time, and it seemed as if the appointed hour might never arrive. And so Niohuru, like all the others, waited for the accelerator car to arrive, and for his turn to board.

The accelerators, which spun down slowly to a relative stop, carried passengers to and from the orbital track of the habitat ring that coursed like a circular railroad through the living rock of Zhurong. Here, on the lowest and outermost level of the habitat ring, rotational forces generated simulated gravity; at the other end of the accelerator, out nearer the moon's surface, was the hangar bay, where dozens of orbital craft waited in microgravity.

Once they reached the hangar bay, they'd board one of the craft, and there they would wait again, this time for the craft to slip out through the twin locks that led to the vacuum beyond, then wait still more while they maneuvered into position over the drop zone.

Waiting. It seemed all that Niohuru had done for months, first for the troop carriers to reach Fire Star, then for the rest of the Ninth Brigade to assemble in Zhurong, then for the orders to move into position. Waiting, just like all those long, pointless nights back in Northern Capital, waiting for something exciting to happen.

The difference was, this time Niohuru was certain that excitement would, in short order, be the very last thing he would find lacking.

Even so, had it been up to him, Niohuru would already be out in the field of combat, along with the rest of the Bordered Yellow Banner's Ninth Brigade, who had gone down to the planet's surface almost two days before, to take part in the ground offensives of Operation Great Holdings. But the Third Battalion had been given other orders. Once the first waves of the ground-side invasion established beachheads on the lowlands west of Bao Shan, the Third was to parachute from low orbit behind enemy lines, and then attack the Mexic line from the rear.

Niohuru glanced around at the men surrounding him, all of them from the First Raider Company. Most of them were tall, Niohuru's height or even taller, their profiles made broader by the bulk of their armored surface suits. Besides Niohuru and a few other new additions, the rest of the company were battle-hardened veterans, even those who had only been in theater for a matter of mere months before Niohuru arrived. From the stories that Niohuru had heard, back on Earth or in transit aboard the troop carrier, a reinforcement trooper such as himself had better odds of dying within his first week of combat than he did of surviving the first month, and if he survived to the end of two months, his chances for long-term survival improved astronomically.

In the last two days, in training drills and mission briefings, Niohuru had seen other members of the Third Battalion, and to a man they had been precisely the kind of soldiers whom he had dreamt of serving alongside. Proud in bearing, the heirs of a long-tradition of martial service to the emperor, dating back to the first days of the Clear Dynasty and beyond. True bannermen, the kind featured in dramas and victory songs.

Not so the men of the First Raider Company who surrounded him now. And much less so their commander, Captain Hughes Falco.

En route from Earth, Niohuru had heard accounts of victories won by the First Raider Company from other bannermen returning to active duty. The First Raiders, or the "Falcon's Claws" as they were called—Falcon being the meaning of their commander's given name in the Briton tongue—had in the two years since their founding covered themselves in more glory than entire brigades had done combined. The Falcon's Claws were invariably given the toughest assignments, the missions with the longest odds on success. That they survived at all with such relatively low casualties was itself cause for comment, but that they achieved their objectives with such a high rate of success was remarkable.

Niohuru had arrived on Zhurong, eager to meet his new commanding officer, and see just what sort of man he was.

Niohuru had seen, and he still wasn't sure just what he thought of it. He wasn't pleased, though, that much was certain. He just didn't think there was much to be done about it.

As if in response to his unspoken thoughts, Niohuru could hear the voice of Captain Hughes coming down the line, addressing each of the men in the company by name.

Niohuru's childhood tutor, the Nipponese bannerman, Etsuko, had always talked about the noble traditions of the Eight Banners, and had instilled in young Niohuru above all a deep and abiding respect for the value of protocol and etiquette, and the proper observance of both.

Hughes, Niohuru had learned shortly after their first meeting, clearly put no stock in any of that. Niohuru had been alarmed to discover that Hughes had abolished the traditional officers' privileges, requiring that platoon leaders under his command should dress and act no differently than the men under them, wearing the same uniforms, carrying the same equipment, sleeping in as much or as little comfort, as the circumstances demanded. Hughes had further insisted that all of the men address each other in familiar terms, just as he addressed them, and expected them to address him in return.

From a few meters away, Niohuru could hear the captain's conversation with another of the men. Hughes was walking among them, stopping to chat with this one here, that one there, soothing nerves and giving words of encouragement about the impending operation. He seemed more like one of the men, good natured and smiling, than a battle-tested leader of multiple commendations.

Niohuru looked away, checking the safety on his semi-automatic, feeling for the hilt of his saber.

"Tie," came the captain's voice, approaching. "Are you ready enough for your first drop into live fire?"

Niohuru turned, snapping off a salute.

"At ease, Bannerman," Hughes said with an easy smile. "We're all friends here."

"Yes, sir," Niohuru answered. He tried to keep his face expressionless, but was unable to keep from his voice all trace of his mounting disappointment at the unconventional nature of his new commanding officer.

Hughes arched an eyebrow. "Sounds like you disapprove of something, there, Tie." He paused, and scratched his neck, thoughtfully. "Mind giving those thoughts voice?"

Niohuru pressed his lips into a line, still standing at attention. "No, sir."

Hughes glanced around at the other men, still smiling. "Come now, Tie. You've something to say, you ought to say it."

Niohuru's mind raced, wondering how much if anything he should say. "Permission to speak with candor, captain?"

Hughes grinned, glancing at the other bannermen nearby, some of whom began to chuckle. "You're new to the unit, Tie, so let me explain. Unless you get orders *not* to speak with candor, which may happen from time to time, you're free to assume that permission is already granted."

Niohuru nodded. "Well, captain…"

Hughes raised a finger. "'Falco'," he corrected.

Niohuru cringed, but gave a slight nod. "*Falco*," he went on. "I simply… that is…" He paused, taking a deep breath. "Well, I just don't know that I'm entirely comfortable…"

"Yes?" Hughes made a pulling motion, coaxing him on.

"That I'm comfortable with your organizational structure," Niohuru finished, lamely. It was true, so far as it went, but the least of his objections. Hughes, Niohuru had learned shortly after joining the unit, had discarded the traditional organizational table of the Eight Banners. "It seems that you want to treat the Eight Banners like the Green Standard, if you'll excuse me saying so, and I think that's wrong."

Hughes gave a little shrug. "You're entitled to an opinion, one supposes, and I *did* say you were free to speak with candor. Now, please permit me to speak with equal candor." He stepped nearer, and brought his face close to Niohuru's. "I think your opinion in this instance is worth less than ox dung, Tie."

Niohuru pulled his head back, fractionally, but managed to keep from stepping away.

"Why shouldn't we take the lessons of whomever will teach us, eh?" Hughes went on. "I put to you that the Green Standard's unit structure of small fire teams makes more sense on Fire Star than the old Eight Banners' squads. And if the small units make more sense, the Eight Banners would be fool-hardy not to adopt them."

In the old days, the smallest organizational unit in the Eight Banners was a company, with five hundred companies to a banner. That changed in the days of the Tongzhi Emperor, who restruc-tured the companies into platoons, and the platoons into squads, the smallest functional unit of the time.

Now, though, Hughes was breaking each squad into smaller units, which he called combat cells. Every cell was composed of three bannermen, armed with semi-automatic rifles and equipped with a specialty in one of three areas-demolition, sabotage, and field medicine. The First Raider Company had three rifle platoons made up of such combat cells, and a heavy weapons platoon armed with light mortars and machine guns.

"Look, Tie, I know that you're fresh from ban-nerman training, and your head is full of tradition and protocols and etiquette." Hughes frowned with distaste. "But that red rock down there doesn't care about your protocols and your manners, and it doesn't give a damn about your traditions. We can't fight effectively on Fire Star with tactics and struc-tures last updated during the First Mexic War. We're not fighting *that* war anymore, we're fighting *this* one."

The captain straightened and, even though he was only a centimeter or two taller than Niohuru, in that instant Hughes seemed to tower over him.

"You're going to have to relearn the gentle art of combat, my friend. There aren't any support teams in the First Raider Company, no rearguard and no base. My raiders don't use any weapon that can't be carried by a single man, and carry with them everything they'll need on the march. We're organized for long, swift patrols, and can stay weeks at a time in country."

Niohuru had asked about that two days before, when first he'd heard about Hughes's unorthodox tactics and strategies from the other members of the unit. Typically the raiders carried three days' worth of oxygen, water, and food, and were resupplied by aerial drops every three days from overflying planes.

"Like it or not, Tie, you're one of the Falcon's Claws now, and there's no retreat to safety in the rearguard when we get battered or tired. You'd best stop fretting about the way tradition says fighting *ought* to be done, and start thinking about *fighting*, instead."

To Niohuru's surprise, Hughes reached out and laid a comradely hand on his shoulder before moving on.

"You just worry about keeping yourself alive and following orders, Tie," the captain said with a wistful smile, "and let me worry about the wages of bucking protocol."

With that, the captain moved on, addressing the next man in line by name, a smile on his face.

Niohuru still had his concerns, of course, entirely unconvinced, but knew better than to pursue them now. If nothing else, he had wondered what happened if the raiders *missed* one of their drop points when their supplies of air and water ran out, or if the planes for whatever reason didn't make it. But he'd left the question unvoiced, not sure he wanted to hear the answer.

Hexagram 18
Ills to be Cured
Below Wind Above Mountain

Below the Mountain, there is Wind. In the same way, the noble man stirs the common folk and nourishes their virtue.

It was morning on the second day of Operation Great Holdings, and the forces of the Middle Kingdom had made observable progress. The Eleventh Armored Infantry Battalion had advanced slowly through the maze-like network of agricultural domes and tunnels, and had reached the far side, where a long-disused airfield stood. The long shadow of Bao Shan draped the whole area in darkness, while to the north and south the morning sun pinked the red sands. Even in the gloom Guardsman Carter could see the burnt hulks of cloud-flyers scattered here and there around the pitted airfield, casualties of earlier encounters between the Middle Kingdom and the Mexic Dominion.

At the far side of the airfield stood a tall, slender control tower, ringed at its summit by reinforced windows, and beyond that a line of low-lying structures, though whether storage, habitat, or support structures, Carter couldn't say.

The job of First-Second was to sweep the airfield and perform a visual inspection of each of the structures, to ensure that no Mexica remained in them. The squad was only halfway across the airfield, still in the chill shadow of the looming mountain to the east, when the rain began.

Mortars began to shatter into the tarmac all around them, followed by even heavier shells. Before Carter even knew what was happening, the guardsman next to him evaporated into a cloud of red mist when a mortar shell caught him square in the chest, the mist immediately freezing into a rain of tiny rubies when it hit the cold, thin air surrounding them.

"Take cover!" shouted Corporal Eng, diving behind the nearest of the wrecked aircraft, his words all but indecipherable through the heavy interference.

Carter broke left, taking cover behind another of the husks. As soon as he crouched behind it, a shell slammed into the wreckage from the other side, rocking it back and forth as if it were buffeted by a high wind.

Disjointed syllables burst through the static, as the corporal shouted orders to the rest of First-Second, but Carter couldn't make out their meaning.

There were a few other men crouched behind the wreckage with Carter, though he couldn't see their faces through their helmets, and wasn't sure who they were. He still had his carbine at the ready, its stock against his shoulder, the barrel pointed at the ground. Another shell hit the wreckage, even harder this time, another buffet of strong wind.

Carter chanced a quick look around the wreckage, seeing if he could spot where the artillery was coming from. Through the muffling effect of his helmet and the thin air, he could faintly sense the crumping sounds of heavy guns from somewhere ahead of them, and reasoned that they must be firing from emplacements on the far side of the structures. But how were they hitting the First-Second with such accuracy?

A glint caught his eye, to the right and overhead. It was sunlight glancing off the reinforced windows atop the control tower, as the mountain's shadow slipped slowly toward the east.

Carter thought he saw movement behind the windows, but couldn't be sure.

He wished Ears was with him, sniper-rifle in hand, but the Arabian was pinned down on the far side of the airfield with Corporal Eng.

Raising his rifle, bracing himself against a pitted hole in the tarmac, Carter sighted for the windows high overhead. He took a breath, let it out halfway, and then squeezed the trigger.

He fancied he could see a flash as the shot spanged off the window, but even if the shot impacted, it didn't leave any mark. Thirty seconds later an even heavier shell rocked the wreckage behind which he crouched, threatening to topple it over on him.

Carter was sure he had it. There was a Mexic observer up in the control tower, spotting for the artillery beyond the structures.

Still crouched down, he tried to call for the corporal, for Ears, even for the other guardsman at his side, but it was no good. The jamming interference was simply too great. He supposed the spotter must have a hardline of some kind running down through the tower and out the back, perhaps even the remnants of the original communication system built by the Middle Kingdom designers. Either way, Carter couldn't get a word through, but the inerrant shots of the artillery suggested strongly that the spotter could.

A mortar shell arced high overhead, plunging almost straight down onto the head of the guardsman crouching beside him. Carter was thrown to one side, bits of quickly freezing viscera draping over his shoulder. He scrambled back behind the cover of the wreckage, wondering absently if the dead man had been a friend.

Surprisingly, Carter felt no fear, not anymore. Nor did he fret about whether he'd have to kill, as he'd done from time to time since first enlisting with the Green Standard back in Tejas. Did a surgeon worry himself about cutting out diseased tissue to save a dying patient? Then why should he feel any remorse about taking out the Mexica who infected this red world like a cancer? If he'd have been able to put a bullet through the reinforced window and into the brainpan of the Mexica calling in these strikes, he'd have done so in an instant.

He tried calling the corporal again, with no luck, then squeezed off another half-dozen rounds at the windows atop the control tower, without effect. Whatever it was, some transparent alloy or ceramic or whatnot, it was too durable for his carbine to penetrate.

Carter was about to chance running into the open to rejoin the corporal and tell him about the spotter in the tower when the crawler-tank crunched up behind him.

Moving on massive treads, the segmented body of the crawler-tank was surmounted by a mobile turret, from which extended the bore of a heavy-caliber cannon. The crawler was one of several such mechanized units attached to the Eleventh Armored Infantry, and had been following behind the First-Second all morning, bringing up the rear. On seeing the squad taking the heavy shelling, apparently the crawler-commander had ordered the vehicle to advance, evidently hoping to help take out the artillery emplacement.

Which struck Carter as a fine idea. The problem was, the cannon was pointed in the wrong direction. As the treads crunched up and onto the airfield, cracking the already pitted tarmac, it fired off a round at one of the structures on the far side, the shot blowing a hole in a building already riddled, injuries of previous hostilities. For a single moment, Carter almost allowed himself a sigh of relief, seeing the flashing bore of the cannon, feeling the faint wind of the shot as it passed.

Then a heavy shell slammed into the tarmac only a few meters from the crawler.

The artillery was zeroing in on the crawler-tank, but the crew had no idea about the spotter. So far as Carter knew, *nobody* but him had any idea.

It was time someone else knew.

"Ahoy the crawler!" he shouted into his helmet mic. "Ahoy the crawler!" He waved his arms. "Up in the tower!" He pointed. "A Mexic spotter!"

He was shouting himself hoarse for all the good it did. The crawler's crew couldn't hear him any more than the corporal and the others, the airwaves bathed in static.

"Goddamn," Carter cursed, and sprang to his feet. Keeping as low as possible, he sprinted out toward the crawler, getting beside it, as close to the grinding treads as he dared.

"Hey, in there!" he shouted, pointlessly. Then he banged on the hull with the butt of his carbine's stock. "Hey! I'm talking to you!"

Still nothing but static bled from his helmet radio.

The crawler continued to creep forward, centimeter by centimeter. Another flash and a sound like distant thunder, and another shot ripped from the cannon's bore, slamming into another already badly-shelled building.

"Aw, hell," Carter swore in English. He straightened up, swinging the carbine over his shoulder, and sprinted around to the front of the crawler. He got in the line-of-sight of the forward viewports, and started waving his arms. "Up there!" he said, pointlessly, but exaggerating his lip movements as much as possible. He gestured to the control tower with frantic motions, then mimed holding a remote-viewing mirror before his eyes. "Spotter!" he mouthed the word in Official Speech with broad lip movements, like he was speaking to a deaf man.

The crawler continued to creep forward, centimeter by centimeter. Carter waved his arms frantically, trying not to care that the massive vehicle looked about to run him down.

Then, just as it seemed that there was no hope, Carter taking one last reluctant step backward and waving his arms in front of the viewport, a hatch on top of the crawler swung open, and a man in an armored surface suit stuck his head up. He was shouting something, moving his lips in as exaggerated a manner as Carter had done, but Carter still couldn't quite work out what was being said.

"What?" Carter shook his head

The crawler-crewman repeated himself one last time with mounting annoyance.

"Get. Out. Of. The. Way!!"

"Oh," Carter said, but too late. In the next instant, the turret atop the crawler swiveled to the right, the cannon's bore swung upward a few degrees, and another shot blasted out of the bore, whistling right over Carter's left shoulder.

The shot hit the control tower halfway up, taking a huge chunk of masonry with it.

Carter didn't have time to enjoy the sight, diving to his right, just beyond the oncoming path of the crawler.

The cannon swung up another few degrees, and another flash bloomed at the bore's tip as a new shot slammed into the tower, this time only a handful of meters below the windows. Still more masonry flew off in all directions, and the tower began to sway.

The crewman, still sticking up out of the hatch, turned a smile to Carter, giving a thumbs-up. Then he mouthed, "Thanks!"

One final shot was all it took, reducing the top of the tower to dust and raining debris.

The artillery shots continued to fall, after a brief interval, but they were nowhere near as accurate, landing nowhere near the crawler or any of the guardsmen.

Of course, it was in *that* moment that the interference abated, if only slightly.

"Move out!" came the voice of Corporal Eng over the radio. "Let's get those blood-hungry bastards!"

No longer pinned by the rain of shells, the men of First-Second raced forward over the tarmac, pouncing for the structures beyond. Carter took a moment to get back onto his feet, and once he'd regained his balance and got his carbine unslung and ready, he was pounding right after them.

HEXAGRAM 19
OVERSEEING
BELOW LAKE ABOVE EARTH

Above the Lake, there is Earth. In the same way, the noble man is both inexhaustible in his powers to edify others and feel concern for them and limitless in his practice of magnanimity and protection towards the common folk.

Nothing had gone right that morning. Thanks to the pilot's foul-up, coming in too high, too fast, when the sun had risen over the Tamkung Plain, blazing dimly around the bulk of Bao Shan in the east, Niohuru had found himself in the wrong place entirely.

The mission plan had called for the orbital craft to launch from Zhurong moonbase and skim the atmosphere. When they were just a few dozen kilometers over the planet's surface, the hatches were to open and the men of the First Raider Company were to dive out into the black night air.

In jump training back on Earth, Niohuru had never imagined that he'd be coming in this high, this fast. The high-altitude-low-opening jumps they'd made in bannermen training had typically been made from craft flying some ten thousand meters above the Earth's surface. Now, they were starting from a point several times that high.

Fire Star had a thin atmosphere that consisted mostly of carbon dioxide, at a pressure about one percent that of Earth's. With its lower gravity, though, the red planet had an atmospheric scale height almost twice that of Earth's.

The ground was alarmingly close before the mission plan allowed them to open their chutes, giant sails measuring some fifteen by thirty meters, all but invisible against the night sky. As large as they were though, they could only slow the jumpers' descent so far, and when Niohuru finally hit the ground, he was traveling at a rate of roughly six meters per second, and if he'd not rolled with the impact as he'd been trained to do, he would have broken both of his legs, armored and insulated surface suit or no.

Niohuru didn't know then that the pilot had fouled things up. All he knew was that nothing, and no one, was where it was supposed to be.

The First Raider Company's orders were to come down a few kilometers behind enemy lines and attack the Mexic defenses from the rear. The plans for the ground invasion called for a two-pronged attack from the east, one to the north and one to the south, dozens of kilometers apart. When the orbital craft had left Zhurong, word was that the offensive was proceeding on an acceptable timetable, establishing twin beachheads that had already begun to push together, the northern line pressing south, the southern pressing north.

If the First Raider Company were successful in securing the area in between, as they'd been ordered to do, then the two offensive lines would be joined in a single combined beachhead.

The problem was, First Raider Company wasn't anywhere near where it was meant to be.

Niohuru had studied the surveillance photos of the terrain, memorizing the landscape of the drop zone. They were to have inserted on the western edge of a domed settlement at one hundred-forty seven degrees west longitude. Instead, he found himself east of a terraforming complex. As he freed himself of his harness, collapsing his parachute, he studied the surrounding landscape. He was atop a wide, rectangular structure a hundred meters on a side, that rose a meter or two off the red sands. Only after a moment did he recognize it as the cap of an enormous underground water reservoir, a veritable lake hidden beneath his feet.

And instead of being surrounded by other bannermen of the so-called Falcon's Claws, more than two hundred-fifty of them altogether, Niohuru found himself all alone. Even if he *wasn't* under orders to maintain radio silence, the jamming interference pouring down from the Middle Kingdom planes in flight would have prevented him from contacting anyone. For the moment, he was on his own. Ditching the parachute and harness, hiding it as best he could in the shadow of the reservoir, Niohuru headed east, looking for the rest of his unit.

The sun had just begun to burn around the edges of Bao Shan in the east when Niohuru caught sight of another bannerman, a few hundred meters away to the north. Crouching low, his semi-automatic loaded and ready in his hand, he hustled over, hoping that he didn't encounter any Mexica.

Niohuru only narrowly avoided getting shot as he came upon the other bannerman, but just before squeezing off a round the other had recognized that the figure racing toward him wasn't a Jaguar Knight looking to rack up a capture or kill, but one of his brothers-in-arms. The bannerman was a Han whom Niohuru had seen on Zhurong, but whose name he didn't know.

As Niohuru drew near, the Han bannerman slung his own semi-automatic over his shoulder, and then touched his fists together, knuckle-to-knuckle. Niohuru slid to a stop before him, and then the two leaned in together, touching faceplates.

"What's your name, private?"

"Niohuru."

"Cong," the other bannerman answered. "This is one rutting dream of a drop, isn't it?"

"What happened?"

The other bannerman had been on enough high-altitude insertions to have worked out for himself what had gone wrong, and explained how the pilot had dropped them at the wrong altitude and speed. Rather than coming down in close proximity, the men of the First Raider Company had been spread across several kilometers, maybe more, overshooting the target drop zone.

"What do we do?" Niohuru asked, trying to project a confidence he didn't feel.

A smile split the Han's face, his eyes flicking over Niohuru's shoulder. "We do what *he* tells us." The bannerman pulled away, and pointed past Niohuru, where a quartet of bannermen approached. Even at this distance Niohuru could recognize the bannerman in the lead as Captain Hughes Falco.

In short order, Hughes had gathered another three bannermen, bringing their total number to nine. They found a depression in the ground, a low gully or the weathered remains of some ancient erosion, and using hand signals Hughes instructed them all to activate their radios, set to the lowest broadcast strength.

"Look, men, this is a royal rutting mess, but we've still got a job to do." Broadcasting at the lowest power, obscured by the ridge of red stone around them, Hughes was gambling that the Mexic wouldn't pick up their transmissions, but given the circumstances he had deemed it necessary to break radio silence to formulate a new plan. "It's like this. If I'm reading the terrain right, one of the forward lines of the Middle Kingdom forces is a few kilometers *that* way"—he pointed to the northeast—"and the other line is right over *there*"—he pointed to the southeast. "We're a few kilometers too far west and south, but we're still in the general vicinity of the line of defense the Mexica have supposedly set up in the middle. So here's what we're going to do."

The plan was distressingly simple. Keeping close, they were going to head northeast, nearer their original destination, and accomplish as many of the mission objectives as possible. Hughes divided them up into combat cells of three men each, with Hughes taking command of one, the Han bannerman with another, and a Nipponese bannerman with the third. Niohuru was assigned to Hughes's cell.

They headed out, keeping as low to the ground as possible, moving as quickly as they were able, both of which attempts were complicated by the low gravity, which meant that running was almost impossible, their steps instead sending them in loping bounds. Still, it was nearly an hour after they started out that they first encountered the enemy.

Ahead of them to the left, facing east, was a battery emplacement in a trench. Two lines of supply pipes coming from the east converged at the trench, so that the battery sat at the point of a V-shape run. A hundred or more meters east of the emplacement was a rocky ridge that rose little more than a meter above the red sands.

Hughes flashed hand signals, too fast for Niohuru to follow, and the men moved into action without question or complaint. It was only after they began to shift into position that Niohuru worked out just what the orders had been.

One of the combat cells crawled forward on their bellies, to the east of the rocky ridge, making their way all the way across the battery emplacement's field of fire to the supply pipe that marked the northern boundary of the killing field. The other cell crept in from the south, taking up a position hidden by the southern supply pipe, coming as near to the battery emplacement as they dared. Finally, the third cell under Hughes's command followed the first in crawling north along the eastern side of the rocky ridge, but instead of continuing on, stopped halfway, opposite the battery emplacement itself.

A small angled mirror, periscope-like, gave Hughes a more or less unobstructed view of the emplacement without revealing his position. Niohuru pulled his own mirror from a pouch on his thigh, fitted the rods into place, and rolling over onto his back, held the mirror's edge just over the rise of the ridge. It took a bit of adjustment, seeing the tiny image inverted and then working out what he was seeing, but after a moment Niohuru adapted.

The combat cell on the left, at the southern side of the field, had crept nearly up to the first gun in the battery. And then, as if in response to some unspoken signal, the three of them hurled grenades into the trench.

The explosions were all but inaudible, and if not for the smoke billowing up from the trench Niohuru might not have known they'd happened. The combat cell on the right was clearly aware, because as soon as the grenades had detonated, the three men of that cell rose up from hiding and started firing down into the trench with their weapons, laying down flanking fire.

As Niohuru watched, a few of the Mexic warriors within the trench came into view, racing first one way and then the other, trying to deal with the grenades falling from one direction and the flanking fire pelting down on them from the other.

Then Hughes tapped Niohuru's shoulder, impatiently flashing more hand signals Niohuru appeared to have missed the first time around. Then the captain was on his feet and up and over the rise, pounding toward the battery emplacement with his semi-automatic firing in one hand and his saber in the other, charging ahead in a frontal assault. With the other two cells still laying into the trenches, Niohuru saw the whole operation as a smoothly-running machine, every component knowing their place, overseen by the tactical mind of the captain himself. And despite himself, Niohuru had to admit that, however unconventional the captain's strategies and behaviors, if this was anything to go on, Hughes's approach appeared to get results.

Niohuru jumped up and over the rise, only a few steps behind the third member of the cell, firing his own semi-automatic again and again, his war cry echoing around inside his helmet, unheard by anyone but himself.

HEXAGRAM 20
VIEWING
BELOW EARTH ABOVE WIND

The Wind moves above the Earth. In the same way, the former kings made tours of inspection everywhere and established their teachings in conformity with their viewing of the people.

It was late afternoon on the second day of Operation Great Holdings, and *Fair Winds for Escort* was limping back to base after another bombing sortie. The other bombers in the squadron had already headed back, as per orders, but Amonkar and her crew carried the additional burden of doing an aerial inspection for the high command, and so were returning to the east by a more roundabout route, escorted by a pair of Dragonfly rotary-winged fighters.

"Everybody alright back there?" Amonkar called over the hardline, keeping the plane at a steady trim.

"Are you sure these flight suits are insulated properly?" Nose Gunner Siagyo replied, peevishly. "Because my rutting nipples are freezing off!"

"Don't worry, my darling," Bombardier Mehdi answered, "I shall warm them for you when we return to base."

"What about me?" Navigator Geng asked in mock distress.

"You can *both* lick me warm if that's what it takes," Siagyo answered, her tone suggesting she was only half-joking.

Amonkar couldn't help but smile. She knew that back home in Bhopal, as little as a year before, such loose talk between men and women would have made her blush and avert her eyes, shocking and importunate. But now?

"Listen," Co-pilot Seathl said, "if you monkeys help get this crate safely back on the ground, and keep us from getting shot at another rutting time, I'll service *all* of you."

Amonkar glanced over at her Athabascan co-pilot, who came from one of the northern districts of Khalifa. Not a Muslim herself, Seathl had still been raised in a culture which prized much about Muslim belief, albeit in a far looser and more liberal interpretation than that practiced half a world away in Arabia. To hear Seathl curse and swear and speak so openly about things that, only a generation or two before, her grandmothers would have cringed to discuss with their own husbands, suggested to Amonkar that something strange and unexpected was happening.

Perhaps even strangest of all, it was clearly happening to Amonkar herself, as well.

But there would be time to consider the sociological implications of women serving in the Air Corps at some later time. For the moment, they had far more pressing concerns.

"Stow it, all of you," Amonkar said, reluctantly putting an end to the banter. "We need to tighten up and keep on the alert, as we're not back home yet. When we're wheels down and back in the warmth and pressure, I'll joke along with the rest of you, but until we do I want eyes, hands, and minds on the job. Understood?"

"Yes, pilot," came the ragged chorus over the hardline.

"Co-pilot, confirm course and speed," Amonkar said. "I don't want us to fly over a single square centimeter of Mexic territory more than the flight plan demands."

Seathl bent down to confer with Navigator Geng below her, while Amonkar continued her visual inspection of the landscape below them.

It would be for the tacticians, generals, and strategists to determine the successes and failures of Operation Great Holdings. Or perhaps it would even fall to historians to decide when all involved were dead and buried. But from the cockpit of *Fair Winds for Escort*, it certainly looked to Amonkar as if the forces of the Middle Kingdom had made measurable advancement. In two days they'd already managed to push incursions dozens of kilometers into formerly Mexic-held territories to the east, recapturing farms, plants, and settlements. Of course, those structures not already damaged by previous hostilities in months and years past were badly shelled and abused during the course of the current offensive, so the gains were more symbolic than anything else. But they still represented the first time since the previous year that the Middle Kingdom had managed to retake territories once the Mexica had been allowed to become deeply entrenched in them. Small steps, to be sure, but measurable.

Of course, if these were the first small steps, then the road that lay ahead was a long march indeed. Even flying as far west as she'd done in several bombing runs, Amonkar hadn't got nearly so far that she could even glimpse the crater strongholds of the Mexica to the west, out on the other side of the Tamkung Plain. And if she could not see them yet, flying as high and as fast as she was, then how long would it take for the troops on the ground to advance far enough that *they* could see the strongholds for themselves? Only then would the attempt to recapture those craters begin, and at what cost in time, armament, and lives?

Amonkar couldn't worry about that now. She would leave such questions for generals and admirals to wrestle. For her, all that mattered was her crew, and getting them home safely after completing their mission.

Of course, what her crew did or didn't do to or with one another when they arrived was *their* concern...

HEXAGRAM 21
BITE TOGETHER
BELOW THUNDER ABOVE FIRE

Thunder and Lightning. In the same way, the former kings clarified punishments and adjusted laws.

By sunset of the second day of Operation Great Holdings, the principal operational objectives had been largely accomplished. The Mexica had been pushed back from the western slopes of Bao Shan, driven from the loose network of terraforming facilities, agricultural domes, airfields, and residence compounds that they had held for longer than the Middle Kingdom cared to remember. As the Mexic had used these sites as a staging ground for attacks on Middle Kingdom settlements to the east of Bao Shan, the strategic importance of their recapture was all but incalculable.

The three arms of the Middle Kingdom military—the Air Corps, the Green Standard, the Eight Banners—had worked together like teeth on the same jaw, biting deep into the Mexic flank. In the process, however, the forces of the Middle Kingdom had sustained heavy casualties, particularly on the part of the ground forces of the Green Standard and the Eight Banners. The early indications were that the losses sustained by the Mexic forces were equally as heavy, but for those who had lost their brothers and sisters in arms, that came as cold comfort at best.

Still, the Mexica were far from defeated. Operation Great Holdings was a victory, but it was only one battle, not the war. Even as the Middle Kingdom forces solidified their forward line on the western slope of Bao Shan, shelling continued from the west, flashing on the horizon like brief glimpses of sunlight, the ground underfoot shaking with the vibrations of distant impact, feeling like far-off thunder. To the west, tracer fire lit up the sky, brief fast-moving constellations against the cold Fire Star night. The Mexica, having fallen back to the edge of Tamkung Plain, had re-entrenched, and every centimeter the Middle Kingdom would push west from this point on would be won at a high cost.

For the moment, though, the orders were to reinforce and hold the line, which meant that the newly-recaptured areas would have to be secured. Beginning on that second day and continuing into the third, guardsmen and bannermen had swept through the compounds and structures abandoned by the Mexica, ensuring that no enemy remained behind, nor had they left any explosive devices or booby traps in their wake. Once their commanders were satisfied that the area had been secured, technicians and artificers were sent in to get the structures habitable once more. Under the watchful eye of their guardsmen escorts, they set to work repairing any damage incurred in the recent fighting or in earlier engagements, repressurizing the interiors of habitats and hangars, bringing heating and ventilation systems back online.

The work took several more days, during which time most of the Middle Kingdom forces slept in temporary shelters, when they slept at all. But finally enough of the structures were certified as safe and secure, and were designated as temporary barracks, mess facilities, surgical units, and so forth. The aircraft of the Interplanetary Fleet Air Corps were set up in makeshift hangars, ground crews set to work on repairing and refueling them as needed, while from the rearguard sections east of Bao Shan new men and materiel were brought up to reinforce the new forward line.

Every man and woman of the Middle Kingdom forces knew that, sooner or later, the orders would come down from on high to press further to the west, to drive still deeper into Mexic-held territory. For the moment, though, the soldiers and airmen of the Dragon Throne were to be given some brief respite. For many, this was the first time they had removed their cumbersome surface suits for more than a few moments in days, and the first time they had luxuriated in fully heated air, in even longer.

Hexagram 22
Elegance
Below Fire Above Mountain

Below the Mountain, there is Fire. In the same way, the noble man clearly understands all the different aspects of governance and so dares not reduce it to a matter of passing criminal judgment.

As Niohuru finished his ablutions in the makeshift bathing facilities, he tried not to breathe too deeply the odor of the chemical toilets in the adjoining latrine almost overpowering. He pitied the bannerman who had been unlucky enough to get the nearest pallet, the last picked of the bunch.

The First Raider Company had been billeted in a hastily patched-up greenhouse facility, and with more than two hundred-fifty men in the Falcon's Claws to be housed, the available accommodations were strained to their limits.

After toweling off, and pulling on his fatigues and shoes, Niohuru headed back to the greenhouse's far end. While the rest of the Falcon's Claws had been helping themselves to a second serving of fish stew and rice, Niohuru had hurried to the greenhouse to select a pallet for himself, one a comfortable distance from the chemical-smell of the latrines. If the others were too busy sating their appetites, and ended up too near the funk, that was their lookout.

As he made his way through the haphazard arrangement of pallets, each occupied by a bannerman, most crowded with piles of gear, soiled clothing, and armor, Niohuru tried to remember how efficient a machine the First Raider Company was in combat.

He'd fought along with them for the first time only days before, and had seen just how elegant the Falcon's Claws could be when engaging the enemy, not a step out of place, not a movement wasted. Combat for them was almost a dance, each bannerman knowing his place and his movements, all directed by the hand of Captain Hughes.

How jarring, then, to see them sprawling unwashed, unshaven, their uniforms shabby and their personal effects in such disarray. Most of the men in the First Raider Company had been fighting on Fire Star for years, some for nearly the whole of the Second Mexic War, and it seemed at times as if they had forgotten everything that they had ever learned about protocols and etiquette back at Hangzhou Garrison.

Still, he couldn't help noticing the loving care with which some of them were cleaning their semi-automatic rifles, or honing the blades of their sabers with whetstone and oil. They might have poor grooming and even poorer personal habits, but it couldn't be said that the Falcon's Claws didn't have impeccable weapons discipline.

When Niohuru reached the far end of the green-house, he thought for a moment that he'd got turned around. Then he saw his armor and gear shoved off to one side against the nearest wall, a considerable distance from the spot where he'd left it carefully arranged beside his pallet—the pallet now occupied by an enormously tall, well-muscled Ethiop, who stretched out at full length with eyes lidded and head pillowed on his hands.

"Excuse me," Niohuru said, his shadow falling over the Ethiop's face. "I believe that you are on my pallet."

After a moment's pause, the Ethiop opened one eye, remaining otherwise immobile. "Are you speaking to me?"

Niohuru nodded, and pointed at the pallet before him. "That's my pallet."

The Ethiop smiled slowly. "I did not see your name upon it." His grin widened. "My mistake."

Niohuru looked around, searching for corroboration. On the other side of the Ethiop was a pallet upon which sat Cong Ren, the bannerman whom Niohuru had first met following the disastrous parachute drop on the second day of Operation Great Holdings.

"Cong," Niohuru called over to him, "you saw that this pallet was mine when you arrived."

Cong, running a whetstone along the edge of his saber, didn't look up. "This is between the two of you, leave me out of it."

Niohuru made a dismissive noise, and looked back down at the Ethiop. "Well?"

The Ethiop's smile began to fade. "Well, what?"

"Are you relinquishing my pallet or aren't you?"

With a sigh, the Ethiop lifted up on one elbow, and craned his neck to look back the way Niohuru had come. "I think there is a free pallet over by the latrine."

Cong snickered, his eyes still on his saber.

Niohuru's hands balled into fists at his sides. He could well imagine the giant bannerman remaining behind for second or even third helpings of fish stew and rice, and when arriving to find all but the most undesirable of pallets taken, simply claiming Niohuru's as his own while Niohuru was grooming himself. This was *far* from the kind of etiquette Niohuru had come to expect from the Eight Banners, and exemplary weapons discipline or elegance in combat be damned.

"Barbarian," he cursed beneath his breath.

Moving with blinding speed, the Ethiop leapt to his feet, eyes narrowed and jaw set, towering over Niohuru.

"Repeat," the Ethiop said in measured, barely restrained tones. "Repeat what you just said."

Niohuru hesitated for a moment then puffed out his chest, head held high. In haughty tones, he answered, "I called you a barbarian."

The Ethiop, teeth clenched, took a deep breath in through flaring nostrils, and then out again. His hands curled at his sides, as though grasping the very air.

"My name," the Ethiop began, his voice rumbling like distant thunder, "is Axum Ouazebas, and I have the blood of kings in my veins." He leaned in close, bringing his face only centimeters from Niohuru's. "I will *not* be insulted by a puffed-up"—he poked Niohuru in the chest with an outstretched finger—"little"—he poked Niohuru again—"daisy."

Niohuru trembled with constrained rage, teeth gritted. "And *I*," he said, batting the Ethiop's hand away, "am a proud son of one of the Eight Great Houses, and I say *that*"—he pointed at the pallet beside them—"is *my* pallet."

Axum sneered, and in a lightning fast move reached forward and grabbed hold of the front of Niohuru's tunic. "Well," he said in a menacingly quiet voice, "do you intend to take it from me?"

Before Niohuru could react, Cong began coughing loudly. In between the hacking noises, Niohuru distinctly heard Cong say, "Falco!"

Axum still held Niohuru's tunic-front, and Niohuru's hands were balled into fists and readying to strike, but they turned as one when they heard the voice of their commander, Captain Hughes Falco, calling out.

"Oh, good!" Hughes shouted, navigating around the maze of pallets and making his way toward them. "Tie, Ouazebas, I was *just* looking for you two."

Axum released his hold on Niohuru's tunic, while Niohuru cringed. Even knowing the stiff penalties in the Eight Banners for altercations between soldiers, he'd allowed the Ethiop to goad him into anger. Just being involved in the beginnings of a scuffle such as the one Hughes had caught them in was sufficient grounds for a punishment detail at least, and the lash at worst.

Niohuru hung his head, ashamed, fearing the worst.

Hughes reached them, and stopped almost within arm's reach. Smiling broadly, he said, "Good news. I'm putting you in a combat cell together."

"*What*?" they both said, in perfect unison.

"It's simple," Hughes said, crossing his arms over his chest. "Tie, you're rated as a field medic, right?"

Niohuru nodded, blankly.

"And Ouazebas is a sabotage expert."

Axum drew himself up straighter, chin up. "The best in the Falcon's Claws."

Hughes gave Axum an indulgent nod. Then, with particular emphasis, he said, "I'm *sure* that there will be no trouble, and that you two can get along with one another. Correct?"

Niohuru and Axum looked to one another, then to Hughes, both wearing expressions that intermingled confusion with horror.

From his pallet a short distance away, Cong looked up from his labors to laugh.

"I wouldn't laugh if I were you, Ren," Hughes said, glancing his way. "Isn't your specialty demolitions?"

Cong put down his whetstone and nodded.

"Then you're in the cell, too."

Dropping his whetstone onto his pallet, his face screwed up in disgust, Cong sulked.

"Well, I'll leave you to it," Hughes said, turning to leave.

Niohuru, perplexed, raised his hand, like a schoolboy waving for his tutor's attention. "Captain Hu... that is, *Falco*?"

Hughes paused, looking back over his shoulder.

"Yes, Tie?"

Niohuru looked over at the Ethiop beside him, and then back to Hughes. "Is that it? I mean, will you not be disciplining us?"

Axum, teeth clenched, whispered out of the corner of his mouth. "Keep your mouth *shut*."

Hughes turned to regard them, his arms crossed. "Disciplined for *what*?"

"Well," Niohuru said, with a faint shrug, "for our altercation?"

"Altercation?" Hughes threw back his head with a bark of laughter. "You've still got all your teeth, no blood's been spilled, I haven't lost a man." He shook his head, grinning. "I don't know if getting your fatigues rumpled is exactly an 'altercation,' Tie. But if you feel like you need to be disciplined, I expect that being lumped with these two"—he gestured to Axum and Cong—"will be punishment enough."

Niohuru looked from one to the other. He would be putting his life in the hands of these men, and taking their lives in his own.

Hughes turned to walk away, but before going, he paused. "You'll find that not everything is quite so grave and serious as regulations might suggest, Tie, and that not every offense is a capital one."

With that, the captain walked away, leaving Niohuru with his new cellmates. He looked up to find the towering Axum looking down at him.

"Well?" Niohuru said. "Are you going to give up my pallet or not?"

Axum grinned, then roared with laughter, slapping Niohuru on the back. "You know, Cong, I think our little daisy is not so bad, after all."

Cong sneered. "Well, he's not getting *my* pallet..."

≡≡

HEXAGRAM 23
PEELING
BELOW EARTH ABOVE MOUNTAIN

The Mountain is attached to the Earth. In the same way, those above make their dwellings secure by treating those below with generosity.

They were nearing the bottom of the last unbroken bottle of lychee wine when Amonkar decided that they should take a walk while they still could.

Neither she nor Geng had been imbibers in civilian life, neither of them having so much as a drop of alcohol in all their young lives. Seathl, for her part, had got an early start, ignoring all the Quran's strictures against intoxicants while drinking with her roughneck friends in Khalifa, and now she was helping her two crewmates make up for lost time.

When she'd first taken a drink, during leave from flight training back on Earth, Amonkar couldn't help but feel guilty. The ancient Hindi scriptures, after all, listed drinking as one of the five heinous crimes, right after murder and adultery. There had, of course, always been exceptions made, and the dramas she'd watched as a girl were full of references to warriors, nobles, and kings quaffing tankards and mugs, raising glasses in toasts, and so forth. Still, in taverns and inns in Guangdong she'd always felt as if she were committing some trespass, breaking some rule, and that at any moment her parents would burst through the door and denounce her as a harlot and drunkard.

Since she'd flown over the battlefield repeatedly, and pitted her life and those of her crewmates against the enemy time and again, it seemed that a drink was *exactly* what she needed. And when Seathl turned up a case of lychee wine left over from before the Mexica had driven the colonists away, in it three bottles left miraculously unbroken, Amonkar had been the first in line.

They were dressed in fatigues, sweat glistening on their foreheads from the over-hot air blowing down on them from the ventilation systems overhead, but it was worth it just to be out of their flight suits for a change, just to be able to *breathe*. The rest of the crew were dispersed with the rest of the airmen around the makeshift barracks set up for the Air Corps in a disused storage hall, but Amonkar, her copilot, and her navigator had snuck off together, like schoolgirls sleeping over. Geng had found a relatively isolated side corridor for them to set up their sleeping pallets, somewhat secluded from the clamor and clatter of the hall, and with a bottle for each of them they'd stretched out, their shirts open at the neck and their feet bare, laughing and giggling as they grew progressively more and more intoxicated.

Nearly all the lychee wine was gone when Amonkar finally lurched to her feet. With one hand on the wall for balance, she tugged on her shoes gracelessly with the other.

"Where are *you* going?" Geng asked, wiping her mouth with her sleeve.

"I miss my plane," Amonkar answered simply, as if that was all the response needed. She stomped her left shoe against the floor a few times, to jam her foot into place, and then straightened, with visible difficulty. "Been on the ground too long, and I miss my plane."

Seathl grabbed the bottle from Geng, took a long pull, and rose unsteadily to her feet. "I'm up for a walk."

The navigator shrugged, and climbed to her feet as well. "I've got nothing planned," she said with a bleary grin.

It had only been the day before when Amonkar and the others had helped shepherd the Deliverer *Fair Winds for Escort* into the makeshift hangar at the disused airfield. Like the storage hall where the airmen had been billeted, the hangar had been selected because it had survived the bombings and firefights relatively intact, and could be connected by pressurized tunnels with the nearby structures.

But with kilometers of tunnels, both above ground and subterranean, and dozens of reclaimed structures, it was the work of more than an hour for the three women to find their way back to the hangar. They were still drunk by the time they reached it, but they could feel sobriety encroaching, and resented it like an unwanted guest.

There were a few other Deliverer-class aircraft in the enormous hangar, the rest of the room taken up by Dragonfly and Hornet rotary winged fighters, but even lined up alongside identical bombers, Amonkar would have known her plane in an instant. Would have known it, that is, under anything resembling normal circumstances.

"What have they *done* to her?"

Geng stepped over and took hold of Amonkar's elbow. "Arati, are you alright?"

Amonkar turned to look at her navigator with wide eyes and a stricken expression. "No, I am *not* alright!" She turned and pointed at *Fair Winds for Escort*. "Just *look* at her!"

Having taken some damage from enemy fire during the recent hostilities, the Deliverer was being tended by ground crews. The thin covering which served as the bomber's skin has been peeled back, like bark from a tree, its skeleton of aluminum exposed.

"They're fixing her up, skipper," Seathl said, stepping forward to stand on Amonkar's other side. "Looks to me like these folks know what they're doing." She pointed with her chin to the hangar's far side, where ground crewmen were putting the finishing touches on repairs to another Deliverer's outer hull.

Amonkar turned to her co-pilot, still wearing a horrified expression. "And I was just relaxing and... and *drinking*... while my plane is stripped down to bolts and struts?"

Seathl and Geng exchanged confused glances. "It's really not that bad, Arati," the navigator began, somewhat bewildered. "She just took a few shots and needs patching, that's all."

Then big fat tears poured down Amonkar's cheeks, and her knees buckled. If not for the two women on either side taking her weight, she would have fallen sprawling on the floor. As it was, they barely managed to keep her upright.

"Is there a problem over there?" the foreman of the ground crew called over, lifting a welding visor and peering out from under *Fair Winds for Escort*.

"No problem!" Seathl called back, as calmly as possible. She managed to turn Amonkar back around the way they'd come. "Come on, Geng," she said under her breath, then called back over her shoulder, "No problem at all!"

The two managed to maneuver Amonkar out of the hangar and back into the tunnels before the pilot had another outburst. They snaked their way through the tunnels back to the makeshift barracks, and on to their pallets in the side corridor, without running into anyone they knew, and without being stopped by anyone curious as to why the woman between them wouldn't stop crying.

Only back in the seclusion of their isolated corridor did they pause to catch their breath. At length, Amonkar's crying jag seemed to abate somewhat, and Seathl and Geng managed to get her attention again.

"I never took you for a weepy drunk, skipper," Seathl said, handing Amonkar a cloth.

Amonkar blew her nose like a trumpet, then dabbed at the corners of her eyes. "I know, it's just... my plane... seeing it like that..."

Geng reached out and put a hand on Amonkar's shoulder. "I don't have Seathl's long experience with different flavors and varieties of drunkenness, but I know that what's *really* bothering you isn't the plane."

Amonkar blinked a few times, looking from one to the other. She wiped her eyes again with the back of her sleeve, straightened up, and visibly tried to regain her composure.

"No," she said, shaking her head. Her voice was strained, but under control. "You're right. It's not."

Seathl quirked an eyebrow. "Then what?"

Amonkar settled herself, taking a deep breath through her nostrils, then letting it out slowly through her lips. "It's just..." She blinked hard, rolling her eyes up to the ceiling and willing the tears not to fall. "We spend so much time training, and flying, and training, and simulating every combat situation imaginable, and then when we get up there and it's really happening, it can just be too…"

"Too real?" Seathl finished for her.

Amonkar nodded. "I can't help thinking about all those targets we bombed. There were people down there, surely, or we wouldn't have been given those targets. Can you imagine what those bombs must do to a human body when they hit?"

Geng narrowed her eyes. "Can you imagine what the Mexica can do to a human body when they get hold of it?" She didn't mention the stories of the prisoners used for sacrifice, of countless lives put under the obsidian blades of the Mexic priests. She didn't have to mention it, since they'd all heard the stories more times than they cared to remember.

"I *know* that," Amonkar snapped, "but this wasn't the Mexica doing it. It was *me*."

"It was *us*," Seathl corrected. "And we were doing what we were ordered to do. And if we hadn't done it, more innocent men and women might have ended up as Mexic prisoners."

"If people like us weren't up *there*"—Geng pointed to the roof overhead, indicating the skies beyond—"then none of us would be down *here*"— she pointed to the makeshift barracks beyond their corridor. "I don't know if the Mexica are kept up at night by the guilt of the horrible things they do to people, but I don't much care. What I *do* care about are the people in my crew, the rest of the Air Corps, the ground-pounders, the civilians, and the emperor, in that order. If I can do something to keep any or all of them safe and secure, I'm going to do it, and a good night's sleep be damned."

"So it bothers you, too?" Amonkar asked.

"Of course," Seathl answered, slapping the pilot's shoulder. "What did you think, we were automata?"

"No," Amonkar said with a weak smile, "I just…" She shook her head. "I don't know what I thought."

"Well," Seathl said, "want to know what *I* think?"

Amonkar raised her eyebrows.

Seathl grinned, and said "I think it's time for another drink."

Geng clapped her hands, and stood. "We passed a crate of Kentuck whiskey on our way back here. If we're lucky there just *might* be an unbroken bottle or two in there."

"Well," Amonkar said, "what are we sitting around here for? Navigator, set course." She reached a hand up to Seathl. "Co-pilot, help your drunken pilot to her feet."

"Yes, pilot," the two said, snapping off ragged salutes.

HEXAGRAM 24
RETURN
BELOW THUNDER ABOVE EARTH

Thunder in the Earth. In the same way, the former kings closed the border passes on the occasion of the winter solstice, and neither did merchants and travelers move nor sovereigns go out to inspect domains.

The floor beneath Guardsman Carter's feet rumbled, and for a moment he thought it was the Mexica launching an attack. Then he heard the squawk of the crawler-tank driver calling the all-clear over his helmet radio, and realized he was just feeling the vibrations of the passing crawler patrolling the outer perimeter.

Of course it couldn't have been an attack, Carter thought. He couldn't be that lucky.

Not that he *wanted* the Mexica to attack, not really. He just wanted something, *anything*, to help him stay awake, and he found it hard to imagine drowsing while someone was shooting at him. As it was, Carter was struggling to remain conscious and in full control of his faculties. What only made matters worse was the fact that the rest of the First-Second squad was working so hard to head in the other direction.

Sentry duty wasn't a punishment. Carter's name had just come up in the rota, and it had been his turn in the barrel, as the joke went. He was inside the pressurized zone, at least, but it came as small comfort. It meant that he could keep the faceplate visor of his helmet lifted up, and hopefully get a breath of fresh air instead of his suit's reclaimed and recycled tanks, but by the same token it meant that he was indoors in the warm ventilation in a suit better designed for the cold unpressurized outdoors. He was already sweltering, sweat pooling down in his boots, but regulations said that all sentries had to wear their suits, on the off chance that they'd be called upon to go out onto the surface.

Never mind the fact that *no one* was to be out on the surface tonight. That was the whole reason Carter was on sentry duty in the first place, guarding one of the locked-down airlocks, making sure no one from the inside tried to get out. His orders were to stand on duty, from the beginning of the sixth watch to the end of the eighth, rifle in hand and saber at his side, and basically just stay awake. He couldn't help but envy the mechanized patrols out on the surface, making sure no one from the outside tried to get in. At least they were nice and cool in the pressurized cabins of their crawler-tanks, and had their crewmates onboard to share a bit of conversation. Who did Carter have?

Not that Spitter, Moonface, and Ears were much for conversation, but they were better than nothing. But they, along with the rest of the First Squad-Second Platoon were back in their billet, getting royally hammered on double rations of wine while huddling around mahjong tiles or bone dice, or else just singing out-of-tune songs in a dozen different languages. The orders had come down that morning from Captain Quan, the stern head of Fourth Company, that the unit was to get a day of rest, in recognition of their valued efforts in the recent engagement.

No rest for Carter, of course. By the time he was relieved when the chimes rang the ninth watch, he'd barely have time to get back to his pallet and catch a few moment's sleep before the All-Wake was sounded in the morning. And considering that Captain Quan had *also* ordered that their day of rest would be followed by a full day of close-combat drills, to keep their battle readiness honed, Carter was sure he wouldn't be getting any rest then, either.

Carter shuffled his feet, thinking that getting the blood flowing might help him remain alert. But that only served to remind him how hot and stifling his surface suit was. Instead, he tried a bit of mental exercise, thinking to keep his mind alert and active.

He tried mentally reciting passages from the Five Classics, the Four Books, from the Canon of Filial Piety. That only made matters worse, and his eyes droop even more. Then he tried totting up all the days and nights since he joined the Green Standards, working out just how long since he'd been a free man.

It had been well over a year since he'd left home, he realized. Nearly a year and a half, in fact. It would be winter back home in Tejas, near year's end. Maybe even Yuletide already. The last Yule, he'd been on Taiwan Island, and had done little more to mark the season than sing a few carols with a handful of other Vinlanders and Europans who observed the old traditions.

Carter wondered what his family were doing, his parents and his sisters. Probably sitting around the Yule tree, drinking mulled wine and finding new ways to snipe at one another while sounding polite. Or it would be evening, his mother having spent too much time preparing the dinner, and then his father would have fallen asleep on the sitting room couch, snoring away while his sisters played chess. Or maybe, if he'd got the counts of days and weeks wrong, it might be even later in the year than he thought, and the family would be gathered at the ringball courts with the rest of the Duncan populace, watching the local team play their rivals from the next township over. The winners would go on to the regional championships in Brazos after the new year's celebration, and the players' families would caravan down to cheer them on.

The years that Carter had played for the team, he'd always been assigned to defense, using elbows, knees, and hips to keep a rubber ball from bouncing onto their side of the court, and while he was a good enough defender, he was lousy at offense, and could never have led the team to victory by knocking the ball through the ring on the opponent's side of the court. Lucky for Carter, and the team, his classmate Clement Ross was a dab hand at shooting, and together they'd led their team to the championships two years running.

Carter was wondering when he would ever be back home again, and what his return might be like, when his reveries were interrupted by the sound of footsteps. He looked up the corridor, and in the dim light saw a man in fatigues approaching.

His first thought was that it was Squad Leader Corporal Eng come to check on him. Then he allowed himself to entertain the fantasy that his relief had been sent early and that he would be allowed to go join the revels back in the billet, however briefly.

As the man stepped into the pool of light around the sealed airlock, though, Carter saw the rank character stitched onto the man's tunic, and knew that it wasn't Corporal Eng. And unless the Green Standard was assigning lieutenants to sentry duty, it wasn't likely to be Carter's relief either.

Remembering himself, Carter snapped to attention, shoulders back, his hand on the barrel of his rifle, its butt resting against his right foot.

"At your ease, guardsman," the man said, stopping directly in front of him.

It was Lieutenant Seong, Corporal Eng's superior officer, in command of the entire second platoon of the Eleventh Armored Infantry's Fourth Company.

Carter relaxed only as much as was needed to turn his head and eyes toward the lieutenant, not willing to take any chances.

Seong chuckled, a tight smile curling the corners of his mouth. "Relax," he said. "I'm not on inspection, just coming back from a stroll."

Carter let out the breath he'd been holding, and nodded. "Thank you, sir."

The lieutenant was silent a moment, studying Carter's face thoughtfully. "Guardsman Carter, isn't it?"

Carter tried not to panic. There was no reason that Seong wouldn't recognize all seventy-odd men under his command on sight. There was no reason in particular for the lieutenant to recall the *last* time that he and Carter had exchanged words.

"Yessir," Carter said with a nod.

The lieutenant's smile broadened. "Don't need any more lessons on how to take an enemy-held structure, I hope?"

Carter cringed, his smile growing brittle. "No sir," he said, too quickly. "That is, I think that…"

Seong shook his head, chuckling. "Don't worry, Carter, I'm just having fun with you. The fact that you've stayed alive *this* long is to your credit."

"Thank you, sir," Carter answered, a little uncertainly.

Seong narrowed his eyes, giving Carter an appraising look. "Vinlander, aren't you?"

Carter nodded. "From Tejas, sir."

"I was stationed there a few tours, in Tejas, before being transferred to Fourth Company. My first posting out of Taiwan Island was to patrol the Mexic border, in fact." Seong smiled. "I've a lot of good memories of Tejas, Carter, a lot of good memories." He fell silent a moment, a wistful look on his face. Then he turned his attention back to Carter. "You play ringball, guardsman?"

Carter blinked, startled. "Um, I..."

"Ringball," the lieutenant repeated. "They played a lot of it in Tejas, when I was there."

Carter grinned, and nodded. "Yes, sir," he said. "I've played a bit of it."

"A fine sport, ringball." Seong scratched his chin, thoughtfully. "If we get a chance, maybe we can rig up a court here, see how the game can be played at one-third gravity. What do you think about that?"

"Um..." Carter wasn't sure how to respond. "Sure, I suppose..."

Seong reached out and slapped Carter on the shoulder. "Well, keep it up, guardsman. And don't look so glum, you won't be on sentry duty forever, and there'll come a time when you'll long for this kind of peace and quiet." He chuckled, ruefully. "Not that *I* want to switch places with you, of course..."

Then the lieutenant continued on up the corridor, passing out of the pool of light and back into gloom.

☰ (hexagram symbol)

HEXAGRAM 25
NO ERRANCY
BELOW THUNDER ABOVE HEAVEN

Thunder going on everywhere under Heaven. In the same way, the former kings brought about prosperity, for they nurtured things in accord with the seasons.

"Come on, you layabouts," Captain Hughes called from the doorway as the men of the First Raider Company were finishing their morning meal. "You're coming with me."

All around Niohuru, the other men of the Falcon's Claws grumbled, hunched over their still only half-eaten bowls of rice. Most were still somewhat groggy, after double rations of rice wine the night before, looking even more unkempt and disheveled than normal.

"All of you, on your feet," Hughes continued, his grin broadening. "I've got a present for you, and you'll think it's your birthday come early."

With scarcely concealed scowls and a fair amount of mumbled complaints, the men of the First Raider Company shuffled from the improvised mess into the maze of pressurized tunnels that connected the buildings housing both the Third and Fourth Battalions of the Bordered Yellow Banner's Ninth Brigade, along with elements of the Fourth Division of the Green Standard's First Army.

Unlike the more lax attitudes common in the First Raider Company, the rest of the bannermen in the compound held etiquette and protocol in high regard. Superior officers did not fraternize with those under their command, and bannermen did not mix with soldiers in the uniform of the Green Standard.

The ensign of the Bordered Yellow Banner was hung at the entrance to each of the structures given to the bannerman, a yellow field bordered in red, upon which was emblazoned a dragon. The structure to which Captain Hughes led the men of the First Raider Company, though, was unmarked and unadorned. When the door was opened, and the air within escaped into the pressurized tunnel fitted over the entrance, Niohuru could detect the mingled scent of motor oil, petroleum, and human sweat. Shouting voices and the banging of metal on metal could be heard, occasionally punctuated by the low animal roar of engines.

The room was enormous, and must once have been a hangar used to house aircraft. On one wall were enormous doors designed to roll up into the ceiling, and enormous vents in the ceiling appeared capable of both evacuating the air in the space when the doors were to be opened, and replacing the air and repressurizing the hangar when the doors were closed. It would have been an inefficient and time-consuming procedure, Niohuru was sure, but was likely the only way to get the large planes into a completely pressurized environment so that they could be depressurized and repaired.

But there were no planes in the hangar now. Instead, there was a small fleet of crawlers, unloading large crates. Dozens upon dozens had already been unloaded, and gangs of technicians were in the process of uncrating and assembling the contents, small vehicles in various stages of completion. Arranged in neat rows on the opposite wall were more than two dozen of the small vehicles, each identical to all the others.

"Well?" Hughes said, hands on his hips and a smile on his lips. "What do you think?"

The men of the First Raider Company drifted into the hangar, moving over towards the rows of vehicles. They were small, each of them little more than a chassis on four oversized knobby wheels, an engine, a steering wheel and pedals, three seats, and a pair of machine guns mounted front and back.

"I give up, Falco," shouted one of the bannermen, leaning down and looking at the driver's controls. "What is it?"

"It *looks* like a four-wheeled speeder," said another, his Official Speech laced with traces of a Quangdong accent, "but I've never seen a speeder body so scrawny."

"Or with such overfed tires," laughed a Nipponese bannerman.

Hughes dismissed their jibes with a wave. "It's a rutting rover, you mental deficients.

Bannerman Cong, the demolitions expert in Niohuru's combat cell, went over and rapped on the exposed frame of the nearest rover. "When does the rest of it get put on?"

Hughes laughed. "I know, I know, they're hardly armored at all, but they move like greased weasel dung."

Bannerman Axum, the third member of Niohuru's combat cell, glanced at the others standing near him. "Is it the weasel that is greased, or the dung?"

"Why not both?" answered another.

Niohuru ignored the others, and stepped closer to one of the rovers for a better look. It was hardly bigger than the one-manned three-wheel speeders that Niohuru and his friends used to race all over North Capital, from the Great Bell Temple to the Fishing Terrace to Sandy Mouth. Niohuru thought about the other spoiled children of the Great Houses, and for the briefest moment wondered what they were doing at that moment.

"I've had these rovers specially built to my specifications," Hughes continued, pacing along the line, a hungry look in his eyes. "There's not another vehicle quite like them, not on Fire Star, not on the Moon, and not on Earth."

Niohuru leaned in to get a better look at the controls. Despite what Hughes was saying about the rover's uniqueness, the steering, acceleration, and brakes all seemed virtually identical to that of any speeder Niohuru had ever driven.

Of course, no speeder Niohuru had ever driven had come equipped with heavy-caliber machine guns on pintle mountings.

"All things have their season," Hughes went on. "There are times to walk, and there are times when walking isn't enough. There are times to run, and there are times to *ride*. Now that the initial phases of Operation Great Holdings have been completed, it's time for the First Raider Company to boost its mobility."

As the Falcon's Claws drifted in and around the parked rovers, they began to climb into the driver's seats, or into the passenger or rear seats to test the movements of the mounted machine guns.

"I know you won't be surprised to hear that I disagree with much that Master Sun says in *The Art of War*," Hughes said, resting his hands on the front tire of a rover, "but the author was right when he said, 'One who sets his entire army in motion to chase an advantage will not attain it.' We have an advantage right now, with the Mexica in an entrenched position, their access to resupplies and reinforcements strained. But if we sent the whole weight of the Middle Kingdom forces in theater after them at once, we'd just be like a tidal wave crashing against rocks."

Hughes patted the rover's tire affectionately, like a man petting a dog.

"The rest of the rovers should be uncrated and assembled by first light tomorrow, one for each combat team in the rifle platoons. We've borrowed a few bombers and crews from the Air Corps, and with the rovers outfitted with chutes, we'll drop combat cells and their wheels behind enemy lines. It's time for the First Raider Company to do what we do best, and leave the head-on engagement to the rank and file."

The other bannermen began to look with new appreciation at the rovers, knowing now that they'd be taking them on raiding runs in a matter of days. Niohuru, for his part, was less than enthused by the idea, and his distaste showed in his expression.

"Tie?" Hughes asked, seeing the look on Niohuru's face. "Do you have another... concern?"

Some of the other bannermen chuckled, remembering the previous times the captain had invited Niohuru to express his "concerns," but Niohuru paid them no mind.

"Yes, sir," Niohuru answered. "Doesn't Master Sun also say that, though a smaller force may make an obstinate fight, in the end it will always be captured by the larger force?"

Hughes laughed. "Well, I *did* say that I disagree with much that Master Sun says. But in this case,

I'll let the master's own words be my answer. 'When campaigning, be swift as the wind; when raiding, be like fire.' A raiding force of two hundred men, well armed and highly mobile, can be that kind of fire, and attack places where two thousand men could never go. It isn't a flight of arrows that takes the target's center, it's the one arrow that hits the mark. I'm talking about precision raids, each combat cell a single arrow flying unerring at a target."

Hughes paused, grinning.

"We'll be in and gone before the blood-hungry bastards even know we're there."

HEXAGRAM 26
GREAT DOMESTICATION
BELOW HEAVEN ABOVE MOUNTAIN

Heaven located within the Mountain. In the same way, the noble man acquires much knowledge of things said and done in the past and so domesticates and garners his own virtue.

Unlike the Earth with its sole natural satellite, Fire Star had two moons. The larger and nearer of the two orbited more than nine thousand kilometers above the surface of the red planet, while the other, roughly half its size, followed an orbit nearly three times as distant. The larger moon was so close to the surface of Fire Star, that its course was below the synchronous orbit radius, moving around Fire Star faster than the planet itself was revolving. Twice a day it rose in the west and set in the east, unlike the smaller moon that followed a more stately course from east to west.

To the early settlers on Fire Star, it seemed as if the two moons were constantly hurtling themselves at one another, day after day. Accordingly, the settlers named the larger moon Zhurong and the smaller Gonggong, after the mythical god of fire and his son the water god, about whose battle across the heavens many songs had been sung and stories told.

To those within the command center deep within Zhurong, the commanders of the Eight Banners and the Green Standard, the admirals of the Interplanetary Fleet, it seemed that war across the heavens had never ended, and sometimes seemed that it never would.

The war between the Middle Kingdom and the Mexic Dominion had been fought these many years in the vacuum surrounding Fire Star, in the skies of the red planet, and on the blood-colored sands themselves. The collective attentions of the Middle Kingdom strategists had been divided among these various domains and theaters of operation since the beginning of the war, years before.

Now, though, all attention was on the red sands, and on the actions of the ground forces and the airmen who supported them.

It had been some months since a covert operation—a joint effort between the Eight Banners, the Green Standard, and the Interplanetary Fleet, overseen by the watchful eyes of the Embroidered Guard—had temporarily cut off the Mexic supply lines. In a few months' time, the Mexic resupply ships that had left Earth shortly thereafter would reach Fire Star. When they arrived, they would find an Interplanetary Fleet blockade in place, every available vacuum craft and amphibious vehicle arrayed against them.

If the Middle Kingdom forces were to succeed in gaining complete control of the planet's surface, the Mexic supply convoy would not be able to touch down unmolested. They would be forced to fight their way to the surface, or remain in vacuum and fight until their supplies of ammunition, air, and water ran out, or else head back to Earth and hope that their supplies were sufficient for the return voyage.

By the time the early stages of Operation Great Holdings had been completed, the majority of the Mexic ground forces were spread across the Tamkung Plain, with their strongholds being the former colonies of Ruosi and Zijun, pressurized domes built inside a kilometer-deep crater. The advances made by the Middle Kingdom since the launch of Great Holdings had pushed a few thousand meters into the eastern edge of the Mexic-held territory, but the vast remainder of Tamkung Plain and the crater colonies remained in the enemy's control.

The stakes were simple, their meaning stark. If the Middle Kingdom succeeded in overrunning Tamkung Plain and retaking Ruosi and Zijun before the supply ships of the Mexic Dominion arrived, then Fire Star would belong once more to the Dragon Throne. With the planet completely held and fully defended by the armed forces of the Middle Kingdom, there would be no possibility that any Mexic vacuum fleet, however large, could retake it.

On the other hand, if the Middle Kingdom *failed* to retake the crater colonies and the majority of Tamkung Plain before the Mexic resupply arrived, and the Mexic ships were able to break the Interplanetary Fleet's blockade, then there was no reason to suppose that the Second Mexic War might drag on interminably, with no clear chance for victory in the foreseeable future.

If the Middle Kingdom were to retake Fire Star and scour the Mexic off the planet once and for all, it would need to be done now.

HEXAGRAM 27
NOURISHMENT
BELOW THUNDER ABOVE MOUNTAIN

Thunder going on under Mountain. In the same way, the noble man is careful with his language and practices restraint in his use of food and drink.

Pilot Amonkar eased back on the stick, pulling *Fair Winds for Escort* up towards the thin, wispy clouds overhead. It had been days since the bomber had flown, and like her pilot it seemed somehow tentative, uncertain, but still eager to get up and into the open skies. They had rested for long enough, and it was time to push on.

Fair Winds for Escort was part of a squadron of Deliverer-class light bombers that had been sent out to "soften" the enemy in advance of ground forces moving out. For the better part of a week the forces of the Middle Kingdom had reorganized and resupplied after the initial push of Operation Great Holdings, during which time the Mexic Dominion was able to re-entrench themselves. The main line of defense was now a perimeter along the eastern edge of the Tamkung Plain, a corridor of minefields, tripwires, and deadfalls, covered by gun emplacements and armored divisions to the west. If the Middle Kingdom intended to retake the Tamkung Plain, they would first need to cross this perimeter.

"Do you have to *jostle* so much?" moaned Tail Gunner Xiao over the plane's hardline.

Amonkar could hear in her helmet's speakers the tinny sound of Co-pilot Seathl chuckling, and the stifled laughter of Navigator Geng down below.

"Maybe if you didn't drink so rutting much," Nose Gunner Siagyo replied, "you wouldn't feel so queasy."

Amonkar and Seathl exchanged a look. Both knew that what was *really* bothering Siagyo was the drunken pass Xiao had made at her the night before, well in his cups. Or the fact that, if she hadn't been stone-cold sober, she might have fallen for it. But with orders that they were to suit up and fly the next morning, the rest of the crew had abstained, leaving the plane's tail gunner as the only one to overdo it, drinking not only his own nightly ration of rice wine but that of several of his crew-mates as well.

Xiao belched loudly, the liquid sound echoing in everyone else's helmets.

"Eighteen hells, Xiao!" Bombardier Mehdi objected. "I can almost *smell* it..."

"Stow the chatter, people," Amonkar scolded, cutting in on the line. "Xiao, are you alright back there?"

Another stifled eructation, and then Xiao answered, "Yes, captain, I'll be alright." He moaned softly, then added, "Just try to fly her straight, won't you?"

Amonkar didn't want to smile, but couldn't help herself. "I'll do what I can."

When Xiao had arrived at the morning mess looking like he'd been beaten with a bag full of cats, holding his head with one hand and his belly with another, Amonkar had initially said that he would be grounded, and an auxiliary member of the ground crew tapped to stand-in as tail gunner for the run. Amonkar didn't want to pull an inexperienced replacement into any live-fire mission, but a healthy but inexperienced gunner was better than an experienced gunner who couldn't see straight.

Xiao, though, wouldn't hear of it, and had insisted that he was fine. All he needed, he said, was a few cups of tea and he'd be right as rain.

Sure enough, when the crew of *Fair Winds for Escort* had gathered in the hangar to board, Xiao had looked, if not exactly bright-eyed and well-scrubbed, at least awake and alert. Once they were airborne, though, came the groans and complaints which, while initially amusing, soon began to grow a bit stale.

"How's our position, navigator?" Co-pilot Seathl asked over the hardline, craning her neck to look out first the starboard and then the port side windows, checking their alignment with the other dozen bombers in the squadron.

"Coming up on target," Geng replied, after conferring with the nose gunner and bombardier.

The clouds above were high and thin, like Earth's cirrus clouds but far higher than any terrestrial clouds could fly. The sun was at their back, rising in the east, with the Mexic-held lands before them still touched by the shadow of Bao Shan. Their advances and gains since Great Holdings began, every meter fought and bled for, seemed so small a space, when viewed from this high vantage. On the ground, it was easy to fool one's self into thinking that real progress had been made, but up here among the clouds it was clear that they still had far to go.

"Incoming hostiles!" called Nose Gunner Siagyo. "Starboard front."

Amonkar tightened her grip on the stick, looking ahead and to the right. There, coming up from below, she could see a phalanx of Mexic fighter planes, their hulls painted to resembled enormous white- and black-feathered birds of prey, their noses constructed to resemble wicked beaks, their landing gear and low-slung weapons grasping talons.

"Eagle Knights," Seathl said, managing to turn the mere name into a curse.

"Make sure our escort sees them," Amonkar said, maintaining a steady course and heading.

"Oh, they see them," Seathl said with a grin. On either side, above, and below them, flew rotary-winged Dragonfly fighters in a diamond formation, prepared to run interference as necessary for the bombers.

Suddenly, tells screamed on proximity alarms, as a thick black cloud erupted just ahead of and below *Fair Winds for Escort*.

"We're taking flack," Siagyo called in an even, calm voice. If there was ever a portrait of grace under pressure, the diminutive Nipponese nose gunner was it.

"Approaching target," Navigator Geng said, with somewhat more strain than Siagyo was showing.

Another black cloud erupted ahead to port as more surface-to-air rounds exploded before them.

Amonkar was forced to roll *Fair Winds* slightly to port, then back again to correct, hit by the concussive force of the anti-aircraft round. If the air through which the blast had propagated had been any denser, they might have been unable to remain aloft at all, and as it was they were in for some turbulent flying.

Through the deck-plates beneath her feet, Amonkar could feel the faint vibrations as the nose and tail gunners unleashed their machine guns on the approaching Eagle Knights. If the Mexic fighters pulled too high, out of range of the gun turrets on the Middle Kingdom bombers, then the Dragonflies would step in and take up the slack. But whenever the Eagle Knights dipped low enough, the bomber's gunners were ready, and willing, to open fire.

Amonkar noticed, though, that when the nose gunner's machine gun fell silent and still, as the Eagle Knights soared out of range, she could still feel the distant vibrations of the tail gun being fired. It was possible that there were Mexic fighters coming around behind them and in range, but it seemed too early for the Eagle Knights to have a chance for that kind of maneuver.

"You alright back there, tail gunner?" Amonkar called.

Before Xiao could answer, Navigator Geng cut in. "Over target!"

"Bombardier," Seathl shouted, contravening protocol but too elated to care, "to your duty."

"First bomb is away," the Persian Mehdi replied. Then quickly, "Second bomb is away."

Amonkar watched the horizon, waiting to hear the tail gunner give the status of their bombing's accuracy at any moment. As the seconds mounted, she began to worry.

"Xiao?" she called over the hardline.

The response from the tail turret was a loud rumbling mixed with a hacking cough and the sound of liquid smacking into something solid. Then more hacking, quickly stifled, the sound of distant thumping, and then silence.

"Xiao?" Amonkar called again.

Only silence was the answer.

Overflying enemy territory, with the Dragonflies darting and buzzing around them, keeping the Eagle Knights' attack off their back, having to swoop and dive occasionally to avoid the worst of the surface-fired flack, *Fair Winds for Escort* and the rest of the bomber squadron wheeled around and returned the way they had come, making another bombing pass on the Mexic perimeter as they went.

In all that time, there was still no word from Tail Gunner Xiao. With the plane in flight, there was no safe way to reach the tail turret, even if all of the other crewmen weren't required at their posts, which they were.

It was only when the bombers had touched down again on the makeshift runway, and were wheeled into the hangars set aside for the Air Corps' use, that they learned the reason for Xiao's silence. They had expected to find the turret compromised by enemy flack, or pierced by rounds fired from the Eagle Knights, but to their surprise the turret was whole and unbroken. Strapped into his seat at the tail gun controls, though, Xiao was still and lifeless, the inside of his helmet's faceplate caked with a lumpy, irregular dun-colored substance. When the helmet was removed, out wafted the strong stench of stomach acids and bile, and it was clear what had happened.

From that point onward, the standard orders for all flight crews was no alcohol or intoxicants of any kind within eighteen hours of a scheduled mission.

There was no way of knowing if Xiao would be the last to get sick in his helmet, aspirating on his own vomit, but even so, no one was in a hurry to be the second to die by those means.

HEXAGRAM 28
MAJOR SUPERIORITY
BELOW WIND ABOVE LAKE

The Lake submerges the Tree. In the same way, though the noble man may stand alone, he does so without fear, and, if he has to withdraw from the world, he remains free from resentment.

The magic number, Carter had learned, was thirty.

You had to stay thirty centimeters away from the probing area. When probing, you prodded the ground at thirty degrees. And you checked the meter-wide path thirty times, once every three centimeters, before moving forward six centimeters and starting the whole thing over again.

Which meant flinching thirty times for every six centimeters of ground gained, hoping that the next probe didn't result in the red sands exploding in your face.

The Second Platoon of Fourth Company had been detailed to act as sappers, clearing lanes through the minefield that divided the Middle Kingdom forces to the east with the forward line of the Mexic-held territory to the west.

Eventually, if the Middle Kingdom retook this region, the whole minefield would have to be cleared. At the moment, though, their orders were only to clear an assault footpath, one meter wide, through which the Middle Kingdom ground forces could cross the minefield and establish a bridgehead on the far side. Then, once the footpath had been expanded a few meters on either side, the crawlers and armor of the Eleventh Armored Infantry Battalion would advance and breach the minefield, assaulting the Mexic main line of resistance directly.

Carter's world had shrunk to the few centimeters in front of him. Crouched low to the ground, with his head down, he couldn't see much more than that. He tried not to think about what might be flying directly overhead, or about what lay a few hundred meters ahead, behind the embankments and ridges on the minefield's far side.

The first step was to check the area immediately in front of him for tripwires. Then, he looked for disturbed dirt. If he didn't find any, he used the bayonet at the end of his carbine to probe the area, sticking its blade six centimeters into the ground at a thirty degree angle, checking for resistance, then carefully pulling it back out and probing again about three centimeters to the right. If he made it all the way from one side of the one-meter path to the other, he marked the boundaries left and right with colored plastic stakes, then moved ahead six centimeters and started probing again, moving from left to right.

In the best of conditions, he'd be lucky to cover fifty or sixty meters in a day, creeping along. But these were far from the best of conditions, with machine gun and small arms fire from enemy strong points on the other side of the minefield kicking up red dust all around him, and shells and mortar bombs crashing down on all sides. From time to time, smoke grenades were lobbed ahead of him, the smoke sent billowing up to hamper the enemy's observation and target acquisition, but even in the thin air the winds were blowing enough to chase the smoke away after just a few moments, and then the shots would start pocking around him again. The ground troops behind him were laying down suppressing fire, targeting the suspected sniper and gun placements on the far side of the minefield, but that just meant bullets whizzing overhead from the *other* direction as well, which was hardly comforting.

There were two basic varieties of mines they were ordered to watch out for the anti-armor type, intended to damage the massive crawlers and other mobile armor, and the anti-personnel mines intended to take out foot soldiers like Carter. Of the two, the anti-armor mines were the priority, since they were designed to inflict serious damage on a steel-plated crawler. But even though the anti-armor mines were larger, containing anywhere from five to fifteen kilograms of explosive materials, they weren't Carter's primary concern, at least as far as his personal safety was concerned. The anti-armor mines were mostly detonated by force, and in the low Fire Star gravity Carter could probably jump up and down on a buried anti-armor mine without setting it off. Which was why his greater concern was the second variety, the anti-personnel mine.

Anti-personel mines were smaller, perhaps a few hundred grams of explosives, and activated by force or tripwires. There were three major types of anti-personnel devices, the blast mines, the fragmentation mines, and the bounce mines.

Blast mines, buried beneath the surface, detonated when someone stepped on them, the foot obliterated and fragments of bone sent upwards, destroying the leg. The effects of the blast mines were localized, though, usually only injuring the person who tripped it. If he inadvertently set off a blast mine with his prodding, so long as he was thirty meters back from the upwards blast he could escape serious injury.

Fragmentation mines, on the other hand, were trickier, though usually easier to spot. They were typically mounted on plastic stakes a few centimeters above the ground, and activated by tripwires. When they were triggered, they didn't just explode upwards like blast mines, but sent hot metal fragments out in all directions at high speed, with enough force to drive a few millimeters into armored steel plate. If he failed to notice a tripwire and set off one of those, thirty meters wasn't going to be far enough away to escape injury.

Worse yet, though, were bounce mines. They were buried beneath the ground, like blast mines, and triggered when someone stepped on them. But rather than just exploding upwards, they instead jumped up to groin height before exploding, sending metal shrapnel out in all directions.

To make matters worse, the Mexica had a reputation for often laying mines of one type in combination with others. Anti-personnel mines might be planted near anti-armor mines, and blast or bounce mines might be buried around the stakes of fragmentation mines with tripwires.

So it was thirty centimeters out, thirty degrees in, thirty times across before advancing six centimeters, with smoke obscuring his vision, and small arms fire and mortar shells kicking up the red sands around him when the smoke cleared. The whole time praying that he didn't get shot in the back by friendly fire, or get sniped by a Mexic rifle from one of the forward strong points. There were other sappers advancing, he knew, spread out a dozen or more meters apart on both sides, but each of them was essentially alone, in a world a few centimeters deep and one meter wide, with bullets racing overhead in both directions. Each of them alone, and knowing that they might get shot at any moment, or else be laced with shrapnel if they happened inadvertently to set off a bounce mine with their probing.

There was no point in being afraid. Fear wasn't going to help matters at all, Carter knew. Still, he couldn't help flinching every time the point of his bayonet slid into the red dirt. He might not be afraid to die, but it wasn't something he was looking to do either.

Carter reached the right side of the path, having found no mines along the way. He marked it with a colored plastic stake, crept forward six inches, and started again at the left.

Thirty out, thirty in, and thirty across. And again, and again.

HEXAGRAM 29
THE CONSTANT SINK HOLE
BELOW WATER ABOVE WATER

Water keeps coming on. In the same way, the noble man consistently practices virtuous conduct and constantly engages in moral transformation.

As the rover bumped along the rough ground through the fog-wrapped night, Bannerman Niohuru wished for the hundredth time that the driver's seat was better padded. Even through the sturdy material of his armored surface suit, he could feel every jostle and jar through the hard, unforgiving metal seat.

While the rest of the Middle Kingdom ground forces were engaged in a frontal assault on the Mexica's eastern perimeter, the First Raider Company and their vehicles had been dropped behind enemy lines in the dark of night, to harass the enemy's rearguard and disrupt Mexic supply lines. At the moment, though, visibility obscured by heavy clouds, Niohuru and the others could see no evidence of the enemy, rearguard or otherwise.

The nocturnal clouds on Fire Star, so much like terrestrial fogs, were markedly different than the daytime clouds. Unlike the thin, wispy cirrus-like clouds that drifted sometimes as high as one hundred kilometers above the surface, the nighttime clouds dropped toward the surface just as the temperature dropped, growing thicker and heavier as they fell. In the dead of night, they could be as much as five times thicker than the daylight clouds, a heavy mist hugging the surface like a fog.

But while the low-lying nocturnal clouds had been a valuable asset and ally when the Falcon's Claws had made their night drop behind enemy lines, once their rovers were unchuted and ready to roll, it had tended to work against them.

They were driving with no other Falcon's Claws in sight. They had jumped in over an area several dozen kilometers in length, each combat cell given a different target and operational objectives. They were to carry out their missions well before dawn crept over the hump of Bao Shan in the east, and then regroup to the south, in the untenanted southern reaches of the Tamkung Plain.

Niohuru's combat cell had been given orders to destroy a water reservoir which orbital surveillance had located, some dozens of kilometers behind enemy lines. Niohuru was behind the rover's wheel, with Bannerman Axum in the passenger seat beside him, his hands on the forward-mounted machine gun, and Bannerman Cong in the backward-facing seat behind them controlling the rear-mounted one.

"Distance to target?" Niohuru asked into his helmet-mic, his voice scarcely above a whisper.

Beside him, Axum held up two fingers. *Two kilometers.* At their present speed, they'd be there in a matter of moments.

Their helmet-radios' broadcast settings were set to the lowest power, the signals traveling only a matter of meters before becoming diffuse. There was still the possibility of interception by nearby Mexica, though, and so while not maintaining radio silence, they were operating under strict radio discipline, transmitting to one another only when absolutely necessary. And when transmissions were necessary, they spoke with economy, employing code words for key operational elements.

Those were their orders, at any rate. Niohuru was quickly discovering, though, that the standard code words were employed far less than the more colorful alternatives his cellmates preferred.

Axum kept his eyes on the cloud-veiled darkness before them. They were driving without lights, steering only by the instruments on the rover's dashboard—compass, tachometer, and speedometer—and the dim light of the twin moons overhead. "Contact?" the Ethiop called out.

"No sign of dung-eaters," came Cong's clipped reply.

Axum checked the action of his machine gun's receiver assembly. "Bring them on."

The sound of Cong's chuckling buzzed over the radio. "Too rutting right."

From behind the faceplate of his surface suit's helmet, Niohuru glared at the pair. Before he could criticize their poor radio discipline, Axum reached out his arm, pointing ahead of them.

"Target," he said simply, a smile faintly visible through his own faceplate.

Looming out of the mist before them was a large cylindrical structure, wider than it was tall, with heavy pipes running to and from it at ground level.

Niohuru let up on the rover's accelerator pedal, letting the vehicle coast forward on its oversized knobby tires for a distance. Finally, it came to a stop, a few dozen meters from the base of the structure.

As he turned to the others, expecting to have to scold them for unnecessary transmissions, Niohuru saw Axum touch his fists together, knuckle to knuckle. Then Axum and Cong leaned together, the left side of one man's helmet coming into contact with the right side of the others. When Niohuru sat motionless for a brief moment, Cong crooked a finger, impatiently motioning him over.

Niohuru leaned forward until his helmet's faceplate rested against Axum's on one side and Cong's on the other. With their helmet-radios' broadcast capabilities switched off, they could speak freely, the vibrations of their voices transmitted through the faceplates and into the air inside the other men's helmets.

"Seems a damned shame to waste all that water," Cong said, his voice buzzing inside Niohuru's helmet.

"It will make a nice explosion," Axum ventured.

Cong's lips curled up in a wicked grin. "It will, at that."

Their orders were to locate and destroy the water reservoir under whose shadow they now sat. Like Cong, though, Niohuru questioned the wisdom of destroying so precious a resource. With water in as short supply on Fire Star as oxygen, and just as valuable, it seemed needlessly wasteful.

"Are we certain this is the right course?" Niohuru asked, giving voice to his concern. "What will happen when the Middle Kingdom retakes the Tamkung Plain, and there are no supplies of water or air for us to capture?"

Cong's grin faded, and in the dim light he fixed Niohuru with a hard stare. "That's a worry for tomorrow, daisy," he said, employing the nickname Niohuru had come so quickly to despise. "For the moment, our worry is simply defeating the enemy."

Niohuru drew his lips into a line, giving the barest of nods, careful to keep his faceplate from breaking contact with theirs. "Of course," he said, momentarily shamed. Niohuru knew he *had* to learn to fit his priorities to his circumstances, and adapt to the realities of the battlefield. Too often he had caught himself thinking like a rank novice. For all their lack of polish—and their poor discipline, radio and otherwise—the other two men in his combat cell were battle-hardened veterans, who knew that there was a time for laxity, and a time to be serious.

"I believe I know where best to inflict damage on the reservoir," Axum said thoughtfully. "I was tasked with incapacitating several of this type last year, and had the opportunity to try several alternatives to determine the best."

Cong grinned. "Just tell me how much explosive is needed and where," he said, indicating the closely packed cases of demolitions on the floorboards beside him. "I'll take care of the rest."

To Niohuru's surprise, he found himself grinning as well. "Let's get to work."

HEXAGRAM 30
COHESION
BELOW FIRE ABOVE FIRE

The bright ones act as a pair. In the same way, the great man continuously casts his brilliance in all four directions.

The sun was setting, a faint bluish hue on the western horizon, but huddled on the eastern side of the ramparts, all that Carter could see was the cold black of night overhead. It had been cloudy the last few nights, a low-lying fog-like mist blanketing the surface, but tonight the only clouds were higher up and clustered off to the north.

Carter thought it might have been two days since he and the rest of the Second Platoon had been sent out as sappers onto the minefield, but he couldn't be sure. The days had run one into the other, spending every moment of daylight out on the minefield, probing for mines and marking clear lanes, then returning with nightfall to the sparse comfort and only relative safety of the temporary pressurized shelters just behind the front lines. In the deadly monotony Carter had lost track of the days. All he knew for certain was that it was night now, and that for the moment, at least, he wasn't getting shot at.

That wouldn't last, of course. But he was enjoying it for the moment.

At the western edge of the minefield was a natural ridge, rising and falling irregularly like waves lapping at a beach, at places only a meter or so above the lowlands to the east but elsewhere rising as high as four or five meters. It was where the ridge rose highest that the Second Platoon had established a bridgehead, sheltered by the natural ramparts from the Mexic guns on the other side of the ridge, both the heavy anti-armor guns which were keeping the Middle Kingdom crawlers from venturing out onto into the open, and the small arms and mounted machine guns which had pocked the ground all around Carter and the other sappers for several days now. A complete catalog of losses and casualties would have to wait until the battle was done, but Carter had seen at least half a dozen sappers cut down by Mexic bullets in the last days, and half as many more obliterated by shrapnel from fragmentation and bouncer mines.

Having reached the relative safety at the other side of the minefield, hidden for the moment from

Mexic fire, Carter had hoped for a brief respite. But he should have known better.

Carter was coming to dread Corporal Eng's smile. The broad shouldered, round-faced Eng was everyone's friend, always mixing with the men and getting their measure, laughing and joking with them. But there was one smile in particular that never seemed to reach his eyes, a smile he only used when he was about to give you some really bad news, or tell you something you really, *really* didn't want to hear. It was a smile that promised another joke about the farmer's lusty daughter or an invitation to a round of mahjong, but instead delivered some kind of odious work detail or a dangerous mission or damned-near-impossible-to-achieve operational objectives.

Corporal Eng was smiling that precise smile when he called all of First-Second together, as the last bluish hue of the setting sun faded somewhere beyond the ramparts at their back.

There had been sixteen men in Second Platoon's First Squad when they set foot on the eastern side of the minefield days before. Now there were only twelve. Neither Carter nor any of the other three members of his fire team had been hit, though, by bullet or bouncer mine, which was some comfort, he supposed.

This close to the Mexic main line of resistance, radio communication was out of the question, and so instead Corporal Eng gave them their marching orders through a combination of hand signs and ideograms scratched out in the dirt with the point of his bayonet, illuminated by the faint glow of his helmet's external lights.

The situation was simple. Sometime after dawn the following morning, the Middle Kingdom crawlers at the other side would start crossing the minefield, following the paths carved out by Carter and the other sappers. When the crawlers reached the ridge to the west, assuming they hadn't all been taken out by Mexic anti-armor fire along the way— and assuming the sappers had done their jobs and cleared the paths completely through the mines— then the minefield would be breached and the assault on the Mexic main line of resistance would begin in earnest.

Those were two significant assumptions, though, that the Mexic anti-armor guns wouldn't take out the Middle Kingdom crawlers and that the sappers had cleared good paths. About the latter, there was nothing more for them to do but wait for first light and hope that their hard work had paid off. About the former, there was still one more thing that could be done, but only the men of First-Second were in a position to do it.

The Middle Kingdom crawlers had so far been spared the worst of the Mexic anti-armor guns, the width of the minefield outranging even the farthest reaching Mexic guns. But as soon as the crawlers rumbled out onto the minefield, hoping against hope that the mines in their path had been cleared, they would be driving right into the range of the anti-armor guns, which was bound to take its toll.

First-Second's assignment was simple, in description, at least. Under cover of darkness, they were to sneak round the rampart at the their back, ranging ahead toward the Mexic lines, there to locate and "paint" the enemy firing positions with markers. Operating independently on timers, each marker would, as the sun rose in the east, ignite a flare, burning blinding bright and sending up a column of thick, colored smoke. As the Middle Kingdom crawlers ventured onto the minefield, their gun crews would use the lights and the columns of smoke to target the enemy gun emplacements and fire.

Assuming enough of the Mexic anti-armor emplacements were taken out, the Middle Kingdom crawlers would be able to advance with only small arms and machine-gun fire to oppose them.

Corporal Eng, through that empty smile, had explained that they had a rough idea where three of the anti-armor guns were placed, and were sending a fire team to locate and paint each of them. Carter's fire team, who had been among the first across the minefield and into the bridgehead, was given the task of painting the gun furthest south, off to the left of their current position.

So with the sky now fully dark and filled with stars overhead, Carter and the rest of his fire team moved off to the south, following the ridge and keeping low, out of sight. They worked in pairs, leapfrogging bases of fire, covering all angles of possible attack. First Carter and the African grenadier Moonface would advance, covered by the Arab rifleman Ears with his sniper rifle and the Rossiyan gunner Spitter with his machine gun, then Ears and Spitter would advance while Moonface with his grenade launcher and Carter with his carbine covered them. They were not friends, the four of them, but in much the same way that they leapfrogged one position after another, so they had leapfrogged being acquaintances and rivals to being something nearer brothers. They didn't always like one another, and sometimes hated one another, but they *needed* each other, and could work together in perfect coherence like a well-timed machine.

By dawn, with any luck, they'd be on their way back to the bridgehead, in one piece, having left the marker behind in the close vicinity of the southern anti-armor gun—as close as they could get it in the dark of night without being spotted, at any rate. And as the Middle Kingdom crawlers began their slow crawl across the minefield, and began to exchange fire with the gun emplacements, now targeted and spotted for their convenience, maybe *then* Carter and the others could catch a few moments to relax and recuperate.

It wasn't likely to happen, but that didn't stop Carter wishing.

Hexagram 31
Reciprocity
Below Mountain Above Lake

The Lake is above the Mountain. In the same way, the noble man receives others with self-effacement.

Niohuru licked his dry lips, trying not to check his chronometer again for another few minutes, at least.

The First Raider Company was still behind enemy lines, now formed up in an irregular column and heading south. It was nearly three days since they and their rovers had made a night drop behind the Mexic perimeter to the east, three days in which they'd performed a series of quick hit-and-run attacks on Mexic positions from the rear. So far, they'd exchanged fire with Mexica in a number of limited skirmishes; there'd been no casualties among the Falcon's Claws, and only minor injuries.

The worst encounter led to one of the knobby-wheeled rovers being rendered incapacitated, which had simply necessitated three other combat cells being temporarily expanded to four members, with each of the three men squeezing onboard other rovers, lending their semi-automatic fire in support of the two mounted machine guns.

By any measure, the raiding foray had thus far been a successful one, with the Falcon's Claws dealing blows to the Mexic supply lines and rearguard for three straight days.

Unfortunately, as all of the men in the First Raiding Company were too well aware, they carried only enough supplies of air, water, food, and petroleum to last them a little over three days. If they did not get a resupply, and soon, they would be in considerable trouble.

The cells had rejoined near the end of the third full day. As the sun was just beginning to rise in the east, Captain Hughes had ordered them to form up and head south, where the bombers of the Interplanetary Fleet Air Corps were scheduled to make a supply drop. They had several hours to cover nearly one hundred-fifty kilometers. Already their water supplies had dwindled to nearly nothing, and they only had air enough to last into the next day. Their petroleum supplies would last a little longer, but if there were none of them left breathing by that point it hardly seemed to matter.

They were cutting it fine, in short. Niohuru had learned that was standard operating procedure in the Falcon's Claws. Still, he couldn't help checking his chronometer, working out how much time remained before the gauges spiked into the red.

As the sky pinked in the east, the southern horizon was broken by a line of ridges and hillocks, the start of the irregular landscape that marked the boundary of the Tamkung Plain. Even as the sun crept higher, long shadows still spilled across the irregular terrain. In some places, only at noon with the sun at its zenith, would sunlight hit the ground.

The rough terrain didn't serve only to block the sun, but blocked vision, as well. The Falcon's Claws were wary as they moved further south. The only thing worse than being out in the open with no cover, Niohuru had found, was being undercover and unable to see what was around the next corner.

Midmorning, at about eleven degrees north latitude, they came upon a network of yardangs, ridges left behind by countless millennia of wind erosion. The yardangs with their stream-lined sides looked something like long, thin overturned boat-hulls, highest and broadest at the northern end where they faced the prevailing winds, becoming lower and narrower as they progressed toward the leeward end.

The tops of the yardangs rose several meters above the eroded ground, too high for Captain Hughes to see over, even when standing on the shoulders of his rover's driver.

Beyond the network of yardangs and out of sight was the ridge atop which the Falcon's Claws were to wait for their supply drop, scheduled to coincide with a bombing run the evening of that day. But with ridges on either side of them obscuring what might lie ahead or to the left or right, they had no way of knowing what might be waiting for them.

"We could go around," one of the bannermen put forward, when Captain Hughes put the matter to the Falcon's Claws, opening the matter up for debate.

Another shook his head, the motion visible even beneath his helmet and surface suit. "We don't have sufficient petroleum."

"We cannot simply ride in blind," still another responded. "The dung-eaters might not know our location exactly, but they are sure to know that we are heading south, and may have radioed ahead to others lying in wait."

"But they can't have enough men in the area to cover every rutting channel through the yardangs," Cong put in, pointing to the seven or eight channels visible from where they stood.

"So we are simply to gamble?" Axum asked. "Picking a path and hoping it is not the one in which an ambush waits?"

A few more suggestions were offered, but Niohuru's attention had drifted. He was feeling his way around the edges of an idea, considering it from all angles before suggesting it. Finally, in a brief lull, he spoke up.

"Divide," he said simply.

Hughes turned to look in his direction. "What was that, Tie?"

Niohuru took a deep breath, pausing before answering. "Divide our forces. If the only path forward is through one of these channels, and an ambush might wait behind any one of them, it seems only reasonable that we should divide our number, sending only a percentage of the total into each pass. Then, even if more than one of the channels is guarded on the far end by Mexic forces, others of us will make it through clear, and hopefully be in a position to return once resupplied and give aid. Best-case scenario, none of us encounter the enemy, but if the Mexic are out there, this way at least we increase the odds of someone making it through to continue the mission."

Behind his faceplate, Hughes smiled. "Good suggestion, Tie. That's operational thinking, putting the mission ahead of the men."

Niohuru averted his eyes, self-conscious. "It is nothing remarkable, captain." He paused, then quickly corrected himself. "*Falco.*"

Hughes turned to address the others. "That's enough discussion. I propose we go with Tie's plan, any serious objection?"

Beside Niohuru, Cong began to grumble.

"Any *serious* objection," Hughes repeated. Silence was his answer. "Alright, then. Form up in five columns of seventeen rovers each, and prepare to move out." He caught Niohuru's eye. "Keep it up, Tie."

Within moments, the First Raider Company had grouped as ordered, and each of the five columns turned away from the others, entering five widely spaced channels into the yardang network.

Niohuru's rover was near the rear of the column of seventeen, heading into the channel on the farthest left. Once they had passed between the massive yardangs on either side, there was nothing to see but the pink sky overhead, the rock looming to left and right, and the rear end of the rover in front of them, barely visible through the clouds of dust and sand kicked up.

For nearly an hour the column advanced, slowly progressing deeper into the yardang network. Niohuru wondered how the other columns were progressing, wondering whether they had run into any Mexic forces. The thick rock of the yardangs was interfering with their ability to transmit radio signals from one column to another, and any attempt to increase their broadcast strength to overcome the interference would certainly be picked up by any nearby Mexica, who might use it to triangulate their position. So they were forced to advance in silence, able only to wonder at the state of the others, and to worry whether any of them had entered an ambush.

As the ridges on either side began gradually to grow shorter, though, Niohuru suddenly had worries of his own to occupy him.

Pouring over the tops of the yardangs on either side, their surface suits painted with bright, fantastical designs, came a detachment of Jaguar Knights, the elite ground forces of the Mexic Dominion.

With their helmets shaped like jaguar's head, the faceplates held between massive jaws, the Jaguar Knights carried fire-lances from which shot streams of burning liquid magnesium, or rifles not unlike the Falcon's Claws' own semi-automatics, or else just shouted imprecations while waving clubs lined with razor-sharp obsidian blades.

"That's it?" Cong asked, from behind Niohuru.

Niohuru saw what he meant, even while flinching as a Mexic bullet spanged off the front frame of the rover. There were only a dozen or so Jaguar Knights on either side, easily outnumbered and outgunned by the fifty-odd bannermen in the seventeen rovers. The Jaguar Knights had waited until more than half of the column had passed their position before leaping out, but now that they had revealed themselves the bannermen had stopped in their tracks, swiveling their machine guns and preparing to open fire.

It didn't make any sense. The Mexica would have seen better results from opening fire upon the bannermen from hiding, using the high walls of the yardangs for cover. By revealing themselves, they'd only encouraged the bannermen to stop and open fire, when it was clear how few Jaguar Knights there were on hand.

Unless, of course, their intention was to make the bannermen stop...

Niohuru's eyes widened, as he threw his rover into reverse. "Fall back!" he shouted over his helmet-radio. "Fall back! It's a trap!"

On the passenger seat beside him, Axum sighted along the barrel of his machine gun. "Of course it is a trap, daisy…"

"No," Niohuru said, cutting the Ethiop off with a wave of his hand. He pointed at the dusty ground before them, on which the other rovers still parked. "*That* is the trap."

As if in response, the ground erupted with a plume of smoke and dust as explosives buried beneath the surface were detonated. They were mines, not keyed for weight but for remote detonation. The Mexica's plan had been to get as many of the rovers to stop above the explosives as possible, to increase the detonation's toll.

"Eighteen hells!" Cong shouted, looking back over his shoulder as the rover nearest the blast blew up off of the ground, spinning several times in midair before landing wrong-side up, crushing the driver and passengers underneath.

"Bastards!" Axum shouted, firing his machine gun at the Jaguar Knights who even now were retreating back beyond the tops of the yardangs, where they could return fire from cover. The Jaguar Knights were moving with a swift, merciless precision, doubtless seeking reciprocity for the attacks performed by the Falcon's Claws in the days past.

"It looks like they only hit one of us," Niohuru shouted, squinting through the dust and debris as he continued to drive the rover backward away from the blast. From what he could tell, there were a half-dozen or so other rovers reversing and heading back the way they had come, along with him, and the rest were powering away toward the channel's leeward end on the far side of the blast. "No, make that two," he said. Gripping the wheel, he glanced over his shoulder at the others. "Should we return fire? If we routed the Mexica, maybe we could check for survivors?"

Tightlipped, Axum shook his head.

"You heard the captain," Cong responded, eyes dark and narrowed. "The mission comes before the men. Besides, there's no hope for those poor bastards. Anyone that has a rover dropped on them isn't getting up, one-third gravity or not."

"We don't have enough air to stand and fight," Axum said, his voice barely above a whisper. "If we stay, we all die."

"Drive back the way we came," Cong said, refusing to meet Niohuru's gaze. "With any luck we'll have enough petroleum to join up with one of the other columns and continue with them. They can't *all* have been hit."

Niohuru nodded. He continued to drive in reverse until they were outside the range of the Jaguar Knights' rifles, then maneuvered the rover around, a task complicated by the nearness of the yardangs on both sides and the half-dozen other rovers crowded before and after. The sun appeared above them, shining on them for a moment before dipping beyond the yardang to the west, like the sunlight shining down into an open grave.

HEXAGRAM 32
PERSEVERANCE
BELOW WIND ABOVE THUNDER

Thunder together with Wind. In the same way, the noble man takes a stand and does not change direction.

"Tighten up," crackled the voice of the squadron leader over the radio, buzzing in Amonkar's helmet speakers. Of the other members of the *Fair Winds for Escort* crew, only she, Co-pilot Seathl, and Navigator Geng were currently wired to hear the outside broadcasts, everyone else on the bomber communicating over the plane's own hardline system. "You've got your targets."

Fair Winds for Escort was on another bombing run. With the ground forces of the Middle Kingdom making significant inroads into the eastern perimeter, and with Middle Kingdom raiding companies hammering from behind the Mexic lines, the bomber squadrons and their fighter escorts had been ordered to turn their attentions from the main line of defense in the east to the Mexic rearguard to the west.

"Crossing line of engagement now," Navigator Geng called over the hardline. They were now over Mexic-held territory once more.

"Look alive back there," Amonkar called to the crew. "No hostiles spotted yet, but it's only a matter of time. Siagyo, you awake down there?" Amonkar tapped her boot against the deck-plate, as if the nose gunner could hear her over the roar of the Deliverer's engines.

"Can't I nap, captain? I was having a good dream last night and want to get back to it."

Amonkar smiled, but ignored her. She already had an idea what sort of dream the lusty Siagyo might consider "good," and didn't need any visual imagery to go along with it.

"How about you, Lambert? Comfortable back there?"

"Y-yes," stammered Tail Gunner Lambert, her voice quavering. "I'm fine, just… just fine."

Amonkar's smile faded somewhat. "You just point and shoot when we tell you, tail gunner, and you'll do fine."

"Yes, my captain," Lambert replied, overly formal.

Amonkar suppressed a weary sigh, then exchanged a meaningful glance with Seathl beside her.

The new tail gunner on *Fair Winds for Escort* was a Francois woman who had only been on Fire Star a matter of days before she was tapped to man the vacant tail turret. Lambert was fresh out of flight training, one of the replacement units sent to reinforce the front lines after the losses of the first days of Operation Great Holdings. She had been cross-trained to work either as a nose or tail gunner, or as a bombardier, so certainly knew her way around a Deliverer-class bomber. But she had not seen any combat before signing on with Amonkar's crew, and it showed. It was hard to remember that only a matter of weeks before, neither Amonkar nor Seathl or any of the other members of the *Fair Winds for Escort* crew had been in combat either. But those first long days of Great Holdings had turned them all into hardened veterans in short order. Or so they thought, at any rate.

"Bombardier," Amonkar went on, calling across the hardline, "are the packages ready for delivery?"

"As always, o captain," the Persian Mehdi responded, his smile audible in his voice. "Just give the word."

She couldn't help but feel for the bombardier. When they'd first crewed up *Fair Winds for Escort* before leaving flight training, the crew complement had been equally divided between the sexes, three men and three women. When Bosch had scrubbed out, and Seathl brought in as the new second seat when Amonkar was bumped to pilot, there were four women to two men. Now with Lambert in the tail turret, the only man left onboard was Bombardier Mehdi.

When Lambert had appeared in their billet, a broad smile had crept across Mehdi's gaunt face, and he'd joked that it seemed as though he should have better luck with women, being the only man in the crew. Then Seathl had made an off-hand comment about it clearly being dangerous to be a man onboard *Fair Winds for Escort*, but that had only served to remind everyone what had happened to the *last* tail gunner, and the laughter had quickly died away.

"Distance to target?" Amonkar asked, glancing over at the co-pilot. Before Seathl could relay the request to the navigator, Geng piped up with a response.

"Should be any minute now, Arati."

Seathl looked over to Amonkar and shrugged. "A few minutes, I suppose, skipper."

Amonkar nodded, her lips drawn into a line. Discipline onboard the ship had never been the best, but so long as the crew had got their jobs done, Amonkar hadn't minded. Perhaps it was the addition of a new crew member who still observed all of the spit-and-polish protocols of flight training school that had reminded Amonkar just how far she'd let things slide. Maybe it was time to tighten the reins a bit, after all. She liked the fact that she and her crewmates had become friendly—and in fact that she considered two of them actual *friends*—but protocols had been put in place for a reason, not least of which that a captain had to know who would be answering questions, and to whom questions should be directed, since in the heat of combat, crosstalk could lead to confusion, and confusion could lead to mistakes. Fatal mistakes.

Their target was an ammunition dump, well behind the enemy's main line of resistance. Orbital surveillance had provided longitude and latitude, and enough description of the structure's appearance that they should be able to spot it.

"There it is," Seathl said, pointing ahead as they neared the target's coordinates. She leaned forward to peer down through the forward windshield. Then, quickly, she reared, "Whore-son mother-raper!"

Amonkar leaned forward, trying to see what had set the co-pilot off. "What is it?"

"Look!" Seathl said, jabbing a finger at the structures ahead of and below them.

There was the ammunitions dump, just as their mission briefing had described. But what the briefing *hadn't* covered was the structure next to it, apparently hastily constructed, with symbols of some kind crudely painted on the roof.

"That one on the left is the Nahuatl glyph for 'medicine' or 'healing'," Seathl said.

Amonkar's eyes narrowed to slits as she nodded. "That *would* be fitting, considering."

Considering that the symbol painted next to the Nahuatl glyph was a crude red crescent.

"Is it a *hospital*?" Siagyo called over the hardline.

"Looks like," Amonkar answered absently, all thought of protocol forgotten. Then, in a voice barely above a whisper, she added, "Eighteen hells, it *is* a hospital."

The Red Crescent had first been used to symbolize emergency medical workers hundreds of years before, when Turkiye had waged war on Ellas, before either of them became satellites of the Dragon Throne. It was recognized throughout the Middle Kingdom and her allies on two planets and a handful of moons. So far as Amonkar knew, it wasn't used in the Mexic Dominion, but apparently the Nahuatl glyph served the same purpose there. The presence of both the "healing" glyph and the Red Crescent was to make absolutely sure to anyone who saw it, Mexic or Middle Kingdom, just what the structure below was.

"A rutting hospital," Seathl swore. "Next to an ammo dump."

The Mexica had intentionally put a strategic military target, a prized ammunition dump, next to a hospital, or more likely the other way around. Doubtless they had counted on the sympathy and sentiment of the Middle Kingdom bomber crews not to target a structure housing wounded and convalescing Mexic warriors.

But if the ammunition dump *wasn't* hit, it could be used against Middle Kingdom troops, who would fill other hospitals, somewhere else.

"So what do we do?" Seathl asked, glancing over at Amonkar.

"What *can* we do?" Amonkar answered.

She had been given a mission, and she was going to carry it out. She'd been forced to accept the possibility of incidental casualties when she first ordered a bomb dropped from *Fair Winds for Escort*'s hold, and the sure knowledge that unarmed enemies might be hit was not much worse than the assumption of the same had been these last days.

"Arati, are you sure?" came the voice of Geng over the hardline.

Amonkar set her jaw. She had already made this decision, days before, knowing she'd have to face it sooner or later. And having made the decision, she was going to stick with it.

"Bombardier," she called over the hardline, "prepare to drop."

Seathl gave her a close look, then nodded and turned back to her controls. The others kept silent, each at their duties.

Amonkar knew that they had all made the same decision themselves, one way or another. And having already chosen their path, all that remained was to follow that path through to the end.

HEXAGRAM 33
WITHDRAWAL
BELOW MOUNTAIN ABOVE HEAVEN

Below Heaven, there is the Mountain. In the same way, the noble man keeps at a distance the petty man, whom he does not overtly despise but from whom he remains aloof.

On the fourth day of the assault, the armies of the Mexic Dominion retreated before the advancing forces of the Dragon Throne, surrendering the eastern border of the Tamkung Plain and falling back to reinforced positions in the west. With its final operational objectives complete, therefore, Operation Great Holdings was officially completed.

These last actions of Great Holdings, the concerted push from the east into the Mexic-held territories between Bao Shan and the Three Purities Range, the culmination of so much expenditure of blood, effort, fuel, and munitions, were devoted entirely to retaking a small strip of land that was only a few hundred meters wide from east to west, running a few hundred kilometers from north to south. Located at the escarpment where the kilometers wide region of furrows and ridges extending out from the western slopes of Bao Shan met the smooth unbroken expanse of Tamkung Plain.

Having resupplied and reorganized in the captured complexes of hangars, habitats, and greenhouses after the first days of Great Holdings, the forces of the Middle Kingdom had thrown themselves in an all-out assault against the Mexic main line of defense, combined with bombing runs and raids behind enemy lines, until the minefields along the escarpment were breached and the Middle Kingdom battered into the entrenched Mexic positions.

The Mexic had broken and run, in their maddeningly controlled and orderly way, pulling back to the west, their lines drawing thinner at the front. The Middle Kingdom, facing only token resistance from the retreating Mexic rearguard, overran the eastern edge of Tamkung Plain, occupying the gun emplacements and defiles from which the Jaguar Knights had shot at them only hours before.

The Middle Kingdom now held the eastern extremity of Tamkung Plain, the final objective of Great Holdings, but it had come at a considerable cost. Thousands of lives had been lost and countless munitions expended in order to gain a featureless strip of land only a few hundred meters wide, a few hundred square kilometers in area, wholly unremarkable but for its strategic importance.

But despite it all, the forces of the Dragon Throne couldn't pause to celebrate their victory or to mourn their dead. For the Tamkung escarpment was merely the next step in a journey that had already taken more than twelve years, and was far from over yet. Their ultimate goal lay at the heart of Tamkung Plain, nearly a thousand kilometers to the west, in the crater colonies of Ruosi and Zijun.

The Middle Kingdom had made considerable progress since the launch of Operation Great Holdings, but that progress had not come nearly fast enough. If they were to reach the crater colonies and overthrow the Mexic strongholds before reinforcements and resupplies arrived from the Mexic Dominion, they would need a bold strategy, decisive action, and good fortune.

Unfortunately, what they got was Operation Great Strength.

HEXAGRAM 34
GREAT STRENGTH
BELOW HEAVEN ABOVE THUNDER

Above Heaven, there is Thunder. In the same way, the noble man will not tread any course that is not commensurate with decorum.

Deep within the Zhurong moonbase, the final plans for the next major offensive had been taking shape since before the first morning of Operation Great Holdings. The commanders of the Eight Banners and of the Green Standard, along with the admirals of the Interplanetary Fleet, had pored over orbital surveillance, monitoring Mexic troop movements, evaluating the strengths and weaknesses of the enemy position. When the Mexic forces retreated before the Middle Kingdom assault at the Tamkung escarpment, the final decisions were made, and the orders sent by coded transmissions to the commanders on the ground.

It was a bold strategy that, if it worked, would speed the Middle Kingdom towards victory, ensuring the defeat of the enemy in a fraction of the time that more conventional methods would require. If it failed, however...

When the orders were received by the ranking officers on the ground, some called the strategy a bold move, while others considered it the potentially decisive operation of the entire Second Mexic War. There were, however, those nay-sayers who whispered that the plan was dangerously overconfident at best, and wasteful if not borderline suicidal at worst, but such objections were rarely voiced in the open.

The strategy called for the ground forces to make a rapid advance, pushing through the weakest point of the Mexic line. The advancing phalanx of Middle Kingdom infantry, supported by the bombers and fighters of the Air Corps, would drive deeper southwest into Tamkung Plain, like an arrow shot directly towards the crater colony of Ruosi. The Mexic Dominion, with their forces stretched thin along the eastern main line of defense by their recent retreat, would be ill-equipped to resist the advance, and as a result the Mexic forces would be effectively halved, with part of them isolated south of the Middle Kingdom advance and the other part isolated to the north. The main body of the Middle Kingdom forces could then continue pushing onward towards Ruosi and Zijun beyond, leaving their rearguard to mop up the remaining Mexic forces on their flanks.

So it was that, despite the grumbled warnings and objections of those few nay-sayers in the rear echelon, Operation Great Strength commenced.

Hexagram 35
Advance
Below Earth Above Fire

Brightness appears above the Earth. In the same way, the noble man illuminates himself with bright virtue.

Somewhere behind them, Middle Kingdom artillery and mobile armor still pounded into the Mexic main line of defense, the impacts occasionally felt as slight tremors in the ground beneath their feet, but for Guardsman Carter and the rest of the men of the First Squad of Fourth Company's Second Platoon the main concern wasn't what lay behind them, but what might be ahead that most occupied their thoughts.

The sun had set hours ago, the stars all but hidden by the clouds overhead. They moved in nearly total darkness, watchful for any sign of Mexic resistance. If they *were* to be spotted by the Mexica, the first that they'd likely know of would be a flare lighting up the sky, if they were lucky, and a Mexic bullet to the head, if they weren't.

Carter wasn't sure who he had angered to find himself waist-deep in trouble, kilometers on the wrong side of enemy lines. Maybe it wasn't his own sins he was working off, come to that, but those of one of his comrades. He couldn't help but glance over at the Rossiyan guardsman at his side, a heavy machine gun in his hands. Carter smiled. Yes, it would stand to reason that this was Spitter's fault, somehow.

When the order to march had come down from on high the day before, First-Second had drawn the short straw and ended up as the point troop for the advance. So while the majority of the ground forces engaged in an all-out assault on the Mexic front, as soon as a gap appeared in the line, First-Second drove forward, pushing past and into enemy-held territory. There were others following close behind, if everything had gone to plan, with armored crawlers and support teams keeping the Mexica from pursuing them, but out here in front, with nothing but Mexica on three sides—left, right, and ahead—the men of First-Second were on their own.

Their orders were to advance as far and as fast as possible, setting up a forward post that would then be linked with supporting positions ranging back towards the breach in the Mexic main line to the east. The posts, ranged a little more than a kilometer apart north to south, would be used to set up a corridor driving towards the west into Mexic territory, splitting the Mexica north and south, and creating a thoroughfare directly towards the Mexic strongholds to the west.

That was the plan, at any rate. But even as Corporal Eng was giving them their marching orders, it was clear to Carter that he wasn't the only one to question the strategy's merits.

At the moment, though, larger questions of strategy and tactics were the furthest things from Carter's mind. Like the rest of the men in the squad, his principle concern was surviving the night.

They had come upon a deserted compound, a Middle Kingdom colonial settlement with habitats interspersed with the domes of greenhouses, factories, and bacteria farms. The settlement must have been long since abandoned, since it appeared that not one of the structures was completely intact, all of them shot through with holes, or with crumbling walls, or otherwise unable to be pressurized.

On the northern edge of the compound a rough road of hard-packed red dirt snaked in among the broken structures from the flat expanse of Tamkung Plain to the north, and as it moved through the settlement it angled to the west, continuing on into the night. If this was the track that they'd been shown on the map, it would continue on like an arrow due west to Ruosi.

Corporal Eng motioned the men together, and gave them their instructions by hand signals and gestures. As he'd explained in their briefing the morning before, the fact that the compound straddled the road to Ruosi made it strategically useful. Their orders were to check the compound for any Mexic elements, clear out any of the enemy and gain control of the area, and then use the settlement as a forward base of operations. They carried collapsible tents, that could be fully pressurized in the event that they were able to secure the area sufficiently to set up temporary facilities, to give them a few moments out of their surface suits if possible.

They had managed to check about half of the structures in the compound, all of them empty, when the Mexic crawler rumbled into town, and then all hell broke loose.

"Contact!" shouted somebody over Carter's helmet radio, while he was still checking the interior of a ruined habitat. When he and the rest of his fire team rushed back out into the night, their weapons hot and ready to fire, it was as if the sun had returned from the far side of the sky, a flare blinding bright as it drifted back down to the ground under its wide parachute.

That was the first that Carter and the others saw of the enemy since they'd broken through the breach in the Mexic line. A crawler, flanked by a detachment of Jaguar Knights, none of whom looked as if they'd expected to find anyone lurking inside the long-abandoned settlement.

Before Carter could squeeze off a round with his carbine, the forward most of the Jaguar Knights sent a gout of burning magnesium pouring over the guardsmen on the far side of the road. One of the guardsmen fell to the ground, screaming over his helmet radio, more panicked than hurt, but the rest dropped into defensive crouches and, carefully braced against the recoil, opened fire on the Mexica. Carter didn't wait to get sprayed himself, and joined in.

"Find your targets and open up," he shouted over the radio to Spitter, Ears, and Moonface, who wasted no time in complying.

The Jaguar Knights had been caught off guard, that much was clear. Most had their weapons slung, and many of the rest only carried wooden clubs lined with obsidian blades, vicious and lethal at close quarters but not much good when facing the range of Middle Kingdom carbines. They were a guard detachment, little more than sentries on foot for the crawler they protected, and clearly hadn't been expecting any resistance this deep into Mexic territory.

The fact that the Jaguar Knights had walked into the situation completely unprepared was probably all that saved First-Second from a serious fight. Though the guardsmen outnumbered the Mexica nearly two-to-one in the encounter, the Mexica had a crawler on their side, and though the crawler was a transport and not a mobile artillery unit, it was still equipped with mounted machine guns, which should have more than made up for the Middle Kingdom's superior numbers.

Of course, it was far from the first time that First-Second had gone into combat together, and each man knew his role.

Moonface shot a grenade from his launcher that smacked square into the forward left machine gun turret on the crawler, bending the gun's barrel out of true and nearly cracking the crawler's outer hull in half, cracks spidering out in all directions.

Spitter opened up with his machine gun, sending a spray of bullets at waist height across the nearest of the Jaguar Knights.

Ears crouched, raised the scope of his sniper rifle to his eye, and squeezed off one careful shot after another, taking aim at the faceplates of the Jaguar Knight's outlandish helmets, one of the weakest points on the Mexic armor. The only place weaker was the exposed air hose that led from the air tanks on their back up into their helmet, exposed for several centimeters, unlike the air systems of the Middle Kingdom surface suits, which flowed air from the tanks to the helmet through the carapace seal. Otherwise, the Mexic surface suits were considerably better armored than those of the Middle Kingdom, and notoriously difficult to crack open.

They were not, however, *impossible* to crack open, as Spitter's repeated machine gun barrages and a few grenades from Moonface were able to put more than a few of the Jaguar Knights on the ground, with the rest of the gunners and grenadiers of First-Second doing likewise. With Carter, Ears, and the rest of First-Second's carbines and snipers targeting the Mexic faceplates, the rest of the Jaguar Knights were down in short order.

The drivers of the crawler were safe behind the reinforced armor of the hull, and would likely have driven off, continuing on to Ruosi, if not for a half-dozen well-placed grenades from Moonface and the other three grenadiers in First-Second, which knocked the treads on the port side off their rollers. The crawler dug into the red dirt on one side as the treads on the starboard side continued to churn away, listing in a ragged circle, until finally the drivers gave up and, obviously preferring death to capture, threw open the door and rushed out at their Middle Kingdom attackers, armed with nothing more than obsidian-lined clubs.

In the dramas Carter had watched as a boy; if an enemy had come rushing at a better armed and outnumbering force with nothing but a bladed weapon, the commander of the opposing force would do something noble like order his men to hold their fire, while he went forward to meet the enemy on equal terms. But Corporal Eng wasn't a scripted player in a drama, and he didn't draw his saber and go forward to meet the Mexic drivers one on one. He had remained with his men, firing with his carbine, not ordering the others to hold fire until the drivers had fallen beneath the barrage of bullets. Even if the Middle Kingdom weapons hadn't broken open the drivers' surface suits, and even if their suits' armor had absorbed some of the bullet impacts, they would have been bruised and battered enough that their bones would likely have shattered in several places and their internal organs awash with heavy internal bleeding.

When the last of the Mexic defenders fell, the worst that First-Second had sustained was a bit of bruising, with no serious injuries and no loss of life.

"Tejas," Corporal Eng said over their helmet radios, pointing in Carter's direction, "crack open the crawler and make sure there aren't any more dung-eaters hiding inside."

Carter reached the rear of the crawler, and slung his carbine while Ears, Spitter, and Moonface covered him. It took several moments to work out the unfamiliar door mechanism, and another few moments to wrench the heavy door open

"Um, corporal?" Carter called over the radio, as soon as the door swung open. "You're going to want to see this."

The corporal swore under his breath as he moved to join Carter's fire team. "You may not have noticed, Tejas, but they got a flare up before the shooting started, and we may have company sooner than we'd like."

Carter nodded, and pointed inside the crawler. "I think we've got company *now*, corporal."

Inside the crawler, on the other side of a pressurized cage-wall, were a half-dozen Middle Kingdom colonists—men, women, and children. They had the glassy-eyed look of having been drugged, a tactic the Mexica often used to keep their prisoners tractable and calm. But even underneath the imposed docility, there was panic and fear evident in their expressions. These prisoners knew just what use the Mexica had intended for them, and the use to which they'd still be put if the Mexica got their hands on them again.

Which meant that it fell to the First-Second to get the prisoners to safety, or else they'd end up on the sacrificial altar after all, their life blood spilled out at the end of a black glass blade.

"Eighteen hells," Corporal Eng swore, the barrel of his carbine drooping toward the ground like a detumescent member. "I *knew* this was a bad idea…"

HEXAGRAM 36
SUPPRESSION OF THE LIGHT
BELOW FIRE ABOVE EARTH

The light has gone into the earth. In the same way, the noble man oversees the mass of common folk.

The Mexic crawler which had been transporting the half-dozen prisoners had been too badly damaged in the fire fight with First-Second to be moved, and it appeared that the pressurized cell within was quickly losing air through a series of cracks along the seal with the crawler's inner hull. It was only a matter of time before the cell completely lost pressure and the prisoners within, who were dressed only in tattered and thin shirts and pants, would suffocate or freeze, whichever came first.

It had been Carter's suggestion to set up one of the temporary pressurized shelters that they had brought along. The tents had been intended as their base of operations once they'd cleared the compound of any Mexica, and established a forward position, but they had a much more urgent use at the moment as shelter for the rescued prisoners.

Corporal Eng had quickly pointed out that the shelters wouldn't stand up to a tossed rock, much less a Mexic bullet, and if any Jaguar Knights in the area had seen the flare sent up by the fallen prisoner escorts only moments before, bullets would doubtless be flying again in short order. But Eng allowed that the idea of shifting the prisoners out of the crawler and into something not actively leaking warmth and air was a solid suggestion.

Eng sent out a handful of guardsmen to scour the abandoned structures in the compound, looking for one that was reasonably well intact, and with a large enough interior to accommodate one of the pressure tents. The idea was that the walls of the structure would help shield the tent from view, and from bullets if need be. It was a gamble, but was better than leaving the prisoners to freeze, at best, and to be retaken and delivered to blood-hungry Mexic torturers and executioners, at worst.

Finally, a suitable structure was found, once a bacteria farm, now just a hemispherical dome several meters high at its tallest, with only a bare handful of breaches in its walls, and these relatively small and widely spaced. Even better, it was only a dozen or so meters from where the crawler was parked.

Once one of the pressure tents had been inflated inside the dome, the men of First-Second had to put their backs to it. With the starboard side treads grinding away, Carter and the others were positioned on the port side, pushing to the right and forwards as hard as they were able, trying to compensate for the lopsided propulsion. It was only after more than an hour of effort, and a few twisted ankles and dislocated shoulders, that they got the crawler near enough to the bacteria farm's front entrance. An umbilicus was dragged out, connecting the airlock on the pressure tent to that on the rear of the crawler, and the six prisoners were shepherded through as quickly as possible. When all of the prisoners were safely through the airlock and into the shelter, the umbilicus was recoiled, and the crawler left where it stood.

The prisoners were scarcely aware of their surroundings, still addled by the Mexic drugs which had sedated them, but began slowly to regain their senses, and were ecstatic over their rescue at the hands of the First-Second squad. Like Carter and the others, they had all heard horror stories about what the Mexica did with their prisoners, and had prayed for deliverance.

Now that the prisoners had been delivered, though, there still remained the question of what to do with them. They were safe inside the pressure tent for the moment, but couldn't be left on their own, or they'd be easy prey for the next Mexic patrol to come through. First-Second still had the rest of the compound to check and clear before they could establish the forward post, and there was the strong possibility that more Mexica would arrive soon, drawn by the Jaguar Knights' flares.

In the end, Corporal Eng decided to divide his forces, albeit in unequal divisions.

"Tejas, Spitter," Eng said, pointing to Carter and his Rossiyan gunner, "I want you two to stay close to this dome, keeping watch over the prisoners. The rest of us will sweep out and check the rest of the settlement, and once I'm confident it's clear we'll entrench here and radio back for assistance. With any luck, we'll just sit tight until reinforcements arrive, and then we can call for a crawler to come pick these people up and take them back behind the line."

"And if not?" Carter asked. "If we *don't* have any luck?"

Eng gave him a grim look and shook his head. "I'm trying not to think about those options."

Once the corporal and the rest of the First-Second had moved off, Ears and Moonface tagging along behind another fire team, and Carter and Spitter took up positions on either side of the dome's entrance, their weapons ready, their eyes scanning the darkness around them.

Time passed, and nothing happened. Carter and Spitter stayed at their posts under radio silence. If not for the chronometer on his wrist, which he checked every few moments, Carter wouldn't have had the slightest idea how much time he'd been standing there. It seemed like an eternity, but had been a little less than an hour. Then the shouting started over the radio, and the lights started flashing on the far side of the compound, obscured by the nearer buildings.

"Contact!" "Enemy engagement!" "Taking fire!"

From where they stood, neither Carter nor Spitter had any notion how many Mexic troops were attacking, but it was clear that it was not an outnumbered and unsuspecting prisoner escort. More like the main Mexic column, if the amount of gunfire being exchanged was any indication.

They were far from the battle, which was happening on the outskirts of the colonial settlement, a considerable distance from the bacteria farm dome where the prisoners had been moved. But even at this remove, they could see the flashes of tracer fire, and the bright sunbursts of incendiaries exploding off to the west.

"Fall back!" came the voice of Corporal Eng, crackling over their helmet radios. "Fall back!"

Spitter had raced around the perimeter of the ruined dome, rushing to Carter's side. "Come on, Tejas," he said, jerking a thumb towards the east. "Time to be getting out of here."

The Rossiyan turned to go, but Carter reached out and grabbed hold of his elbow before he could move. "What about the prisoners?" Carter glanced towards the entrance of the ruined dome, the pressure tent all but invisible beyond the shadows within. "We can't just *leave* them here."

Spitter shrugged, his lips pursed, then tugged his arm from Carter's grasp. "The corporal says fall back, I fall back."

Carter scowled. He suspected that the gunner was right, but wasn't about to agree. "Fine," he said at length, exasperated. "You go." Spitter began to turn. "But I'm staying here," Carter quickly added.

Spitter paused, glancing back over his shoulder.

"You go ahead," Carter said, more an order than a suggestion, "and tell Corporal Eng that I've stayed behind with the prisoners. I'm not leaving them alone."

The Rossiyan gave him a quizzical look, then shrugged again. Without another word he took to his heels, pounding off towards the east.

After the gunner had retreated after the others, Carter checked the gauges on his forearm. He had several hours' worth of air reserves left, but not enough to last until the Middle Kingdom forces returned. *If* the Middle Kingdom forces returned. And standing out in the open, he was more likely to be spotted from a distance.

He moved through the entrance into the vast interior of the dome, and then to the airlock of the temporary shelter. The prisoners inside were gathered around a small heating unit, which generated as much light as heat, warming hands, faces, and feet as best they could. Carter tapped the controls on the airlock, cycling it open, and then moved inside.

When the airlock had cycled shut, and the door to the tent's interior had opened, he raised his visor, cutting off the flow of oxygen from the tanks at his back into his helmet. This way, at least, he was able to breath. If the Mexica *did* discover them inside the dome, though, he wouldn't be able to shoot back without puncturing the tent's walls, so he'd need to stay in the airlock, ready to close his visor and cycle the airlock again to get back outside and return fire, if the need arose.

He hoped the need *wouldn't* arise, of course. Which meant that the light and heat of the heating unit would have to go off.

"I am sorry," he said in his most formal Official Speech, "but the enemy might see the light, and might have instruments to detect the heat source. We will have to hope that enough warmth remains in the floor to keep us from freezing through the night."

The six prisoners looked to Carter, their eyes wide, their expressions mingling faint hope and naked fear. He realized that he was the only thing standing between them and the terror of the executioner's blade and the sacrificial altar.

"Don't worry," he said, more informally. "It will be dawn soon, and then we can turn the heat back on." He paused. It would still be a risk, presenting a thermal profile against the cold, thin air of day, whether warmed by the sun or not, but if they waited too long they'd simply freeze to death. He tried as comforting a smile as he was able, then added, "Just a little while longer. And I'm sure the others will be back for us before long."

The six prisoners looked to him, as the heating unit was shut down, and the faint light began to fade. Then they sat in the silent darkness, Carter and the strangers, waiting. Though whether they waited once more for salvation, or waited for their inescapable doom, none of them could say.

HEXAGRAM 37
THE FAMILY
BELOW FIRE ABOVE WIND

Wind emerges from Fire. In the same way, the noble man ensures that his words have substance and his actions perseverance.

By the time dawn peaked through the cracks in the bacteria farm dome overhead, Carter had got to know the rescued prisoners better than he'd intended. He had originally said that everyone would have to remain silent, out of the remote fear of the Mexica outside detecting the sound of their voices, but as the cold and dark hours of the night crept by, slowly and more slowly by the moment, he knew that silence was becoming unbearable. Only by whispering to one another, almost as though assuring each other that they were not alone there in the dark, were any of them able to make it through the night.

There were two men, three women, and one little girl in the temporary shelter with Carter. In the dim light he could barely see them, but the image of their drawn, hungry faces and thin, emaciated limbs, first glimpsed when he'd cranked open the rear door of the Mexic crawler, was embedded in his memory.

The relationship between the prisoners was difficult to work out at first. They all huddled together, as much for the sense of security as for warmth, though one of the women and one of the men seemed to take particular care of the little girl. The man and woman, he eventually learned, were the girl's parents, a husband and wife who had come to Fire Star with one of the later waves of colonists, shortly before the Mexic attack twelve terrestrial years before. The little girl, whose name Carter never learned, had been born a few years later.

Carter tried to imagine what it would be like for the girl, having known nothing but this unending war for her entire life. Did she think that stories of peace, of living without the threat of constant danger and death hanging always over their heads, were nothing more than fairy tales to sooth children at bedtimes?

He couldn't even begin to guess what such a childhood must have been like. But the fact that the little girl was one of the quietest of the six, silent, reserved, almost stoic while the adults around her whimpered and trembled, suggested something about the effects of such an upbringing on a young mind that he didn't care to contemplate.

The other man and the other two women were unrelated and unconnected to one another, so far as Carter was able to determine. They had been part of a refugee train of colonists fleeing from the northern reaches of Tamkung Plain, trying to reach the strongholds of the Middle Kingdom armies deep within Tianfei Valley. But Tianfei was far to the east and south, beyond Bao Shan and the Three Sovereigns range, and even if they hadn't been captured by Mexic forces *en route*, it was doubtful that they would have made it the whole distance.

Carter had been on Fire Star for—how long, now? Weeks? Months? It was hard to say. But this was the first time that he'd spent any time with those they'd ostensibly come to protect, the Middle Kingdom colonists.

He realized that, since arriving on the red planet, he'd been thinking of the colonists purely in the abstract, as nameless, faceless people whose lives and hardships he never really spent any amount of time thinking about. Even when he'd first seen the prisoners inside the Mexic crawler, they'd been drugged and disoriented, not quite able to focus their gaze on him, more objects than individuals.

As dawn broke, though, and the light gradually filtered through the sundered dome into the transparent walls of the pressure tent, he could see their faces, their huddled forms. For hours in the darkness he'd been listening to their voices, hearing their whispered prayers to all the gods, saints, and ancestors for deliverance, their stifled sobs, their muttered words of comfort to one another. And through it all, listening to them, he had kept silent, sitting inside the airlock, his eyes on the dark night out there beyond the dome's ruined entrance, watchful for any sign of Mexic approach. He had not spoken to the prisoners, after telling them to extinguish the heating unit and to remain silent, and they had not spoken to him.

Now he could see them, and put faces to the voices he'd heard throughout the night. And he came to find that they were no longer anonymous, no longer abstract, but living, breathing individuals depending on him for their survival. A family, a group of frightened and scared people bound together by circumstance and chance, unsure whether they would ever see another sunrise.

And all of them looking to him. Every eye on him, man, woman, and child, in their expressions the dim hope that, with his help, they just might survive.

Carter knew that whatever he did or said would be weighed and measured. If he spoke with despair, they would abandon their last slim hopes. But if he spoke and acted with courage, with conviction, then the prisoners just might be able to cling to whatever small confidence remained in them.

He wondered whether he had strength enough to loan them some, or hope enough to share. Then he caught a glimpse of movement out in the grey light of dawn, beyond the dome's entrance, and it was too late to wonder.

Someone was coming.

Carter started the airlock cycling shut, hearing the hiss of air as the inner door began to seal.

"There's someone out there," he said, checking the action on his carbine, his visor still raised. "I want you all to stay down on the ground, making as little noise as possible. I'm afraid we'll have to wait a little longer to turn the heat back on."

The prisoners glanced nervously at one another as the inner door sealed with a final hiss. As the outer door started to cycle open, Carter reached up and swung his visor closed, then switched on his surface suit's air circulation. As the warmed, purified air hit his nostrils, he realized for the first time how cold and stale the air within the pressure tent had become.

None of the prisoners said a word, until the little girl raised her head and met Carter's gaze. "Where are you going?" she asked, almost casually. "Are the bad men coming back?"

The air was already filtering out of the lock, so Carter had to lean forward, resting his helmet against the inner door. "I'll do what I can to protect you."

Then the outer door was fully open, and Carter moved outside, swinging his carbine up, the safety off.

Taking slow, steady steps, he moved to the dome's entrance. The movement he'd seen had been indistinct, a fluttering of shadows in the middle distance. If he'd been back on Earth, he'd probably have chalked it up to a bird flying past, or perhaps a cat leaping from atop a fence to the ground. But there were no birds wheeling overhead in the thin, cold air of Fire Star, no cats slinking underfoot.

Carter was surprised it had taken the Mexica so long to work their way across the compound to where he and the prisoners were hiding. The disabled Mexic crawler was still parked just a few meters away from the dome's entrance, as sure a signal that the dome should be checked as a red flag fluttering overhead. But it had been hours since the Mexic main column had engaged in the fire fight with the rest of First-Second, and even if elements of the Mexic force had given a chance to the retreating guardsmen, there surely were enough Mexica on hand to search the rest of the settlement.

Reaching the door, Carter hugged the wall, then leaned his head to the side, peering around the edge, keeping the bulk of his body concealed inside.

Off to the south, he could see a column of dust rising up above the habitats and farm domes. A line of crawlers, perhaps? Mexic reinforcements returning after routing the retreating Middle Kingdom forces? It was impossible to say, only that whatever was causing the dust was approaching the colonial settlement at speed.

A flash of movement in the corner of his eye brought Carter back to more immediate concerns. He pulled back inside the dome, dropped to a crouch, then swung his carbine around, sighting around the edge of the entrance, sweeping the rifle's barrel across the open space to the left of the door. There had been something, over behind the nearest of the habitats, just east of the bacteria farm. But what?

The sun was rising in the east, just cresting the tops of the buildings, and Carter squinted, the glare all but blinding.

Just then a figure stepped into the clearing, out from behind the nearest habitat, a black shadow framed against the rising sun.

Carter held his breath, and began to squeeze his carbine's trigger.

"Tejas, you awake?" came a voice crackling over his helmet's radio, startling loud in his ears.

Jerking back, Carter yanked his finger away from the trigger, only a hair's breadth away from having fired.

He lowered his carbine's barrel, but remained hidden behind the wall. He squinted into the glare of the rising sun, and saw another figure step out into the clearing, behind the first. As they drew nearer, now only a handful of meters away, Carter could see that both wore the surface suits of Green Standard guardsmen, one with the markings of a corporal on his carapace.

"Spitter," another voice crackled in his ear, "is there some reason why you're shouting? The radio works just as fine with a whisper." It was Corporal Eng.

One of the surface-suited guardsmen turned to the other and shrugged, and Carter could recognize immediately the Rossiyan's sloppy posture.

"Come on out, Tejas," Corporal Eng said, holding a hand up palm forwards, approaching the entrance where Carter was hidden. "The Mexica pulled out in the night, looks like, after we fell back. There's nobody in the compound but you and your prisoners."

Carter stood, and stepped out into the light, startling Spitter. "Not *my* prisoners, corporal," he corrected, with a slight smile. He slung his carbine on his shoulder, and breathed a sigh of relief as a Middle Kingdom crawler crunched into view behind the other two men, a transport large enough to accommodate all six colonists huddled inside the dome. "They'll be nobody's prisoners again, if I can help it."

≡≡
≡ ≡
≡≡

HEXAGRAM 38
CONTRARIETY
BELOW LAKE ABOVE FIRE

Above Fire and below Lake. In the same way, the noble man differentiates among things while remaining sensitive to their similarities.

It was a simple error of logistics, and while it should have made things *easier* for the men involved, the actual result was far, far more complicated. It was all the fault of the brigade colonels, or so the consensus held. There was a joke that Bannerman Niohuru had heard repeated often through the ranks of the First Raiding Company, that if the generals ordered the Eight Banners to cram dung back *up* their back ends instead of dropping it into latrines, the colonels would be the first in line with corks and shovels.

In hindsight, the problem was obvious. There were simply too few operational objectives involved in Operation Great Strength to go around. Not that the operational objectives were actually attainable, but that was another matter. And with the division of authority and resources at the highest level thrown into mass confusion by the illogic of some of the tactics involved in Great Strength, it was only natural that signals would get crossed, and two units would be dispatched to take the same target.

Ideally, two combat units both assigned to take and hold the same spot of land *should* have meant less work for each unit. But when the two units were the Falcon's Claws on the one hand and on the other the famed Immortals, the Sikh warrior-saints of the Akali Sena, what *should* have happened was quickly a lost, forgotten concern.

As near as could be determined in the aftermath, what had happened was a matter of simple confusion. When the elements involved in Operation Great Strength were given their marching orders, the colonel in charge of the Bordered Yellow Banner's Ninth Brigade handed Captain Hughes Falco and his men of the First Raiding Company the task of taking and holding an abandoned mining operation, located on the southern extremity of the corridor being cut through the Mexic lines, and to keep the nearby habitats clear and unoccupied. At the same time, however, the Akali Sena battalion, which was attached to the Third Army of the Green Standard Army, was ordered to take and hold habitats north of the mining operation.

Hughes had registered a complaint with the battalion lieutenant-colonel that his men had only just returned from a long stint operating behind enemy lines in the final stages of Great Holdings, during which they had sustained a considerable number of casualties. The Falcon's Claws were tired, injured, and not operating at full strength. Hughes complaints were noted, but the orders handed down by the brigade's colonel stood.

The Akali Sena, for their part, had been part of the frontal assault on the Mexic line at the Tamkung escarpment, during which they had suffered nearly as many casualties and during which they had sustained, if anything, an even greater number of injuries than the First Raider Company. As was pointed out by the Sikh warrior-saints to their reluctant allies in the defense of the mines in the coming days, however, the leaders of the Akali Sena did not register any complaints about their orders with their superiors, but set about their task with a will.

With elements of the Eleventh Armored Infantry Battalion of the Green Standard acting as the thin end of the wedge, the forces of the Middle Kingdom drove through the breach in the Mexic lines. The Sikh warrior-saints of the Akali Sena battalion preceded the First Raider Company in the order of march, driving as far west as they were able, following close in the wake of the Eleventh Armored Infantry Battalion's Fourth Company, then turning to the south and approaching the habitats which were their target from the north. The Falcon's Claws, meanwhile, were near the rear of the advance, and approached the mining facilities from the east.

Radio communication was limited, by order of the brigade colonels, the various units communicating only among themselves at the lowest broadcast strengths, with little coordination between the different elements of the advance. The theory was that the less radio chatter, encoded or otherwise, the less chance the Mexica would have to divine the full scope of Operation Great Strength, and greater the chance for surprise. In practice, however, it introduced the possibility that different elements of the advance might be working at cross purposes, when it would have been much more efficient to work in concert.

So while the Immortals were attacking the habitats from the north, the Falcon's Claws were attacking the mining facilities from the east. And where they met, the problems began.

Two groups of highly trained, deadly effective soldiers, both fiercely loyal to the Dragon Throne, both striving against the same enemy. But both, unfortunately, operating under conflicting orders. Without realizing it, these allies would become inadvertent enemies, with almost disastrous results.

HEXAGRAM 39
ADVERSITY
BELOW MOUNTAIN ABOVE WATER

Atop the Mountain, there is Water. In the same way, the noble man reflects upon himself and cultivates virtue.

The mining facilities, which Niohuru and the rest of the First Raider Company had been tasked with seizing, were among the oldest man-made structures on Fire Star. The earliest elements of the facilities had been among the first assembled on Fire Star, by the early Middle Kingdom explorers of the Treasure Fleet, long before colonists first set foot on the world. And from the moment the automated systems were first initiated, until the day the Mexica overran the Tamkung Plain and drove off the Middle Kingdom colonists, the mines were in continuous operation, extracting deposits of carbonates and nitrates from beneath the planet's red soil.

As the Falcon's Claws approached from the east, the first light of dawn pinking the sky behind them, it was clear that the mining facilities had long since ceased to be put to their intended use. For some time now, it was believed, the Mexic had been using the facilities as a munitions dump, the cluster of habitats a few hundred meters away—formerly the residences of the miners and administrators—employed as makeshift barracks for Mexic troops.

The mine was some distance from the Mexic main line of defense—though the line had been gradually approaching from the east in recent days, as the Middle Kingdom pushed the Mexica further and further back to the west—and so intelligence suggested that it was guarded by a relatively small number of troops, perhaps no more than one hundred. Given the strategic importance of the dump, it was perhaps surprising that there were such a small number of defenders, but given the lengths to which the Mexic forces had been stretched in the weeks since the onset of Operation Great Holdings, with no resupplies or reinforcements arriving from Earth, an understandable concession to the realities of the battlefield.

The First Raider Company was operating at considerably less than full strength, fielding fewer than two hundred men, all told, with more than twenty percent of their original strength either sidelined by injuries, at best, or killed in action, at worst. They still outnumbered the Mexic defenders of the mine by nearly two to one, but the Mexica had the advantage of being entrenched in defensible structures, while the Falcon's Claws were having to approach overland, with little cover and without any armored support. The question had been mooted whether they would employ their four-wheeled rovers in the attack, with some of the raiders advancing the argument that an assault on foot, though more time-consuming and draining, could be carried out with more stealth and subtlety. The operational demands of Great Strength, though, called for the mine to be seized in less time than a purely infantry assault would require, and so Captain Hughes had made the decision that they *would* employ the rovers, but primarily as transportation, not as an element of attack.

Hughes had outlined his strategy for the assault before the column set out from the east. The Falcon's Claws would divide into three groups of roughly twenty rovers apiece, and approach the mine at the highest possible rate of speed from the southeast, east, and northeast. With the morning sun behind them, there was the chance that their approach would not be noticed until they neared the mine, but no one was willing to lay odds on the possibility. The three rover groups were to employ a zigzag, serpentine approach, reducing the possibility that the Mexic defenders would be able to draw a bead on them. And then, as soon as they came within sniping range of the mine, the rover drivers were to draw short. The other two banner-men on the rovers were to climb out as quickly as possible, going to ground and finding what cover they could, while the drivers turned and retreated back beyond the range of the Mexic guns.

Then, with the sniper elements of each combat cell of bannermen laying down suppressing fire on the Mexic firing positions, the others would advance, keeping as low as possible, utilizing what-ever cover was available, until they were close enough to employ smoke grenades to cover their final approach and assault the facilities.

As one of the rover drivers in the southeast arm of attack, Bannerman Niohuru Tie had retreated back out of range, and secured his four-wheel rover along with the others, hidden from Mexic view by the buildings of a transport depot some distance from the southeastern corner of the mining facilities. When the mine was in operation, in all those months and years before the Mexic attack twelve years before, the transport depot would have been a hive of constant activity. Empty crawlers would arrive, load up, and leave, hauling the raw material exca-vated from the subterranean passages to the bacteria farms which dotted the northern plains and the southern highlands. Once there, microorganisms would be unleashed on the ore, consuming, digest-ing, and excreting invaluable greenhouse gasses, carbon-dioxide from the carbonates, nitrogen from the nitrates. Stored and subsequently introduced into the red planet's thin atmosphere, these gases would contribute to the gradual thickening of the atmosphere, and the gradual warming of the planet. In all of those early years of colonization, and the nonstop mining and bacteria farming, it was doubtful that Fire Star's atmospheric pressure had increased by more than a tiny fraction of a millibar. And now both mines and farms had stood empty and inoperable for longer than anyone cared to contemplate.

By the time the rovers were safely secured beyond the transport depot, and Niohuru and the other drivers were able to join the others in the assault force, the lion's share of the work to invade and secure the mining facilities had already been completed. Niohuru and the others formed a rearguard, covering the flanks of the assault force, and watching for signs of any Mexic reinforcements arriving, or any Mexic defenders slipping out and fleeing to the east, north, or south.

It transpired that the intelligence reports had overestimated the strength of the Mexic defense, there being only somewhat more than one hundred Mexic warriors stationed in and around the mining facility itself. Despite the slight advantage of being the defenders, facing an assault over open ground, the Mexic found themselves hard pressed to hold off the Middle Kingdom assault. For all that, being perfectly suited as a munitions dump with its large interior spaces, many of them pressurized, the mining facility had not been intended as a defensible stronghold, and there were numerous weak points in the Mexic defenses as a result.

In taking the mine, the Falcon's Claws had sustained only minor injuries, and only two fatalities, while the Mexic defenders had suffered heavy casualties. Those few Mexica who survived the initial assault, following the dictates of their blood-hungry warrior ethic, refused to surrender, and those who did not successfully flee to the west, towards the nearby habitats, stood and fought until the last of them fell.

When, finally, the mining facilities were completely under the control of the First Raider Company, as the sun was setting in the west, there remained only the mopping up operation. Still under orders to remain relative radio silence, with their helmet radios set to the lowest broadcast power, the raiders were unable to signal news of their success to command. Instead, Captain Hughes and the others set out securing the facilities as best as possible, and beginning an inventory of the munitions stored within the dump.

The only remaining operational objective was to clear and secure the habitats to the west, former residences of the long-since-fled miners and administrators, towards which a small number of the escaping Mexic defenders had fled.

Seeing that the drivers had "missed the party," as Hughes put it, Niohuru and a handful of the other rover drivers were sent to check the habitats, and account for any Mexica who might be sheltering there. As the sun set, a dozen bannermen, Niohuru among them, set out towards the west, their weapons primed and ready.

What they couldn't know was that the Mexica who had fled to the west had already long been accounted for, and there were other elements already sheltering in the habitats looming out of the twilight before them.

☵

HEXAGRAM 40
RELEASE
BELOW WATER ABOVE THUNDER

Thunder and rain perform their roles. In the same way, the noble man forgives misdeeds and pardons wrongdoing.

To his surprise, Niohuru found himself wishing that he had Bannermen Axum Ouazebas and Cong Ren at his side. There were times when the differences in temperament and personality among the three members of Niohuru's combat cell led to aggravated clashes, often threatening to erupt into full-blown violence. But when they were in the field, each performing his duties, all such conflicts were forgotten. Like that first engagement after the night drop, when the Falcon's Claws had finally entered into the fray of Operation Great Holdings, the three bannermen had learned to act as a smoothly-running machine, every component knowing their place, every man knowing his role. And however odious Niohuru might find Axum's presumption or Cong's manner when they were at ease in the barracks, now that he was in the field of battle without them, he realized that there was no one else he would rather have at his side.

Pity, then, that Axum and Cong were more than likely at their leisure back within the mining facilities, or else pulling some relatively stress-free sentry duty. Of course, they *had* spent the day exchanging fire with the Mexic defenders, while Niohuru had spent most of the hours since morning driving or walking, either out of the range of the Mexic guns or otherwise hidden from their fire. But at the moment, his muscles already fatigued by the long hours of walking and driving, Niohuru hardly felt that it was any kind of fair trade. After all, it wasn't as if Axum or Cong had actually been *hit* by enemy fire.

The bannerman ahead of Niohuru—who like him had spent the day driving and walking—suddenly drew up short, dropping outstretched to the ground, and raising his left hand in a fist as he fell. It was a signal all of the Falcon's Claws knew well.

Enemy sighted.

Without the need for discussion or delay, Niohuru and the others, already advancing in low crouches, dove forward, pressing their bodies as low to the ground as possible. Niohuru scanned the darkened buildings that hulked on the near horizon, little more than shadowy outlines against the last dying light of the setting sun. He was looking to see if he could spot what the other bannerman might have seen, what trace of the enemy had prompted him to dive to the ground and...

There... Niohuru saw it, a grim smile just turning up the corners of his mouth. A faint flashing in among the shadowed habitats, a glint of metal and movement. Sunlight bouncing off an armored surface suit, perhaps? The angle of incident seemed wrong. Perhaps an artificial light then, used to consult a map, or check a weapon's ammunition? Or perhaps even a signal?

It was difficult to say. All Niohuru knew for certain was that there was *something* moving within the cluster of habitats, and that his orders were to clear them out.

What Niohuru and the rest of the Falcon's Claws did not know, what they *could* not know given the imposition of radio silence and the lack of communication between different elements of the advance, was that the habitat cluster to the west of the mining facility had been the target of the Akali Sena, who had assaulted the habitats from the north that morning just as the First Raider Company had been approaching the mining facility from the east.

There had been nearly a hundred Mexica in and among the habitats when the Sikh warrior-saints attacked, the balance of those whom Captain Hughes had anticipated would be defending the mine to the east. And the reason that these hundred Mexica had not joined in the defense of the mining facilities, as Hughes had expected they would, was that they had been too busy engaged in the ultimately fruitless attempt to stave off the Immortals' assault.

Unfortunately for the Mexica, the communication between the defenders of the mining facilities and those occupied with the defense of the habitat cluster was scarcely better than the communication between the Falcon's Claws and the Immortals. When the mine at last fell to the First Raider Company, and those Mexic not willing to stand and fight to the death turned tail and fled to the west, they had no idea that they were running right into the bullets and blades of the Sikh warrior-saints.

The Akali Sena, for their part, had assumed the fleeing defenders from the east to be ill-advised attackers, a last-ditch attempt to win the habitat back from the warrior-saints. And once the Mexica who had approached from the east had been cut down, the Sikhs lay in wait, watching the eastern approaches warily, anticipating a further attack.

Then, as the sun was setting in the west, a Sikh lookout's eye was caught by a flash of movement out on the red sands, and glimpsed a half-dozen figures quickly drop to the ground and out of sight.

With a series of quick, abbreviated hand gestures, the lookout alerted the rest of the warrior-saints ranged along the western side of the habitat cluster, and the Immortals prepared themselves for a final assault.

* * *

Niohuru and the other five bannermen in the raiding party held still for a seemingly interminable number of heartbeats, then after a quick exchange of hand signals, barely visible in the faint moonlight, they began to creep forward, pulling themselves along with their elbows, their bodies remaining flat against the ground.

They had covered half the remaining distance to the nearest of the habitats, which ranged in an arc from left to right, and Niohuru had just about decided that the Mexic defenders within the habitat cluster had not seen them. They might have maintained the element of surprise, after all.

Then the bannerman to Niohuru's right suddenly reared back as his helmet's faceplate *exploded* with the force of a projectile's impact, and it was clear that any hope of retaining the element of surprise had been long lost.

As the bannermen around him raised the barrels of their semi-automatics to return fire, remaining as low to the ground as possible, Niohuru unclipped a fragmentation grenade from his waist and lobbed it towards the habitats, despite having no idea where the shots were coming from, or even what sort of weapons were being fired.

Ramdas Singh, the Akali Sena lookout, fired his carbine at the indistinct shadows humped along the irregular ground to the east, then flinched back as a grenade exploded behind him and to one side. He checked himself for any impact or abrasion, knowing that even a small rent in his armored surface suit would be enough to bruise him badly, at best, and cause him to freeze to death, at worst, to say nothing of the loss of blood from any cuts.

The lookout allowed himself a brief sigh of relief, muttering the words of a hymn of thanksgiving, but then caught sight of a brother Immortal a few meters away who had not been quite so lucky. Shrapnel had torn the other Sikh's surface suit open, in the process sending a spray of freezing blood out in the cold, thin air that was now drifting down like a crimson snowfall to the hard packed dirt beneath their feet.

There would be time for sabads to be sung later, once the enemy was routed, to celebrate another fallen brother gone to reunite with god, free from the cycles of rebirth. Ramdas Singh had been on Fire Star for nearly ten years, and had attended the funerals of more fellow warrior-saints than he could recall.

For now, though, there were still the Mexica out in the dark to consider.

A pair of Immortals were bringing the chakram-gun up from the rear, setting it up on a tripod a few meters from Ramdas Singh's position. Firing chakrams, flat steel rings about thirteen centimeters across with razor-sharp outer edges, the massive gun was remarkably simple and deadly accurate. Once the slide atop the launching mechanism was racked forward and back, the massive spring inside was pulled back to full tension, while the return motion also dropped one of the chakram discs into place. When the trigger was pulled the spring was released, pulling the disc forward and setting it spinning. The discs flew out with extremely rapid rotations, keeping them steady as they went, and though their forward velocity was lower than that of a bullet from a carbine, the discs were just as accurate, and capable of inflicting devastating damage on the target.

With the chakram-gun set up and ready to fire, the operators looked to Ramdas Singh to help them range their fire, and he pointed out towards the humped shadows out in the near distance, from which the grenades had been thrown. Their fallen brother's life of service had earned him release from the cycle of rebirth, but that didn't mean that the surviving Immortals wouldn't avenge his death.

Niohuru and the other four surviving Falcon's Claws were pinned down, caught in crossfire that appeared to be coming from both the left and right extremities of the habitat cluster. If they tried to pick up and run back the way they'd come, they'd get mowed down in an instant, and if they advanced they'd fare no better. But staying in one place meant that the defenders in the cluster could simply plink shots at the bannermen at their leisure, and eventually they'd all end up like the bannerman who'd taken the shot to the head only moments before.

Something whizzed by Niohuru's left shoulder, just missing the side of his helmet. It was too slow to be a bullet, and far too large, but he hadn't got a good glimpse of it before it flashed by and out of sight in the darkness behind.

Niohuru turned to the bannerman at his left side, to see if he'd seen the projectile flash by as well, and just as Niohuru's gaze fell on him the bannerman floundered as something sliced into his neck, right where his helmet joined his chest carapace.

Pulling himself over to see if he could offer any assistance, Niohuru grimaced when he reached the other man's side and saw that he'd arrived too late. Blood painted the inside of the dead man's helmet, and the oxygen escaping from the severed carapace-seal fogged in the thin air.

Niohuru reached out, brushing his fingers against the edge of the thing wedged into the dead man's neck. It was a metal disc about two handbreadths in width, razor sharp on the edge.

This was no Mexic weapon, Niohuru realized at once. This was a chakram. And the only units he'd ever heard of who used the flying discs were the Sikhs of the Akali Sena. For a moment he considered the possibility that one of their disc-flinging guns had fallen into the hands of the enemy, then rejected the idea out of hand. The so-called Immortals would sooner destroy themselves *en masse* than let their weapons end up in the enemy's possession.

Which meant only one thing. It wasn't the Mexica who were sheltered in the habitats at all. They were facing friendly fire.

He was able to reach the other three surviving Falcon's Claws by radio, to tell them to hold their fire, but when he tried to radio to the forces within the habitat cluster, he was unable to raise them. Still bullets spanged off the rocks around them, still the deadly chakram-discs whizzed by overhead.

They couldn't retreat, couldn't advance, and yet Niohuru knew if they lay where they were, eventually they'd all end up with chakrams buried in them. Their only hope was to convince the Sikhs in the habitats that they were not enemy forces, but on radio silence it was impossible to raise them.

There was only one option.

Niohuru pulled a flare from the pouch at the small of his back, and as he snapped it in half to light it he jumped to his feet, throwing up his hands in surrender.

There was still the chance that the Sikhs might shoot a chakram at him before recognizing he was in Middle Kingdom armor, but Niohuru hoped that he might be able to dodge the relatively slow-moving disc, if so.

The gun crew were readying the chakram-gun for another volley when Ramdas Singh rushed over and pushed the barrel of the launcher towards the ground.

"Do not shoot!" he repeated for the third time, turning his radio up to the fullest broadcast power and hoping the other two had their radios set to receive. "Bannermen!" Ramdas Singh turned and pointed at the figure standing out in the clearing, a flare held over his head, no weapon in his hand. "They are *Bannermen!*"

In the end, there were only three casualties fallen in the misunderstanding, two members of the First Raider Company and one of the Akali Sena. But even those few deaths were deemed too many to fall to friendly fire, and all for the sake of poor planning and miscommunication. Still, it was agreed on all sides that if not for the quick action of Bannerman Niohuru Tie, the death toll could have been even higher.

HEXAGRAM 41
DIMINUTION
BELOW LAKE ABOVE MOUNTAIN

Below the Mountain, there is the Lake. In the same way, the noble man checks his anger and smothers his desire.

Pilot Amonkar Arati kept her hands on the stick, her eyes on the horizon, and tried to keep her attention from drifting. In all her months of training at flight school, of all the dangers and pitfalls of piloting the students had been warned about, no one had ever bothered to mention the principle difficulty with most prolonged bombing operations. Namely, that they were endlessly, tediously *boring*.

One day was the same as another, day after day after day. Out of bed in the morning; bathe, dress, and eat; then, after briefing, they'd crawl into *Fair Winds for Escort* to go out on yet another bombing sortie. With their rotary winged fighter escort and the rest of the bomber squadron, they'd fly out over enemy-held territory, try like hell not to get shot by anti-aircraft from the ground or shots fired from enemy aircraft, and do their best to hit the assigned targets. Then they'd wheel around, perhaps making another bombing run on the return trip, and if fortune was with them they'd land back on friendly soil, taxi into the hangar, and then deplane to go rest up, debrief, and hopefully sleep, to do the whole thing again the next day.

Day in, day out, nothing but the same. For the first few weeks, so much of Amonkar's attentions were focused on the task in hand that she hardly noticed the numbing sameness. And in those first weeks, too, she still felt the thrill and excitement about being up in the air, flying. But as time went on, and she and her crew became even more efficient at their roles, experience helping to smooth out those early jitters and fears, the excitement and thrill began to diminish, week after week after week. It reached a point where Amonkar could scarcely remember being scared, much less being *excited*, but could only recall being achingly, endlessly bored.

Of course, today it was anger that distracted her attention, which was entirely another concern.

When Operation Great Strength had been announced, it had seemed for a brief moment as if real progress might be made, and the boring tedium might at last be ending. But after the first few days of the advance, after the Mexic lines in the east had been broken through, the Middle Kingdom ground forces had driven only so far to the west, able to go no further. The intent had been that the ground forces would create a corridor straight through to Ruosi, when instead they had succeeded only in creating a finger-shaped salient that pointed a few dozen kilometers into Mexic territory before being halted by another mass of Mexica to the west.

Now, several days into Great Strength, the Mexica on the main line of resistance to the east, to the north and south of the Middle Kingdom salient, had regrouped and reorganized, and were now in the process of pushing back. With the hopes of a corridor to Ruosi now little more than a dim memory, the Middle Kingdom ground forces within the salient now found themselves struggling to avoid being overrun by Mexica pushing in from three sides.

The bomber squadrons had been ordered to try to soften the Mexic defenses that had halted the Middle Kingdom advance to the west. Most of their mission time involved flying over friendly territory, from the hangars in the east, coursing west above the Middle Kingdom salient, and then delivering their payloads onto the Mexica to the west. Unfortunately, the Mexic defenses there were not only more than able to stop the infantry advance, but were well-fortified and even better armed, with anti-aircraft emplacements supported by wing after wing of Mexic aircraft. It was all that the Middle

Kingdom bombers could do to verge just over enemy-held territory without being shot out of the sky, dropping their bombs without time to properly sight the target, and then wheel around and head back over friendly soil as quickly as possible. To say that the bomber squadrons' effectiveness was questionable, at best, was putting it mildly.

"Enemy spotted," Co-Pilot Seathl said, so casually she almost sighed in saying it.

Amonkar leaned forward, glancing to starboard out the forward windscreen, just able to make out the specks of Eagle Knight aircraft fast approaching from the east. "Acknowledged."

Seathl continued to watch as Amonkar settled back and checked the instruments. "Three of our escorts are haring off after them."

Over the plane's communications hardline, the voice of Navigator Geng buzzed in their ears. "Is Pak's Dragonfly one of them?"

The co-pilot chuckled. "Why, are you worried you'll lose his affections to some blood-hungry Mexic pilot. I didn't take you for the jealous type, Geng."

"I'm just worried about him," Geng answered.

"Stow it," Amonkar barked, startling the others. "We've got work to do."

Her own reaction surprised her. It had been for a few weeks that Navigator Geng had been seeing someone romantically in what little leisure time was left to them at the end of the day. Pak was a Chosonese pilot of a Dragonfly rotary fighter attached to the bomber squadron's escort wing.

For the last few weeks, Amonkar had hardly given Geng's dalliance with the Dragonfly pilot a second thought. That had all changed that morning, when Geng had announced that she and Pak were to be wed, once the war was over.

In the hours since, Amonkar had simmered with anger. At first, she had chalked it up to a poor night's sleep, then to her dissatisfaction with another day of tedium, but then she noticed that her discontent flared whenever Navigator Geng's voice buzzed over the hardline.

It wasn't until Geng voiced her concern about Pak's safety in combat that Amonkar realized the source of her anger.

She discovered, in that moment, that she thought Geng was *weak*, giving into selfish desires. It was thoughtless, Amonkar felt, to get romantically involved with another when the risk of death was so great, and worse still when both parties were so often at risk. If Geng were to die in combat, her loss would affect Pak's effectiveness in combat. And if Pak were to fall, Amonkar didn't know whether she would be able to count on Geng to perform her duties when asked.

Perhaps most surprising though, was the realization that she had been suppressing her own desires. Without making the conscious decision to do so, Amonkar realized that she was forgoing any attachments until her duty had been fulfilled. When so many of the other airmen had paired off, whether for ongoing relationships like that shared by Geng and Pak, or for brief trysts like those favored by Seathl, Amonkar had remained solitary, isolated. She had not allowed herself even to consider the possibility of entanglements since she'd set foot on Fire Star, all those months before.

Still, now that she paused to reflect, she couldn't help but be reminded of that tall, fair-haired Vinlander guardsman she had met back on the transport from Earth, with the friendly smile and the flashing eyes.

Amonkar shook her head, pushing those thoughts from her, forgetting the heated dreams that occasionally rousted her from sleep, embarrassed and ashamed at her body's own reactions. There wasn't time for romance now, she knew. They had a job to do.

She would have to talk to Geng about this, sooner or later. But for the moment, she would try to keep her attention on the flying, avoiding both anger *and* boredom, and try to get them all back to friendly soil alive.

HEXAGRAM 42
INCREASE
BELOW THUNDER ABOVE WIND

Wind and Thunder. In the same way, the noble man shifts to the good when he sees it and corrects his errors when he has them.

"They're coming in fast," Co-Pilot Seathl said, turned all the way round in her seat, straining against the restraints and looking out the viewports to starboard. At the center of the instrumentation panel before them, the gyro dipped and spun as *Fair Winds for Escort* rolled, pitched, and yawed through the thin Fire Star air, evading enemy fire.

"Keep on them, Seathl," Amonkar answered, hands wrapped tightly around the yoke, keeping a careful eye on their altitude and velocity. Then, under her breath, she cursed, "What's keeping the rutting escort?"

Through the reinforced material of her pressurized flight suit, Amonkar could feel the metal of her seat vibrating each time one of the Eagle Knights' ammunition rounds pinged the outer hull of *Fair Winds*. So far none of the Mexic fire had done any serious damage to the Deliverer's hull, either rebounding off thin armor plating or passing through the bomber's body without striking anything vital, either crew or component. It was only a matter of time before the Mexica would inflict real damage on the bomber and her crew though, no matter how much Amonkar managed to coax the *Fair Winds* into swooping and diving in evasive maneuvers. The bomber squadron's fighter escort would be needed to pry the Eagle Knights off their tail, but so far the escort had failed to reappear.

It was more than a week into Operation Great Strength, and the mission of the bomber squadrons, already difficult, was quickly approaching impossible. The Mexic ground forces had continued to push inwards from the north and south, for eight days straight, and had now all but pinched off the Middle Kingdom salient. At the moment, the only thing keeping the salient connected to the Middle Kingdom-held territory in the east was the continual bombardment of the Mexic forces in the "pincers" by the Air Corps bomber squadrons, of which Amonkar's squad was just one of many. But the bombers' ability even to keep airborne was being severely tested by the Mexic air forces, who had committed the vast majority of their aircraft on Fire Star to this corridor a few kilometers square.

By the day's end, it seemed likely, the advance column of Middle Kingdom forces would instead be an island, surrounded on all four sides by Mexica. But if there was any chance to keep the salient intact, even for a short while longer, the *Fair Winds* and the rest of the light bombers would do what was asked of them.

Of course, if they were all shot out of the sky, there would be no one left to answer the call to action, when it came.

For the first few days of Great Strength, the most dangerous portion of a bombing run was the moment when the plane overflew the western extremity of the Middle Kingdom salient, into the Mexic-held territory and within the range of the ground-based anti-aircraft guns, and into the sights of the Eagle Knight fighters flying patrols north-to-south along the line of engagement.

But with the Mexic forces pushing together from the north and south, far to the east where the salient met the Middle Kingdom main forces, the Eagle Knights had taken to patrolling the entire border of the finger-shaped salient, and at times even dared to overfly the Middle Kingdom-held territory of the salient, passing from one side to the other.

Now, *Fair Winds* and the other bombers in the squad were at considerable hazard almost as soon as they lifted off the runway, forced to run a gauntlet over contested ground, through the swarms of

Mexic fighters who might be lying in wait for them, all to drop a precious few bombs without much hope of hitting the targets in the first place. The overall mission plans for Great Strength still called for western advancement towards Ruosi, even with the danger of their flank falling before the Mexica on either side. It was a failed policy, which everyone but those in command, it seemed, had long realized.

"They're coming back around," Seathl said, leaning forward and looking left past Amonkar to port. "Still no sign of the escort."

"And to think," Amonkar muttered, "just last week I was worried about getting *bored*."

The morning had started like all the other days since Great Strength had begun. An early rise, mission briefing, suiting-up and final ground checks, then *Fair Winds* and the rest of their bomber squadron, accompanied by an escort wing of Dragonfly rotary fighters, had set out over the salient to the targets in the west.

Almost as soon as they'd passed from the Middle Kingdom-held territory to the east to the salient on the west, they'd been attacked by a half-dozen Eagle Knight fighters, swooping down from the north. Their escort had peeled off to engage the Mexic fighters, leaving the bomber squadron to continue towards the west over the salient. With a few kilometers of Middle Kingdom ground forces below them, the bombers would be fairly safe until they reached the Mexic defenses to the west, by which time some of the escort, at least, would have rejoined them. And just to be on the safe side, the bombers were ordered to slow their velocity, to give the escort enough time to catch up, after driving off the Mexica.

Mission parameters, of course, called for at least a pair of Dragonflies to be left with the bomber squadron, flying over friendly territory or not, but in the last week the rotary-winged fighters had been taking heavy fire, and while a thankfully small number had been casualties, there were a number of fighters grounded, whether due to damage to the aircraft or injuries to their crews, and so the escort wing was left short-handed.

And so, as a consequence, *Fair Winds* was left undefended, at least for a short while. But a short while, unfortunately, was all it took.

When the bomber squadron still had some distance to go before reaching their target, still flying over friendly territory, they encountered a second Eagle Knight wing, diving towards them from the south. And without the Dragonfly escort to keep the Mexica off their back, Amonkar and the others had no choice but to rely on themselves.

"One of them's coming in low," Seathl said, sitting back, a grin on her face.

"It's about time," Amonkar answered. Then, over the ship's hardline, she called out, "Gunners, at your discretion."

With a mix of enthusiasm and relief, Tail Gunner Lambert and Nose Gunner Siagyo both called out their ascent. For the long minutes of the engagement so far, the Mexica had remained above the *Fair Winds'* elevation, making the bottom-mounted guns all but useless. Even when Amonkar rolled the craft from port to starboard and back, there was a limit to how far the gun turrets could be angled.

In response, Amonkar had been pushing the bomber to higher and higher elevations, trying to increase the bomber's altitude and get up above the Eagle Knights. Finally, it seemed, one of them might be slipping into the gunners' sights. But would it come too late?

"I got him!" Nose Gunner Siagyo shouted over the hardline. That was one Eagle Knight down, another half-dozen or more to go.

"Captain!" came the voice of Tail Gunner Lambert buzzing in Amonkar's helmet speakers. "We've got craft approaching fast from the east."

Amonkar and Seathl exchanged a glance. "Is it our escort?" the co-pilot asked, knowing the answer already.

"No," came Lambert's answer.

Amonkar's shoulders slumped. She thought they might be able to hold off the rest of the Eagle Knights until the escort arrived, but if more Mexica approached from the rear, she wasn't sure she could keep *Fair Winds* afloat.

"Even better," Lambert quickly added, laughing.

A flash of yellow and black streaked in the corner of Amonkar's eye, and as she yawed the bomber to starboard, she caught the quickest glimpse of a rotary winged fighter painted in stark tones of bright yellow and midnight black. It was a Hornet, a Middle Kingdom rotary fighter, bigger and better armed and armored than the smaller Dragonflies.

"Ahoy the bombers," came a voice speaking Official Speech, crackling over the ship-to-ship radio. "We heard your escort went dancing with someone else, and didn't want to leave you without partners." As Amonkar watched, another yellow-and-black fighter buzzed past, then another, swooping around the bomber squadron like their tiny insect namesakes.

"Well appreciated, Hornets," Amonkar answered.

"Coming up on target now," Navigator Geng said over the hardline. She didn't have to explain what that meant about flying into Mexic anti-aircraft and fighter patrols.

Amonkar's mouth drew into a line. They'd survived this far, only to dive into the biggest hazard zone in the mission.

She shrugged. With any luck, they'd survive to do it all over again.

"Prepare for bombing run," she said over the hardline. "Let's go earn our keep."

HEXAGRAM 43
RESOLUTION
BELOW HEAVEN ABOVE LAKE

The Lake has risen higher than the Sky. In the same way, the noble man dispenses blessings so they reach those below. He dwells in virtue and so clarifies what one should be adverse to.

By the twelfth day of Operation Great Strength, things were not looking promising. The morning of the ninth day, the Mexic forces had completed their pincering move and succeeded in cutting the Middle Kingdom salient off from the main bulk of their forces in the east. Now the ground forces—bannermen and Green Standard guardsmen—who had advanced at speed towards the west the week before—were cut off, completely surrounded by the Mexica on all four sides. Completely cut off, from reinforcements, from resupply, and from the promise of retreat.

As the twelfth day of the operation dawned, *Fair Winds for Escort* was being prepared for another mission. But unlike all the other bombing runs of the previous days, for the first time Amonkar and her crew would be attempting to drop *life*, not death, on their targets.

"Mehdi reports that the packages are loaded and ready, skipper," Seathl said, settling into the co-pilot's seat and strapping her restraints across shoulders, abdomen, and thighs. "We should be ready to hit the runway in a few minutes."

"Acknowledged," Amonkar said absently, checking and rechecking the gauges.

Their mission brief was simple. The ground forces in the "island" that remained of the salient were in need of provisions, with oxygen, water, and ammunition in particular short supply. Several squadrons of light bombers, *Fair Winds* among them, had been selected for the resupply. Once their holds had been cleared of any unused ordinance, and the crews ready and in place, ground personnel in the hangars had loaded supply "packages," each with enough breathable air and drinkable water to keep a platoon on its feet, and enough rifle and small arms ammunition to give them a fighting chance. Whether any of the ground troops would live through what came next though, remained to be seen.

At long last, the Middle Kingdom commanders had decided that the costs and risks associated with Great Strength far outstripped the potential gains, and that with the salient completely cut off the only sensible response was a fast and orderly retreat. In order for the ground troops to retreat to the relative safety of Middle Kingdom-held territory, they would need to punch through the Mexic line surrounding the salient "island." The main force of the Middle Kingdom would pound on the Mexica from the east, trying to push through to the island, but it would fall to the salient ground forces to make sure they were in position and pushing back at the right moment.

"Co-pilot," Amonkar said, having finished the preflight checks of the instrumentation, "do we have our course plotted? I want to know that we're dropping these things where they'll do some good."

"Well, what about it, Geng?" Seathl called over the hardline.

There was only silence in response.

"Navigator?" Amonkar said, thumbing for general transmission.

After a moment, Geng came on the hardline, harried. "Sorry, Arati," she said, sounding breathless, "I was on the ship-to-ship with Pak."

Amonkar scowled. She'd passed up a number of opportunities to talk to the navigator about her relationship with the Dragonfly pilot, and things were only getting worse. There were stiff penalties for abusing ship-to-ship communications frequencies, and if Amonkar were following regulations she'd have to report Geng to their superiors. But that would lose *Fair Winds* an invaluable crewmember, and Amonkar didn't have any illusions about the quality of the back-up airmen waiting on the ground to fill the place of a fallen crewmember. She would let this infringement slide, but she'd have to tackle the issue of Geng's creeping insubordination in the very near future. Of course, it would mean ordering her to break off all contact with the man she'd pledged to marry, since their dalliance was only serving to hinder the efficiency of both and put in jeopardy not only two aircraft, but all of the other Middle Kingdom forces who relied on them.

For the moment though, Amonkar wanted only to get off the ground, and get their mission underway.

"Is our course plotted, Geng?" Amonkar asked, managing to mask her exasperation reasonably well. "The target drops all mapped and ready?"

There was a brief but still excruciatingly-too-long a pause, as the navigator checked her charts and figures, but finally she answered, her tone casual. "Got it, Arati. We're ready to go."

Amonkar sighed, and nodded. "Very well then, let's get on with it. I just hope we don't drop any of these things on someone's head."

"Come on, skipper," Seathl said, as *Fair Winds* taxied out through the open hangar doors and onto the runway. "You've seen ground-pounders in the wild. The bannermen have heads so thick their brains wouldn't even jiggle if one of those boxes bounced off them."

"What about the guardsmen?" Amonkar asked.

Seathl smiled. "Come on, skipper. You know there aren't any brains in the Green Standard at all..."

HEXAGRAM 44
ENCOUNTER
BELOW WIND ABOVE HEAVEN

Below Heaven, there is Wind. In the same way, the sovereign issues his commands and makes known his wishes to the four quarters of the world.

By any objective measure, Operation Great Strength had been a failure. A qualified failure perhaps, in that the Mexic forces were required to expend a considerable amount of manpower and munitions to overrun the Middle Kingdom salient, but when held in the balance against the loss of men and machines on the part of the Green Standard, the Eight Banners, and the Air Corps, it hardly seemed worth the expense.

It came as small comfort to the ground and air forces so sorely taxed in Great Strength, but the generals who had been the architects of the failed offensive already had new plans ready to put into motion.

The war continued, on multiple fronts. In addition to the main line of engagement on Tamkung Plain, bannermen and guardsmen faced Mexic warriors in a variety of theaters of combat, advancing and retreating in a maddeningly slow struggle for dominance. And not just on the planet's surface, but overhead as well. In the skies above, Middle Kingdom airmen and Eagle Knights dove and swooped in dogfights, vying for aerial supremacy. In the cold of space too, near the edge of Fire Star's gravity well, the vacuum-craft of the Interplanetary Fleet exchanged fire with their opposite numbers, ceramic and steel hurtling through the void at incredible speeds, sending salvoes crashing against one another's hulls.

And deep within the Zhurong moonbase, artificers of the Dragon Throne were at work perfecting dread new technologies, which would soon be unleashed against the Mexic Dominion, weapons which had never before been used against their enemies.

HEXAGRAM 45
GATHERING
BELOW EARTH ABOVE LAKE

The Lake has risen higher than the Earth. In the same way, the noble man gets his weapons in order so he may use them to deal with emergencies.

Guardsman Carter woke up screaming, his hair matted to his forehead with sweat. On the cot to the left of his, Spitter groaned in his sleep, objecting to the noise without waking fully, and rolled over on his side. Carter looked to the right, his eyes still wide and startled, and saw the faint light reflecting off the pupils of Moonface. The African guardsman was propped up on one elbow, watching him with a sympathetic look.

"It's over, Tejas," Moonface said, in a low voice. "We're out. Go back to sleep."

Carter nodded, mouth-closed, and lay back on his cot, the fabric beneath him cold with his own sweat.

It had been less than a full day since they'd broken through the Mexic lines to the east at last, and rejoined the main body of the Middle Kingdom forces. Fourteen days since Carter and the rest of First-Second advanced west at the vanguard of the salient, pushing past the Mexic lines and deep into enemy territory. Fourteen days of near-constant fire-fighting, of gaining ground only to lose it the next day, or losing ground only to recapture it once more. Back and forth over the same few kilometers of red soil, made only redder by the blood spilled on it.

Not all of First-Second had lived to retreat back to the east, when the orders had come down at last to give up the futile assault. Not all of them had been welcomed back by those elements of the Eleventh Armored Infantry Battalion lucky enough not to be selected for Operation Great Strength.

Ears had fallen, in those last hours of the retreat. The Arab rifleman of Carter's fire team, who had been with them since they first arrived for basic training on Taiwan Island, had been pulped by a Mexic mortar shell, only bare meters from the safety of the Middle Kingdom-held territory.

And Ears wasn't the only one to fall. Of the sixty-four members of Fourth Company's Second Platoon that had advanced on the first day of Great Strength, little more than half were returning. First Squad itself had lost seven men, down from the full strength of sixteen troops. Among those left behind on the battlefield, alongside Ears, was First-Second's commanding officer, Corporal Eng.

Round-faced, broad-shouldered Eng. When Carter and the rest of the new recruits had shipped out to Fire Star, the corporal had seemed absurdly experienced. He might have appeared somewhat world-weary at times, but Eng was a man who had already seen combat on Fire Star and lived, and if any of the new recruits in First Squad were going to survive the coming months of battle, it would be by sticking as close to Eng as possible, and following his every order.

Now Eng was dead, his faceplate shattered by a Mexic bullet two days before the retreat. Even if his face hadn't been ruined, the bullet driven deep into his brain pan, Eng would have suffocated in a matter of heartbeats anyway, exposed to the thin Fire Star air. That he had died so suddenly had been a blessing, in its way, though Carter was hard-pressed now to see the positive side of it.

The surviving members of First-Second had been leaderless, in those last days, but it hardly seemed to matter. There were so many units operating at half-strength, or worse, all just struggling to remain alive, to keep the enemy fended off however they could, that the field of battle seemed chaotic madness, men searching for whatever cover they could, firing on anything that moved. In the end, Carter and the other survivors attached themselves to elements of Third Company, who thankfully had some small reserves of oxygen and water left over from the last of the aid drops.

Their fire team had stuck together, never out of sight of one another. Carter, Ears, Moonface, and Spitter, each watching the others' backs, sleeping in shifts, side-by-side in their makeshift trenches and bolt-holes, sharing their ammunition and rations between them.

It had seemed, until those last moments of the retreat, that all of them might survive Great Strength, might live to see another sunrise, might once more stand upright without fear of being cut down by enemy fire, surrounded by hostile forces on all sides. It had been almost too much to hope for, and so the four of them had concentrated their attentions on the immediate future, working towards surviving the next few moments at any given time, and letting the longer stretch of tomorrows worry for itself. But as they loped towards the safety of the Middle Kingdom main line of resistance, towards the bulwarks from behind which their brothers-in-arms were laying down suppressing fire, Carter had allowed himself to hope, for just a moment, in his mind's eye seeing an image of himself and his comrades at their leisure, out of their stiflingly-close surface suits, sharing out a bottle of rice wine between them, glad just to be alive. Then Carter had glanced back, for just a moment, like Lot in the old Bible stories his father used to tell, like Orpheus fleeing the underworld, to make sure the others in the fire team were following behind. He glanced back, just for an instant, but long enough to see Ears hit from behind by a Mexic mortar shell, the force of the impact knocking the Arab forwards off his feet.

When Carter closed his eyes, he could still see the image of the Arab's face, his eyes wide with surprise for a brief heartbeat, then forever obscured as blood exploded outwards, painting the inside of Ears' faceplate in crimson gore.

Carter would have gone back. Even as Ears fell to the ground like a puppet with cut strings, lifeless and ruined, Carter would have gone back for him. But Spitter and Moonface had been at his side, and had each taken hold of one of Carter's arms, dragging him toward the gap in the bulwarks, their faces twisted by shouting and pleading, their voices lost over the chaotic maelstrom of chatter on the radio waves.

In the dark gloom of the makeshift barracks, Carter stared up into the darkness. Less than a full day since he and the other survivors of Great Strength had retreated to safety, and it was still sometimes hard to believe. When Carter closed his eyes, it was possible to believe he was still out in the salient, dreaming fitfully in a trench, his oxygen-starved mind conjuring up tantalizing visions of safety and rest. When he opened his eyes again, would he still be in the barracks, safe behind friendly lines, or would he still be out in the killing fields, waiting the Mexic bullet that had his name inscribed on it?

Carter wouldn't sleep again tonight, he knew. He sat up again, swung his legs over the side of the cot, and then leaned over, reaching underneath to the place where his carbine lay. In the darkness, he checked the action, checked the ammunition clip, checked the safety. He had done the steps so often he didn't need his eyes to see, but could feel his way from barrel to stock by touch. When he was satisfied that the weapon was loaded and ready for action, he lay it across his lap. Sitting motionless and silent in the dark, his weapon at the ready, Carter waited for dawn. If he *was* sleeping, if he *was* still on the killing fields, dreaming, he would be ready, when the moment came.

HEXAGRAM 46
CLIMBING
BELOW WIND ABOVE EARTH

Within the Earth grows the Tree. In the same way, the noble man lets virtue be his guide and little by little becomes lofty and great.

Carter closed his eyes, feeling the warmth of sunlight on his bare face and hands, and took a deep breath of fresh air. Beneath the loamy scents, he caught the trace of green freshness, reminding him something of the Nipponese maples of Taiwan Island, something of the pines of his native Tejas.

But the pine was an evergreen, and the Nipponese maple lost its leaves in autumn. Did the trees and shrubs within the subterranean oxygen farm really smell anything like either of them? Likely not, but these were the first living plants this size that Carter had seen since coming to Fire Star, so it was hardly surprising that he'd have an exaggerated reaction to them. Of course, after months of recycled air, reconstituted water, and the stale smell of his own body and wastes trapped in his helmet, it was to be expected that his sense of smell might have lost some of its keenness.

It struck Carter that this was the first intact greenhouse he'd entered since arriving on the red planet. All of the others had been bombed-out ruins, their walls open to the thin atmosphere, any heat or moisture within long since fled. But unlike those others, this greenhouse was deep underground, fed sunlight through a system of mirrors in the branching ducts overhead. Even after the long years of the war, the shrubs and trees planted down here by the colonists had remained vital, green, and growing. While the ongoing war had ravaged the greenhouses on the surface, life down here had been allowed to thrive, undeterred.

"Expecting trouble, Carter?"

As he spun around, startled, Carter's hands flew to the carbine slung over his shoulder, and he trained the weapon's barrel on the figure standing behind him.

"Lieutenant Seong!" Carter started, eyes wide.

"High marks for reaction time, guardsman," the lieutenant said, smiling, "but I think Captain Quan might frown on shooting one of his officers."

Carter gawped at the lieutenant for a moment before remembering he still had his rifle aimed at the man's chest, his finger on the trigger. Blushing red with shame, Carter swung the carbine's barrel to the ground, coming to attention.

"Taking a little stroll, are you?" Seong stayed where he was, a slight smile still tugging up the corners of his mouth.

"Yes, sir," Carter said, in clipped, efficient tones. "I was at liberty, and thought I'd come down to see..."

"It's alright." Seong silenced him with a raised hand. "The greenhouse isn't off-limits—not yet, at any rate—so there's no harm in coming down for a look."

The greenhouse had apparently been discovered still intact and functioning only recently, while First-Second and the others were still engaged in Operation Great Strength. It had been some time since the colonists in this area had been forced out by the oncoming Mexic forces, but by some miracle the automated systems feeding water and heat to the subterranean oxygen farm had remained in operation, and with the ruins of surface structures blocking the only entrance above, the greenhouse had remained hidden ever since. It was only after guardsmen were tasked with clearing the debris, reclaiming the area for the Green Standard's use, that the entrance, and the greenhouse below, had been rediscovered.

In the days and weeks since, once a pressurized umbilicus connected the greenhouse entrance to the barracks above, the oxygen farm had been frequently visited by off-duty officers and troops, hungry for a glimpse of anything living and green. Carter was just the latest, as was evidently his superior officer, commander of the Fourth Company's Second Platoon.

"There's no problem in coming for a look," Seong repeated, "but I wonder whether you came expecting trouble."

"Sir?" Carter raised an eyebrow.

In response, the lieutenant pointed to the carbine in Carter's hands. "You're far behind friendly lines, deep underground, in a network of pressurized structures, habitats, and tunnels. Do you honestly expect to run into enemy activity down here?"

Carter looked from the lieutenant to his own carbine and back again. Seong was dressed in fatigues, like Carter, but unlike him the lieutenant was completely unarmed.

"No," Carter said, almost like one waking from a dream. "But I just.... That is..." He broke off, shaking his head. "After Great Strength I can't..."

Seong held up his hand again, motioning him to silence. "Do you know the Spring and Autumn Annals, guardsman? There is a quotation there that goes, 'War is like a far...'"

"'...those who will not put aside their weapons will be consumed by them'," Carter finished, remembering the phrase from his own studies.

Seong's eyebrows raised in surprise. "You'll forgive me saying, Carter, but you don't strike me as a scholar."

Carter averted his eyes. "I studied for the examinations, but never passed a one. I'm not..."—his cheeks burned—"...not much of a reader, but I can remember things."

The lieutenant nodded, appreciatively. "I'll have to remember that." He chuckled. "If you'll excuse the inadvertent pun." Carter looked at him blankly. "No matter. In any event, I saw you heading down this way, and thought I'd take the opportunity to speak with you a moment."

Carter remained still and silent, at attention.

"I wanted to..." Seong broke off. "Oh, at ease, guardsman. You look as if you're about to seize up." When Carter had dropped to parade rest, the lieutenant continued. "I read the action reports about the first days of Great Strength, when you refused to comply with an order to retreat, and put yourself in harm's way for the sake of a group of civilian prisoners."

Back straight, Carter tensed, dreading the dressing-down he'd been anticipating for more than two weeks now. "Yes, sir?"

"Those prisoners might be dead now, but for you. And if not already dead, they would be living ghosts, simply waiting for death to take them, with no hope for relief or rescue."

Carter drew his mouth into a line. He'd tried not to think about what might have happened to those six strangers—two men, three women, and one little girl—had he and the rest of First-Second not interrupted the Mexic crawler transporting them.

While Carter and the others had done their best to extend the salient to the west, the six rescued prisoners had been transported back to the east, to Middle Kingdom-held territory.

"You disobeyed orders," Seong went on, "put yourself at risk, and six innocents are alive now because of it." The lieutenant crossed his arms over his chest, and tilted his head to one side, studying Carter closely. "For the former, you should be brought up on charges, and subjected to disciplinary action. The effects of the latter, though, tend to mitigate somewhat in your factor, along with two other important considerations."

"Sir?" Carter still wasn't sure whether he was going to be disciplined or not.

"First is that we are too short-handed at the moment to lose any men to the stockade, much less more men to guard it. And there are scarcely enough vegetables needing peeling for you to be much use in kitchen patrol. Second, and more to the point, I have more pressing need for you elsewhere?"

Now it was Carter's turn to cock his head to the side and study the other man. "Pressing need, sir?"

Seong nodded. "I'm sure it hasn't escaped your notice that First Squad is presently without a commanding officer?"

Carter shook his head.

The lieutenant studied Carter's expression. "Tell me, guardsman, do you have a wife back in the wilds of Tejas, I wonder?"

"No, sir."

"No girl waiting on your return?"

Carter shook his head again, while unbidden came the image of a young Hindi girl in his thoughts. Where had he seen her before? Just before the lieutenant spoke again, he placed her as the pilot he had met on the transport from Earth. But why would he think of her?

"I only ask," the lieutenant continued, "because there are those who believe that married men make poor officers, since they are too worried about getting home to their wives, when the war is over." Seong smiled. "Nonsense, if you ask me, since I would argue that a married man just has that much more to fight for, that much more to *win* for. But I was curious, all the same."

"Permission to speak, lieutenant?" Seong nodded, and Carter went on. "Sir, are you asking me...? That is, you don't expect me to..." Carter trailed off, failing to find the words with which to frame his question.

"I expect you to serve the Dragon Throne and the Green Standard, just as you've done since you entered the service. Only now, instead of simply receiving orders, and directing the movements of the three other men in your fire team, you'll be giving a few orders of your own. There's a big offensive in the works, one last big push to the west, and I need a man I can trust in command of First-Second."

Seong stuck out his hand, thumb upwards, and Carter was taken aback a moment, just looking at it.

"A custom I observed while stationed in Tejas, guardsman. I believe you're meant to shake it?"

Carter blushed. He'd seen his father and grandfather shake hands to close a deal and greet friends for years, but so long away from home had all but forgotten the gesture. With an abbreviated nod, he reached out and took Seong's hand in his own.

"I know you're the man for the post, Carter," the lieutenant said, squeezing Carter's fist in his own. "Now I need you to get First-Second ready to fight, and to win." He nodded towards the carbine slung over Carter's shoulder. "But remember to put away your weapons until they're needed, will you? I don't want to see anyone consumed by them."

Hexagram 47
Impasse
Below Water Above Lake

The Lake has no Water: this is the image of Impasse. In the same way, the noble man would sacrifice his life in pursuit of his goals.

Niohuru Tie and the rest of the men of the Falcon's Claws were in their armored surface suits, many of them newly patched and refitted, out on the cold desert east of the Middle Kingdom main line. They stood at the edge of an ancient crater, its edges all but completely eroded by the thin Fire Star winds over untold ages, so that it looked more like an empty lake bed in the middle of a drought than the impact scar of a fallen meteor.

"We owe a debt to our lost brothers." Captain Hughes Falco was broadcasting to the men at low power, his words reaching only as far as them, scattering on the winds beyond. "It's a debt that we'll all be asked to make good, sooner or later."

For the men of the First Raider Company who had fallen in the course of Operation Great Strength, there would be no funerals, not in any traditional sense. There would be no household statues covered in red paper, the mirrors hung with veils. No Taoist monks chanting scripture through the night, keeping vigil by the body, helping smooth the passage of the dead into heaven, past whatever challenges or torments they might face. No sound of flute and gong, nor the smell of incense or of burning joss paper, ghost money reduced to ashes for the dead to spend in the hereafter. Those were observances for those who had died at home, near family that could honor them.

The fallen Falcon's Claws had been left on the battlefield, unburied, impossibly far away from home. There'd been no way to carry them back in the retreat, and no guarantees they'd still be there if the Middle Kingdom were to retake the territory. Everyone knew what the Mexica did with their prisoners, but there were only rumors and suspicions about what they did with the bodies of the enemy dead.

"None of us rushes to his death," Hughes went on, "but neither do we shrink from it. Those we lost on the field of combat saw death coming for them, and stood their ground and met it head on."

Niohuru knew the captain was being poetic, speaking of the dead in grandiose terms, but that wasn't how he remembered it at all. He thought of the bannerman all but beheaded by the chakram of the Akali Sena. Had he seen his death coming at the hands of his brothers-in-arms, felled by friendly fire. Or the bannermen who had been reduced to bags of shattered bones and liquefied organs by aerial bombardment, or those cooked alive in their own surface suits when torrents of burning liquid magnesium poured through broken visors and carapaces and helmets.

Even though the captain's words rang hollow in Niohuru's ears, he knew better than to question them, especially while the memorial service was still being performed.

"None of us wants to die, so far from home," the captain said, turning slowly and looking at each man in turn. "But the emperor calls us to action, and we go where we are needed."

Niohuru remembered the words of Master Kong, who taught that one should not travel far from home while one's parents are still living, since then there would be no one there to bury and honor them when they died. Older people could not show respect to the young, only the young to their elders. Children could perform the rites for their parents, but parents not for their children.

Remembering the faces of those who had fallen, Niohuru couldn't help but think that many of them had been little more than children themselves, just entering manhood. He liked to think of himself as a man fully grown, but had it really been that long since he was playing at games with the other children of privilege in the streets of Northern Capital, without any cares for tomorrow, pursuing only the pleasures of the moment? He thought of the years his parents had lived, and his grandparents before them. Niohuru had scarcely started on the road of life, and if he were to die here, on these red sands, he would have left no children behind to honor him. There would be no one to perform the filial rites for him in death, no one to respect his passing.

No one but his brothers-in-arms, the other Falcon's Claws, who gave each other what respect in death that they could.

"None of us wants to die," Captain Hughes repeated, his voice lowered, "but there may well come a moment when that is exactly what is expected of us. And should that moment come in the course of our service to the Dragon Throne, then there is no higher service we can perform than to step into the fray willfully, shaming the enemy's fire with our courage, and sacrificing ourselves willingly for our cause and for our brothers."

The captain paused, and regarded the ragged half-circle of men.

"But just because we should be *willing* to die, doesn't mean we should be too eager, either. If we can finish this war without losing another of our number, you won't hear a single complaint from me. So remember our fallen brothers, honor their memory, and do your damnedest not to get *yourselves* killed, too."

HEXAGRAM 48
THE WELL
BELOW WIND ABOVE WATER

Above wood, there is water. In the same way, the noble man rewards the common folk for their toil and encourages them to help each other.

When Cong Ren beside him began to snore softly, his head lolling onto his chest, Niohuru nudged him in the ribs, jerking him awake.

"What was that for, daisy?" Cong said with a sneer, crossing his arms over his chest.

Before Niohuru could reply, Axum Ouazebas leaned forward on his opposite side, shooting glares past Niohuru at Cong. "If it had been me, you would have gotten worse than an elbow to your ribs, you snoring oaf. And if I end up with kitchen detail because a member of my combat cell has snored through a mission briefing, an elbow will be the *least* of your worries."

"Quiet," Niohuru said, gesturing to the front of the large chamber with his chin. Captain Hughes Falco had entered the room, and was stepping up to the screen erected before the projector.

"Settle, men," Hughes said, pausing in front of the screen and scanning the room.

The full complement of the First Raider Company had been called together in the chamber. For the first time in weeks, possibly months, they were at something approaching full strength, their numbers swelled by the arrival of new reinforcements. They had arrived only days before, having been already en route from Earth when Operation Great Holdings began.

Bright, eager, and open-faced, the reinforcement troopers were fresh from training, and looking with barely disguised horror and disgust at the unshaven, disorderly, slovenly wretches of the Falcon's Claws.

Niohuru had to smile when he realized that, although it had been only a few months since he'd worn just such a barely disguised expression of distaste, that now he blended in without distinction among the slovenly wretches. He wondered what he would make of himself, if the young reinforcement trooper he'd been only a few months before could see him now. His smile widened slightly, when he realized that he didn't care at all, no more than the reinforcement troops would, should they be so lucky as to live long enough to learn what really mattered.

"Listen up," Hughes went on, when he had everyone's attention. "I know we're still licking our wounds after Operation Great Strength. Eighteen hells, it's only been a few days since we had a memorial to remember our dead. But as much as I'd like to take quite a bit more time to retrain and integrate our latest additions, we're being called up again. We'll be moving out in three days' time, for another big push."

"What fancy codename has *this* poorly-planned disaster been given?" called a voice from the crowd.

Hughes narrowed his eyes, but the corners of his mouth tugged up in a controlled smile. To the continued horror of the reinforcement troops, he didn't call for the man who'd spoken to be lashed, for impugning the honor of their generals, but only chuckled, and said, "It hasn't got one, that I've heard. Which either means that the generals have decided that fancy codenames are ill fortune, or perhaps just that they're not bothering to tell them to us, anymore. For all we know, there *is* a codename for the operation, but we don't have the ratings to hear it."

Hughes called for the lights to be dimmed, and then flipped a switch on the side of the boxy projector, sitting on a crate a couple of meters from the front wall. White light shone from the projector, lighting up dust motes that swirled in the sluggish air, and an image appeared on the screen.

"This is where we're heading, men," Hughes said, thumping the screen with his finger, sending it waving in gentle ripples. "Ruosi."

The image on the screen was a topographical map of the western reaches of Tamkung Plain, with key locations marked in ideograms. Near the center of the map was the symbol for a colony, and the name "Ruosi."

Niohuru knew the name well. He'd been hearing about the place since he stepped onto the transport from Earth, and the name was famous enough that he'd heard it a time or two before ever dreaming of joining the Eight Banners. Ruosi was once a Middle Kingdom colony, a pressurized dome built within a kilometers-deep crater at the western edge of Tamkung Plain. For longer than anyone cared to remember though, it had been a stronghold of the Mexic Dominion forces on Fire Star.

"I don't have to tell you how important Ruosi is to the Mexic forces," the captain went on. "If the Middle Kingdom were able to retake it, and Zijun as well, then all that would remain of the war would be to mop up the scattered elements of the Mexica from here to Tianfei Valley. And then we could all go home again."

From around the room came mutters of approval, and brief wistful looks flashing across unshaven, scarred faces, indulging if for a brief moment in the images conjured by the word "home."

"Intelligence puts a detachment of the House of Darkness in the dome city itself," the captain explained, pointing to the colony symbol. Niohuru wasn't alone in shuddering, remembering the stories he'd heard about the Mexic secret police and intelligencers, the House of Darkness, who also served as ritual torturers and executioners. "And in addition to the usual assortment of Jaguar and Eagle Knights in and around Ruosi, we've learned that stationed outside the crater itself are the habitats of a full division of Shorn Ones."

While the Falcon's Claws exchanged worried looks, some whistling low, the reinforcement troopers looking confused, Hughes flipped another switch on the projector, and the image on the screen changed.

"We're looking at a shot taken from directly overhead by satellite surveillance." Hughes pointed to the curve of a crater in the upper left quadrant of the image. "That's Ruosi to the northwest, and this"—he pointed to a neatly arranged network of boxes linked by bold lines—"is a compound of habitats linked by pressurized tunnels, some above ground and some below." He paused, and turned from the screen to look at the assembled men. "This is the home of the Shorn Ones. Now, the Green Standard is being tasked with taking the dome itself inside the crater, but they won't even get that far if we can't get the Shorn Ones off their back. So our job is to get there and knock the Shorn Ones down."

The waves of ripples through the Falcon's Claws rose and pitched like breakers at high tide, as the First Raider Company reacted to the news. Only the reinforcements, who clearly didn't understand what Hughes was saying, weren't shocked, outraged, or alarmed.

"Settle down, men," Hughes said, "and that's an order."

One of the reinforcement troopers had his hand up, signaling for the captain's attention.

"Yes?" Hughes paused for a moment, searching for the man's name in his memory. "Hideo, wasn't it? What's your question?"

The reinforcement trooper nodded, and then in Official Speech laced with the accent of Nippon, he asked, "Shorn Ones, sir?"

Hughes nodded, thoughtfully, then turned and hit another switch on the projector, and the satellite image was replaced by a representation of a Mexic surface suit. It was enameled yellow, the helmet painted blue on one side, yellow on the other, with a white butterfly painted on the lower half of the helmet's visor. On one hand was a shield emblazoned with a jagged design, and in the other hand was held a club lined with obsidian blades.

"*That*," Hughes said, jerking a thumb at the screen, "is a Shorn One. Now, I trust that everyone of you, from the newest to the most veteran, understands the rudiments of the Mexic military organization?"

There were a scattering of nods from around the room, some more enthusiastic than others.

It had taken Niohuru some time to get a handle on the ways in which the Mexic Dominion organized its military. The Middle Kingdom employed a rational approach, dividing its forces into infantry, marines, and navy, the latter supporting vacuum, air, and sea branches. The Mexic Dominion military, by contrast, was a single body, reporting through a unified command structure, and headed by their elected leader, the Great Speaker. A man or woman might begin a career in the Mexic military as an infantryman, then be transferred to a marine company, and ultimately be assigned to act as an airman.

"While there aren't any functional divisions in the Mexic military," Hughes explained, "there are sects and orders within their military hierarchy. You know the Eagle Knights, those who've scored a high number of kills in air or space. And if you don't know the Jaguar Knights, who get their stripes capturing enemy combatants on land, air, vacuum, or sea, you'll know them soon enough." A few of the veterans chuckled ruefully, somewhat unsettling the reinforcements. "The Shorn Ones are a sect of Mexic warriors. It's made up of those who have captured an *extremely* high number of enemies, killing even more along the way, but who declined promotion to captaincy in order to remain behind as battlefield combatants. This is the lot from which the Chief of the House of Arrows is always drawn, the second-in-command to the Great Speaker, and battlefield commander of the whole Mexic military." His lips curled in a tight smile. "In short, these are some hard bastards, and it's up to us to take them out."

There were grumblings from the Falcon's Claws, muttering remarks about the advisability of sending a little over two hundred bannermen against an entire division of the Mexica's most deadly killers.

"We won't be fighting alone," Hughes said, but before the sighs of relief had even finished, he added, "we'll be fighting alongside the Akali Sena in the attack."

Some of the Falcon's Claws leapt off their benches, faces red and mouths twisting in rage. None of those who had fought in Great Strength could forget the deaths of their two brothers who fell to the chakrams of the Sikh Immortals, and there were many in the room who still cried out for vengeance.

Hughes raised a hand to silence them, his expression hard. "One of the Sikhs fell in that exchange as well, if you'd forgotten. They're no more to be blamed for that rutting mess than we are."

A voice called out from the crowd, "So who *is* to be blamed?"

The captain narrowed his eyes angrily, his lips curling back from his teeth in a sneer. "You want someone to blame? Then blame the rutting Mexica! They're who we're here fighting. And we've just been given the chance to go after the worst of the bastards!" He smacked a fist against the screen, sending ripples waving through the image of the yellow-enameled Mexic surface suit. "So stop your grumbling, pay attention, and we'll be able to repay the blood-hungry bastards for every one of our brothers and sisters who've fallen. Is *that* clear enough?"

The muttering and grumbling were gone, as the Falcon's Claws snapped to attention, all eyes forward, unified by their captain's words.

"Alright, then," Hughes said with a tight smile. He toggled the projector switch, and another image appeared on the screen. "Now *this* is how we're going to do it..."

HEXAGRAM 49
RADICAL CHANGE
BELOW FIRE ABOVE LAKE

Inside the Lake, there is Fire. In the same way, the noble man orders the calendar and clarifies the seasons.

It had been hours since the chimes had sounded for All Quiet, but in the airmen's billet, Amonkar and her crewmembers, Seathl and Geng, were still wide awake, talking in low voices, huddled in a corner far from the rest of the airmen. This was just the latest in a long line of temporary billets for the members of the Air Corps in theater, this one a former greenhouse, hastily patched and repressurized only weeks before, still smelling of rotten leaves, ash, and mould.

"Pass that over this way, Seathl," Amonkar said, reaching out a hand to her co-pilot.

Fair Winds for Escort didn't have a bombing run scheduled for another day and a half, which meant that the crew would be at liberty for another night and a day. And since they didn't have to be anything approaching cogent or coherent the following morning, the three women planned on getting well and truly drunk tonight.

Seathl took a long pull of the jar of rice wine that they'd appropriated from abandoned colonial stores, hidden below an enormous pile of debris since the evacuation of the colonists. Wiping her mouth on the back of her hand, she passed the jar to the pilot.

Amonkar took a healthy swig, the wine sour and biting on the tongue. But as it crept down her throat, she could feel her ears begin to burn, heat spreading like a blush across her cheeks. The wine was long past its use-by date, but it was doing the trick, which was good enough for her.

"Here, Geng," she said, and thrust the jar towards the navigator, who sat cross-legged a short distance away.

Geng accepted the jar absent-mindedly, but stopped and looked for a moment at the jar's mouth before lifting it to her lips. Then, before taking a sip, she handed it on to Seathl. "Not thirsty," she said by way of explanation.

Amonkar and Seathl exchanged perplexed looks, and then turned back to Geng.

"Not *thirsty*?" Seathl said, disbelievingly. "Since when has that stopped you?"

"You've never turned down a drink before now," Amonkar added, "at least not that I can recall."

"I just..." Geng began, and then broke off, averting her eyes.

Amonkar noticed the navigator's shoulders shaking, almost like she was shivering in the cold, or else...

"Geng, are you *crying*? What's wrong?"

The navigator turned, eyes red-rimmed, tears welling in their corners, and gave Amonkar an imploring look. "Oh, Arati..."

Amonkar's thoughts raced. Had the navigator received some bad news about her man, Pilot Pak, and just not told the others before now? Or was it...?

She suspected the truth, before Geng ever spoke, but was afraid to give it voice, for fear that saying it might somehow make it so.

"... I'm *pregnant*!" Geng said, her voice quavering.

"Well, dung," Seathl spat, lip curled in distaste.

Amonkar took a deep breath, letting it slip back out through her nostrils in a long exhale. "Oh, Geng..."

The co-pilot leaned forward, eyes narrowed suspiciously. "How do you know for certain?"

The navigator chewed at her lower lip, looking from Amonkar to Seathl and back again. "I missed my flow without noticing. *Twice.*"

Seathl gaped in disbelief. "*How?*"

Geng offered an uninspired shrug. "I lost track of the calendar. I only figured it out when you started complaining about the shortage of sanitary products. I checked my kit that night, and realized I'd had the same number of napkins for *months*."

Amonkar nodded. She could well imagine losing track of the weeks and months like that, with one day the same as all the others.

"Does Pak know?" Amonkar asked, then quickly added, "It *is* Pak's, isn't it?"

Geng shot her a hard glare. "Of *course* it's Pak's," she answered, her tone sounding offended. "But no," she added, more subdued, "I haven't told him yet. What can I *say* to him?"

Seathl cocked her head to one side, her expression quizzical. "Weren't you taking the cold flower?"

Amonkar's mouth dropped open, and she spun around to look wide-eyed at the co-pilot. "Seathl! I'm... I'm *shocked*!"

The co-pilot gave her a confused glance. "Shocked? Because...?" A slow smile tugged up the corners of Seathl's mouth. "Skipper, just because we don't talk about contraception with *men*, doesn't mean that most women don't use it." She shook her head, scoffing at what she perceived as the pilot's naivety. "The ling hua contraceptive is used by everyone from the emperor's concubines to professional women, from housewives with too many children to prostitutes who don't want any."

Geng shook her head, eyes downcast. "I ran out, not long after I met Pak. I suppose I could have just stopped..." She shook her head. "I just didn't think it would be a problem. It isn't as if... Not *here*, I mean."

Amonkar sighed again, and laid a hand over Geng's. "So what will you do? Will you tell Pak? Will you...?" She glanced down at the navigator's belly. As much as contraception wasn't discussed in polite society, the techniques for terminating a pregnancy were scarcely even mentioned aloud, even among close friends. But Amonkar had heard whispers as a child in Hind, and heard rumors as an adult in service about what went on in other countries.

Geng met Amonkar's gaze, her eyes welling, tears snaking down her cheeks towards her jawline. "Oh, I don't *know*, Arati," the navigator wailed. "I just don't know. What *should* I do?"

Amonkar pursed her lips, her brow furrowed. She knew this was all *her* fault. If she'd ordered Geng to break off her relations with Pak as she'd intended, all those weeks ago, then Geng wouldn't be in her present state. She might resent Amonkar for interfering with her relationship, citing the "course of true love" and such sentimental nonsense, but at least she wouldn't now be at least a month or two pregnant, in the middle of a rutting warzone.

"I don't know," Amonkar answered with another weary sigh. "I honestly don't know."

Whatever Amonkar suggested, whatever course of action Geng chose to follow, one thing was certain. Things would be changing from this point onward, for all of them.

HEXAGRAM 50
THE CAULDRON
BELOW WIND ABOVE FIRE

Above Wood, there is Fire. In the same way, the noble man rectifies positions and makes his orders firm.

Amonkar stood at attention, while the man in Interplanetary Fleet fatigues with the carbine in his arms and the pistol holstered at his side spoke into the radio clipped to his shoulder. She was in a maze of corridors and rooms that had once been a multi-family residence of some kind, but which had been appropriated for the use of the Fleet brass. This was the deepest that Amonkar had come into the complex, and she was starting to feel the walls close in on her.

The guard at the door tilted his head for a moment, listening to the tiny speaker tucked into his ear, and then gave Amonkar a final appraising look.

"Go on through," he said, pulling the door open. "They're waiting."

Amonkar nodded, and walked stiff-legged through the doorway, scarcely able to breathe.

She'd received the summons that morning, hung over and still trying to figure out what to do about Geng. In the first bleary moments after waking in the billet, she had tried to convince herself that the conversation about the navigator's pregnancy the night before had been some drunken dream. But then she had only to exchange a single, worried glance with Seathl to realize it had been all-too-real. Then an adjutant had arrived with a scrolled slip of paper, and in bold-stroked ideograms Amonkar had read the summons to appear before the Interplanetary Fleet admiralty at the start of the next watch.

She hadn't the slightest idea what the summons was about, but harbored dark suspicions.

"At your ease, airman," said the man sitting at the desk, his arms resting on its pitted surface. He was wearing the red surcoat of the Interplanetary Fleet's dress uniform, the insignia of a fleet admiral on his breast. He gestured to the empty chair opposite him. "Be seated, Pilot Amonkar."

Amonkar managed to nod, and slid into the chair, chancing a glance at the silent woman sitting at the admiral's side. She was wearing a plain gray tunic and pants, unmarked and unadorned, and had the look of a schoolteacher or shop clerk. Amonkar wondered who she was, to be seated so casually next to a fleet admiral, here in this heavily secured room.

The admiral regarded Amonkar for a moment, studying her face, and then nodded, seemingly satisfied by what he found there. "I am Admiral Geng, and this"—he gestured to the woman—"is Agent Wu."

Amonkar's jaw dropped, and she forgot all about wondering who the woman might be when she heard the admiral's name. So this *was* about Navigator Geng's pregnancy, then? Was Amonkar to be held to account for her crewmember's moral lapse? And why had Geng never mentioned having relatives in the admiralty.

"Wh-what..." Amonkar began, her voice quavering. "What relation are you to Navigator Geng, if I may ask?"

The admiral cocked an eyebrow, looking perplexed, then shook his head and smiled. "Oh, that's right, I had forgotten your crewmember. We are no relation, so far as I know. It is a common name, after all." He shrugged, a gesture so casual it was at odds with the crisp dress uniform he wore. "We may be distantly related, though, for all I know."

Amonkar opened her mouth and closed it again, head tilted to one side, before answering. "So this *isn't* about..." She paused, considering how much or how little to say. "... about my ship's navigator, then?"

Admiral Geng's lips tightened in a controlled smile, but his eyes narrowed as he shook his head. "I haven't come all the way from Fanchuan Garrison to check on the health of a distant relation, airman."

Amonkar swallowed hard. For the first time, the significance of the insignia on the admiral's surcoat sunk in. This man wasn't simply in charge of the Air Corps elements involved in the frontal campaign. This was a *fleet* admiral, come from Fanchuan Garrison, the seat of military command on Fire Star, and home to the commanders of both the Army of the Green Standard and the Eight Banners, and to the admiralty of the Interplanetary Fleet.

She averted her eyes, studying the pitted metal surface of the desk between them.

"You have come to our attention in recent days, Pilot Amonkar," the admiral continued. "Under your command, *Fair Winds for Escort* has the highest success rate of any of the craft involved in bombing runs in Operations Great Holdings and Great Strength."

Amonkar was a little taken aback. She'd had no idea.

"Tell me, airman," the admiral said, after a moment's pause. "What is your impression of the war?"

"Sir?" Amonkar was confused.

"How do you think the war is proceeding? What are our chances for victory."

Amonkar was unsure how to respond. "Well, sir, it seems like we are making advances." She chewed her lower lip, considering how forthright an answer to offer. "It *does* seem like we spent a great deal of time overlying the same territory, again and again, but it does seem like gradual advances are being made."

Admiral Geng regarded her for a moment, lips pressed together. Then he glanced at the silent woman sitting beside him, her expression unreadable, before answering. "I will be frank with you, airman. The war is not going well. Not at *all* well."

Amonkar's eyebrows raised in surprise. As much because a fleet admiral was speaking to her so candidly as because of the content of his words.

"We can only assume that by this point the Mexic Dominion has reinforcements already en route from Earth, and even if they did not leave until after the destruction of..." He paused, glancing at the woman beside him. Then he amended, "Even if they did not leave until their supply lines were cut off, those reinforcements are bound to arrive on Fire Star within the next two to three months, at a maximum. If the forces of the Dragon Throne are not able to scour the Mexica from the face of Fire Star by the time those reinforcements arrive, there is no *telling* how long the war might drag on."

The admiral paused, taking a deep breath, then letting it out through his nostrils. "What is needed is a swift, decisive victory. One that will not only take out a significant percentage of the Mexic forces, but will also serve to demoralize those Mexic elements who would remain at large for the moment."

The admiral reached underneath the desk, and pulled out a rolled-up map, which he spread out on the desk before him. It showed the western edge of the Tamkung Plain, and in particular the crater colonies of Zijun and Ruosi.

"We are preparing to launch an assault designed to win just such a victory," he went on. He pointed to Ruosi, the southernmost of the two crater colonies. "The lion's share of the Middle Kingdom ground forces, Green Standard and Eight Banners alike, will be moving out in a big push toward Ruosi. They will drive through the Mexic main line of defense *en masse*, and not stop until they have overrun the crater."

The admiral shifted, and tapped his finger on the northern crater colony, only a few centimeters away on the map, many kilometers away in real life. "But before the ground forces reach Ruosi, though, we have something else planned for Zijun." He glanced down at the map, and then up at Amonkar. "And it is this that you and the crew of *Fair Winds for Escort* will be tasked with accomplishing. Operation Double Thunder."

"Double Thunder?" Amonkar repeated. She paused, as the full import of the admiral's words sunk in. "*Just* me and my ship, sir? What kind of operation requires only one bomber?"

The admiral leaned back, and turned to look at the woman beside him. Agent Wu nodded to the general, then leaned forward, elbows on the desk, her fingers laced.

"Tell me, Pilot Amonkar," the woman said, in gentle, even tones, "what do you know about fission bombs?"

HEXAGRAM 51
QUAKE
BELOW THUNDER ABOVE THUNDER

Double Thunder. In the same way, the noble man is beset with fear and so cultivates and examines himself.

Nuclear fission had been at the heart of space travel since the days of the Shangsheng emperor, more than forty years before the Treasure Fleet first set off for Fire Star. While the orbital elevator that would one day rise above Gold Mountain was still being constructed, soon after the Mexic Dominion first launched a man into space, the artificers of the Dragon Throne succeeded in splitting the atom, a feat which previous to then had only been speculated upon.

But while nuclear fission would, in the years to follow, come to be the literal beating heart of space travel, being the furnace which powered every vacuum-craft of the Treasure Fleet and all the craft of the Interplanetary Fleet to follow, its use as a weapon of war had remained, to date, strictly hypothetical. There had been fear in the days of the Shangsheng emperor that the Mexica might develop the technology necessary to create a fission explosive device, and once the Mexic Dominion had successfully sent a man into orbit, there were doomsayers in the Middle Kingdom who speculated that now it was only a matter of time before a Mexic orbital craft dropped a nuclear bomb down on their heads, but the Mexica either lacked the wherewithal or the will to do so, as no rain of fission fire ever came pouring down out of the skies.

With the outbreak of hostilities on Fire Star, the specter of fission explosion devices was again raised, but while such explosives had long since been developed, and had been tested with varying degrees of success in unpopulated regions of the Earth, on the surface of the Moon, and in deep space, they had not as yet been deployed against a living target.

Early in the conflict on Fire Star, the admirals and generals of the Dragon Throne did not know for certain whether their enemies in the Mexic Dominion had successfully developed fission bombs, but the reports from their own artificers were that the fission bombs constructed by the Middle Kingdom had a high failure rate, more often than not failing to do more than provide a small explosion and then leaking radioactive material on the target. The problem involved the timing of the implosive elements, which required exact precision from all sides.

Seeing the possibility of an interminable conflict with an intractable foe, though, the leaders of the Middle Kingdom forces ordered considerable resources to be assigned to the development and perfection of reliable fission explosives. Over the course of the following years, as the war with the Mexic Dominion for control of the red planet raged, slow but steady progress was made, until finally the Middle Kingdom artificers were able to report success. Immediately, the admiralty and generals issued orders that two such implosion-type fission explosive devices be constructed, each with a destructive capacity in the eighty kiloton range.

When completed, the bombs would be deployed in short order, one to each of the crater strongholds of the enemy. It was hoped that, by decapitating the command structure of the Mexic Dominion forces in one blow, the remaining elements of the Mexic military would flounder, and be quickly overrun.

As the work on the second device was still being completed, new information came to light that affected the course of the war. The discovery of the Mexic asteroid stronghold Xolotl, and the recovery of the Mexic vacuum-craft code-named "Dragon," offered an opportunity too great for the Middle Kingdom leaders to pass up. Rather than holding the fission bomb for the attack on Ruosi and Zijun, then, it was instead assigned to Operation Dragon, and code-named Dragon's Egg.

With the first fission device dispatched to Xolotl, work proceeded apace on the construction and assembly of the other fission bomb. And while there was only time for a single bomb to be constructed and used in the mission, the operation to attack the two crater strongholds with nuclear devices was still code-named Operation Double Thunder, even though the eventual "thunder" would only be echoing from one side.

The plans were in place, and with the selection of the Deliverer class light bomber *Fair Winds for Escort* as the aircraft that would drop the nuclear bomb, all that remained was to complete work on the explosive device itself, and the operation would be ready to launch.

With only one of the two crater strongholds targeted, ground troops would be needed to pacify the other, even at a considerable cost in munitions and life. And in the final days and hours before the fission bomb was ready to deploy, still more ground troops would be needed to fight and die, just to keep the Mexica defenders at bay.

HEXAGRAM 52
RESTRAINT
BELOW MOUNTAIN ABOVE MOUNTAIN

Mountains linked one to the other. In the same way, the noble man is mindful of how he should not go out of his position.

"Keep the line together," Carter broadcast over his helmet radio to the guardsman drifting out of the ranks behind him. "Or you're sharing a tent with Spitter tonight."

The guardsman grimaced behind his helmet's visor, but jumped quickly back into position.

It hadn't escaped Carter's notice that they were advancing over the same ground they'd covered only weeks before in the salient of Operation Great Strength. But this time, there was no turning back.

Operation Great Strength had failed for any number of reasons. Too few troops on the ground, spotty air cover, too narrow a field of combat, and a lack of sufficient arms or reinforcements to strengthen damaged lines. Or perhaps it was just a rutting mess from the word Go, and that was an end to it.

This new operation though, the name of which Carter still hadn't learned, looked to be a different sort of beast altogether. Not just a handful of elements, but the full force of the Middle Kingdom armies was pushing forward as one, driving deeper and deeper into Mexic-held territory, spearing towards the west.

They had been pushing forward for several days now, advancing further to the west each day, with the Eleventh Armored Infantry Battalion in the vanguard. And the Eleventh's Fourth Company, including the Second Platoon, was marching in support of the heavy crawler-tanks which were making the advance possible, acting as the thin end of the wedge.

Carter paused, stepping out of line and scanning his gaze up and down the formation of guardsmen, in two lines forming a wake behind the lead crawler. They'd not encountered any enemy resistance since the previous day, and the long kilometers of advancing unopposed were leaving the men sloppy, over-confident.

"Look alive, Bigfoot!" Carter broadcast to the Deutsch guardsman who held his carbine listlessly by the barrel, all but dragging the stock along the dry ground.

As the Deutsch guardsman lifted his carbine, resting the barrel against his shoulder, Carter turned to the African grenadier, Moonface, who just shook his head and shrugged.

Moonface didn't broadcast his opinion of the new troops in First-Second, but then, he didn't have to. Carter knew all too well that the guardsmen who'd swelled their ranks just before setting out on their current operation had been among the least motivated, least aggressive soldiers he'd yet encountered on Fire Star. But in a choice between unmotivated soldiers and going out into combat at only partial strength, Carter was happy to choose a lack of motivation.

First-Second was operating at full strength for the first time in weeks, a full complement of sixteen troops. And instead of fresh reinforcement troops from Earth, who would have to be retrained, untried, and inexperienced, the replacements in First-Second were the survivors of other units decimated in Great Strength, combined with other partial units to create full units. Second Platoon itself was still at partial strength, with only three full squads instead of the original four, but at least now the individual squads would be able to pass muster.

And more, since the reinforcements were experienced veterans, it was only a matter of time before they rose to the challenge. They might seem listless and apathetic now, marching without resistance over enemy ground, but when the vanguard encountered enemy fire, as they had the day before, the veterans would snap to, quickly rising to the challenge. It was only when the challenge had passed, and the danger was no longer immediate, that they seemed to deflate again.

Carter found it hard to blame them. They had seen many of their brothers-in-arms die on the field of battle, and having grieved, had little energy left over for any other emotions.

There were others in First-Second who were dealing with the trauma of combat in other ways, though no less unhelpful, and potentially more worrying.

"Spitter, is there a problem?" Carter changed his pace to meet up with the Rossiyan gunner, who brought up the rear of the column on the left, his heavy gun primed and ready, its barrel tracking the horizon.

At first, Carter wondered whether the Rossiyan had his helmet radio switched off, since he didn't answer or acknowledge.

"Spitter, you see something?" Carter reached out and put a hand on the shoulder of the Rossiyan's carapace.

Spitter spun around, eyes narrowed and jaw set, training his barrel on Carter. A moment later, he relaxed somewhat, eyes widening and mouth dropping open in surprise, and lowered the gun's aim to the ground. "Sorry, Tejas..." He paused, then hurriedly added, "I mean, sorry, *corporal*."

Carter shook his head. He still wasn't used to the new rank, much less to Spitter treating him with anything like deference. "It's just me, Spitter. Now, what's the trouble?"

Spitter looked at him confused. "Trouble?"

Carter nodded out towards the southern horizon, where Spitter's attention had been fixed. "You looked like you'd spotted something."

Spitter arched an eyebrow, then shook his head, lips pursed. "No, didn't see anything."

Carter studied the Rossiyan's expression through his visor. That's what he'd been afraid of. For days now, ever since they'd moved out on this final push, Spitter had been going around with a hair trigger, jumping at shadows, expecting the enemy to jump out from behind every rock and crater at any moment. Spitter's quick reactions had proved invaluable in the recent skirmishes with the Mexica, but Carter couldn't help but wonder what would happen when the Rossiyan reacted too quickly to nothing, and one of his fellow guardsmen paid the price.

Carter nodded. "Okay. Just let me know if you see anything."

Spitter replied with a short nod, then moved off, returning his attention to the southern horizon.

Carter reflexively checked the action of his carbine, confirming his ammo levels for the hundredth time since sunrise. In another few hours, the sun would be setting, and it would be time to stop for the night. The crawlers, like the armored monstrosity he was marching behind, would ring end to end, acting as a bulwark for the pressurized tents arranged within, like a mountain range encircling a valley. Provided the anti-aircraft batteries on the crawlers were able to keep any Mexic aircraft from strafing the site, the infantry within the ring of crawlers would be able to rest relatively secure.

Then, assuming they proceeded at the same rate of speed for another day or so, by the morning of the second following day, they would be able to see Ruosi on the southwestern horizon. And then the final assault could begin.

With the strength of arms, armor, men, and machines on their side, the advantage was with the Middle Kingdom forces. Whether any of them would survive the coming battle to enjoy the fruits of victory though, or whether success would only come at the cost of their own lives, remained to be seen.

HEXAGRAM 53
GRADUAL ADVANCE
BELOW MOUNTAIN ABOVE WIND

Above the Mountain, there is the Tree. In the same way, the noble man finds a place for his worthiness and virtue to dwell and so manages to improve social mores.

"Watch the left flank!"

Niohuru squeezed off a round with his semi-automatic, potting a Mexic warrior in yellow-enameled armor who was about to douse a bannerman in a spray of burning liquid magnesium. The warrior, one of the elite Shorn Ones, went down, his helmet's visor shattered, the burning magnesium painting the red sands, harmlessly.

The bannerman who'd been spared the firelance gave Niohuru a thumbs-up, and returned the favor by taking out another Shorn One with a rapid fire burst, saving Niohuru the trouble of responding to the Mexica's charge.

They were making slow progress, gradually advancing towards the Shorn Ones' compound, but they were being made to labor for every centimeter of ground they gained.

The attack had started at dawn. The Falcon's Claws of the First Raider Company and the Sikh Immortals of the Akali Sena had approached the Shorn Ones' encampment from the southeast. They had come in under cover, hidden behind the yardangs which ranged to the south and east, escaping detection until the moment to strike had arrived. To all appearances, the attack had caught the Mexica unaware.

The enemy had known that the Middle Kingdom forces were advancing, of course, ever since they'd punched through the Mexic lines in the east, days before. But the main body of the Middle Kingdom infantry was very clearly approaching Ruosi from the northeast, making no effort to hide its advance. And with the main body still a day or more away, the Mexica had doubtless assumed that they still had time to gather their reserves before the assault began.

The Mexica had not accounted for a small raider group though, moving fast over difficult terrain. The greater numbers of Mexic troopers in Ruosi meant that the Falcon's Claws and Sikh Immortals hadn't a chance of taking the crater colony itself. However, striking swiftly, with surprise on their side, they did have a chance to occupy the attentions of the Shorn Ones until after the main body was able to attack in the north, possibly even going so far as to defeat the cadre of Mexic elite troops altogether. And considering that the Shorn Ones were evidently the backbone of Ruosi's defense, taking them out of the equation only increased the odds that the Middle Kingdom main body would be able to take and hold the crater colony in the subsequent attack.

That still left the question of the other Mexic stronghold, the crater colony of Zijun, to be answered, but all of Niohuru's inquiries on that count to Captain Hughes had been met with silence. Just what would keep the forces stationed at Zijun, only a little more than two hundred kilometers away, from swooping in and mopping up the battered and fatigued attackers, should the Middle Kingdom be able to take Ruosi, remained to be seen. As far as Niohuru was able to see, the Green Standard and Eight Banners had the will, ammunition, and reserves of strength to take and hold one of the crater colonies, if luck were with them, but not enough left over to defend it against any kind of assault.

It was a question that would have to remain unanswered for the moment. As things stood, it was unclear whether Niohuru or any of the others in the raiding party would succeed in taking out the Shorn Ones, much less whether the regular army was able to take an entire crater.

"Behind you!"

Niohuru heard the voice buzzing over his helmet radio, clipped Official Speech intoned in a strange accent.

"Behind you, Bannerman!"

Niohuru reacted, spinning around, and saw a Mexic warrior racing towards him, an obsidian-edged warclub in his hands. The warrior's helmet was painted yellow on one side, blue on the other, with a white butterfly picked out in white paint on the lower half of the visor. The face behind the visor was all but obscured, all that was visible being a pair of narrowed, angry eyes. The Shorn One had evidently slipped through the advancing line of raiders to Niohuru's right, intent on taking out the Middle Kingdom assault team one man at a time.

Niohuru raised his rifle, aiming the barrel at the Shorn One's chest and squeezing the trigger. Nothing happened. The firing mechanism had jammed.

The Shorn One was only a few meters away now, advancing fast, raising his obsidian-edged club high overhead. There wasn't time to clear the jam and fire again, so Niohuru threw his rifle to the ground, and drew his saber from the sheath at his side. He got both his hands around the saber's hilt just in time to meet the warclub's downswing in a tooth-jarring impact, barely managing to deflect the Shorn One's blow.

Niohuru staggered back, keeping the point of his saber raised, as the Shorn One shifted his club in a backswing. The bannerman parried again, this time on somewhat surer footing, turning the point of his saber in a tight circle around the warclub's head, batting it back to one side. Steel and obsidian slid against one another, sending up a shower of sparks that died quickly in the oxygen-poor Fire Star atmosphere, like a constellation of tiny falling stars that burned out as quickly as they plummeted towards the red soil.

With the Shorn One's club to one side, his mid-section momentarily unprotected, Niohuru turned the point of his saber and lunged forward, driving the steel blade toward the Mexica's abdomen. The Shorn One danced away, swatting at the saber with his warclub, as Niohuru's blade grazed his armored midsection harmlessly.

From the corner of his eye, Niohuru saw other yellow-armored Shorn Ones advancing, crouching, firing, pushing back against the raiders. His engagement with the club-wielding warrior was taking far too long. He needed to put an end to it, and quickly.

Shifting from one foot to another, Niohuru swept his saber sidewise in a two-handed grip, putting all his weight behind the swing. The Shorn One met with a two-handed swing of his own, and saber and warclub rebounded off one another.

Niohuru's gaze slid over the semi-automatic lying in the dirt at his feet. It was useless to him until he'd dealt with the Shorn One, but without it he was beginning to wonder if the Shorn One wouldn't instead deal with him.

Another lunge, another parry, and Niohuru and the Shorn One still faced one another, each with their weapons held in one-handed grips.

"On your right," came the clipped Official Speech in Niohuru's ear. Instinctively, he shifted to the left, and watched as several silver strands whipped past his head, wrapping around the Shorn One's wrist which held the warclub.

Niohuru scarcely had time to notice the Akali Sena beside him, in his hands the hilt of the urumi sword-whip.

"Strike now, my friend!" the Sikh Immortal said, yanking back on the sword-whip, pulling the Shorn One off balance.

In another instant, the Shorn One could have shifted the warclub from his constricted hand to his free one, and renewed the attack, but Niohuru would not give him the chance. The bannerman rushed forward, lunging with his saber, and drove the sword's point through the unprotected fissure between the Mexica's carapace and his armored midsection. It was a thin, flexible band of material, less than a half-centimeter wide, but with the Shorn One for the moment held immobile the gap was enough for Niohuru to thrust the point of his saber through.

The white butterfly painted on the Shorn One's visor was instantly in stark relief as red blood painted the inside of the helmet, arterial blood coughed up as blood poured into a punctured lung. Niohuru shifted the saber's point, driving his blade up and into the Shorn One's heart.

The Mexica toppled backwards onto the red soil, pulling Niohuru's saber and the Akali Sena's sword-whip with him.

"You have my thanks, brother," Niohuru said, as he planted his foot on the Mexica's chest, and wrenched his blade from between the plates of the Shorn One's armor.

"And you already have mine, my friend," the Immortal said, unwrapping his sword-whip from around the fallen Mexica's wrist, coiling it once more. Some five meters long, with a half-dozen razor sharp filaments each scarcely thicker than a human hair, the sword-whip was favored by troops from Hind, who could wield the flexible blades with deadly accuracy.

Niohuru sheathed his saber, and retrieved his rifle from the dust, clearing the jam in a matter of eye blinks. When he looked up, he saw that the Sikh held out his hand, an invitation.

"My name is Ramdas Sing," the Sikh said as Niohuru took his hand. "Your bravery and quick thinking saved even more of my brothers from needless deaths, in the assault on the mining facilities in Great Strength."

Niohuru tightened his grip around the man's hand, recognizing the name. "And I have you to thank for me not being cut in half by a chakram, I think."

The Sikh grinned. "I live to serve."

A Mexic shot whizzed through the air between them, breaking the convivial mood.

Niohuru turned back to face the line of Mexic defenders in their enameled-yellow armor. "Perhaps we should continue this discussion after seeing to the Shorn Ones?"

The Sikh grinned. "I trust that we will both live to exchange pleasantries again, Bannerman Niohuru."

With a grimace, Niohuru nodded, and fired a round from his semi-automatic at a Mexic trooper leaning out from behind cover. "We can only hope..."

☷☳

HEXAGRAM 54
MARRYING MAID
BELOW LAKE ABOVE THUNDER

Above the Lake, there is Thunder. In the same way, the noble man recognizes the flaw by following a thing through to its far-distant end.

At Navigator Geng's insistence, there was a marriage ceremony the night before they set out on Operation Double Thunder. The pilots of the Sixth Squadron's fighter escort acted as the groom's family, presenting betrothal gifts of field rations instead of bridal cakes, jars of fruit wine instead of tea. The crew of the *Fair Winds for Escort* acted as the brides family, distributing the field rations and wine jars to the other bomber crews present for the festivities.

The Sixth Squadron's chaplain, a jovial old Taoist, officiated over the proceedings, which made up in good spirits and laughter what they lacked in proper observance of tradition. The ceremony itself came to an end at the makeshift altar that Bombadier Mehdi and Tail Gunner Lambert had constructed out of old crates and paper clipped from old books and periodicals, at which Geng and Pak offered homage to Heaven and Earth, to their family ancestors, and to the Kitchen God, Zao Jun, asking for peace and domestic tranquility in later life. Then, while the rest of the celebrants made short work of the fruit wine, the newlyweds went off for one last night before the final flight, their bridal bed just a pair of pallets shoved together in the billet, a ragged curtain hung from the ceiling acting as a nuptial chamber, hiding them from the rest of the airmen.

If it had been a wedding back home in the Middle Kingdom, Geng would have woken early the next morning to honor the ancestors at dawn, and then been formally introduced by Pak to the groom's relatives and friends. Instead, long before the eastern sky lightened, she and the rest of the crew of *Fair Winds* were awake, back in their flight suits, and climbing up into their craft through the open bomb-bay doors, trying not to notice the dark shape of the bomb hulking only a short distance away, surrounded by guards.

Amonkar caught the navigator's arm as she climbed up into the belly of the plane. "Geng, it's still not too late..."

Geng met her gaze, cutting off Amonkar's words with a shake of her head. "Yes is it, Arati," she said, quietly. "It's been too late for a good long while now." She paused, and quirked a half-hearted smile. "After all, where are you going to find a better navigator at *this* late date?"

With a final glance, Geng slipped loose of Amonkar's grasp, and disappeared from view up into the bomber.

"You sure about this, skipper?" Co-Pilot Seathl came to stand beside her, helmet cradled under her left arm.

"No," Amonkar said simply. The Flight Group's physician had checked Geng out, and recommended that she not go up on any more bombing runs in her condition, but had stopped short of outright ordering her to remain grounded. And when Geng had learned that there weren't enough qualified navigators to spare a replacement for *Fair Winds*, she'd simply announced that she and her unborn child would be as safe in the air as they would be on the ground waiting for the Mexica to attack, and that was an end to it. "But she's right," Amonkar went on. "At least about not being able to find a good navigator. The rest of the bombers are going to be busy flying decoy missions, or supporting the ground troops attacking Ruosi. There simply isn't the manpower left aside for a replacement." She paused, and then added, "Really, though, there's no reason that Geng won't be able to perform. And they tell me that we won't pick up any significant amount of radiation from the blast, so her baby won't be in any danger. Nor will the rest of us, I suppose."

Seathl just shrugged, and slipped under the open bomb-bay doors. "I hope you're right."

In a quiet voice, scarcely above a whisper, Amonkar answered, "So do I." She shook her head, trying to compose her thoughts. If only the emotional and physical state of a pregnant navigator was all that she had to worry about this morning. Like the rest of the *Fair Winds*' crew, she'd not had a drop of wine the night before, but still had managed to sleep hardly at all, what little slumber she got fitful and plagued by disturbing dreams.

Maybe it was the wedding ceremony itself. Amonkar couldn't help but remember her sister's wedding back in Bhopal. It had been less than a handful of years before, but seemed a lifetime. Even then, helping her sister dress for the ceremony, hearing their mother nattering on about the groom's prospects for wealth and prosperity, to say nothing of the chances for many grandchildren, Amonkar Arati had known that marriage wasn't for her. At least, not for the foreseeable future. She had a different destiny to answer, a different path to follow.

Later, having decided to enlist with the Interplanetary Fleet Air Corps, Amonkar had pledged herself to the emperor's service, and fancied that she was a bride of the sword-father, a devadasi to Khandoba, Siva incarnate, and guardian of the country.

Now, standing on another world, preparing to go into battle for what might be the last time, Amonkar found herself wondering about the fruit of her union with Khandoba. If she truly was bride to the sword-father, what sort of child would they produce together.

Her eyes were drawn to the bulbous, teardrop-shaped bomb sitting on casters a few meters away, surrounded by heavily armed guards, being tended by attentive artificers and technicians. Double Thunder itself.

If Geng lived through the next seven months, and there were no complications or injuries preventing her pregnancy going to full term, she would give birth to a child, one that commingled aspects of mother and father alike.

If Amonkar lived through the next few hours, she would release a fission bomb from her craft's hold, like an egg dropping from its mother, and would give birth to a new brand of horror in the battle-field. Amonkar's grandfather had been a babe-in-arms when man harnessed the power of the atom, but now for the first time it would be deployed as a weapon against living targets.

Amonkar could not prevent a rueful smile from twitching up the corners of her mouth, as she ducked under the bomb-bay doors and climbed into her craft. She was sure that *this* was not the sort of grandchild her mother had dreamt of, all those years before.

䷶

HEXAGRAM 55
ABUNDANCE
BELOW FIRE ABOVE THUNDER

Thunder and Lightning arrive together. In the same way, the noble man decides legal cases and carries out punishments.

On Earth, the sun was just passing from the Grain in Ear position to the Summer Solstice position in the middle of horse-month, in Water-Fowl year, the fifty-third year of the Taikong Emperor.

In Tejas, those who still followed the old Gregorian calendar for religious rites judged it to be the twentieth day of June in the year 2053.

In Hindi reckoning, in the home of the Amonkar family in Bhopal, it was the fifth day of Mithuna, in the year 5154.

In Khalifa, home of Co-Pilot Seathl, it was the fifth day of Du al-Qa`da, in the year 1475.

On the red planet, according to the colonial Fire Star calendar, it was the three hundred and seventh day of the fifteenth Fire Star Year, the last day of the month Xiaoshu. It was the twenty-ninth terrestrial year since man first walked on the face of the red planet, Fire Star, thirteen years since the beginning of the Second Mexic War.

In the still-dark hours of the morning, *Fair Winds for Escort* set off towards the west, accompanied by an escort of six rotary-winged fighters. Their destination was the crater compound Zijun.

The crater had been christened by the early colonists after the courtesy name of the Xin Dynasty-era astronomer Liu Xin. Located roughly fifteen degrees north, one-hundred and seventy-nine degrees west, the crater had a diameter of eighty kilometers and a depth of two kilometers. At its heart, in a network of pressurized domes and habitats, lay the colony that shared the crater's name. The main body of the colony itself was secured under an enormous pressurized dome, and taken with the smaller satellite domes surrounding it covered an area nearly ten square kilometers in extent.

As the sun began to rise, the first light of dawn pinking the skies over Tamkung Plain, *Fair Winds* approached Zijun from the northeast, cruising at an altitude of fifteen kilometers above the surface of Fire Star. *En route* from the Air Corps base in the east, Bombardier Mehdi had armed the fission bomb in the craft's hold, left unarmed to minimize risks at take off.

The rest of the Sixth Squadron, along with the other bomber squads of the Air Corps, were involved in a hundred different raids and sorties in the early morning hours, diverting the attention of the Mexic fighter patrols, distracting the attentions of ground-based anti-aircraft emplacements away from the single Deliverer-class light bomber and its small escort of rotary-winged fighters. As a result, *Fair Winds* encountered minimal resistance in its final approach to Zijun, well within the capacities of the fighter escort and the bomber's own gunners to handle.

A few minutes after the beginning of the First Watch of the morning, Navigator Geng reported that they had reached the target, and Co-Pilot Seathl ordered the bomb-bay doors of *Fair Winds* opened. Bombardier Mehdi made a final check on the explosive device Double Thunder, and then Pilot Amonkar instructed the co-pilot to relay the order to drop the bomb.

Double Thunder fell towards the center of Zijun like an arrow flying unwaveringly towards its target, finally detonating as planned at six-hundred meters above the surface.

So loud was the resulting explosion that it could actually be *heard*, even through the thin atmosphere of Fire Star. Those close enough to the detonation were able to see the blast and hear the explosion at the same time. Of course, any who were close enough to do so were almost instantly swallowed in the subsequent conflagration.

Everything within a two-kilometer radius of the blast was completely destroyed, with severe damage out to a radius of three-and-a-half kilometers, and shattered glass up to thirteen kilometers away.

Those within the Zijun colony who did not perish immediately in the explosion either died soon after as the pressurized domes and habitats were destroyed, suffocating in the explosive depressurization. The hardiest souls in the crater, farthest from ground zero, who were already in pressurized surface suits and not looking directly at the blast, managed to survive the coming days, if badly. The radiation sickness which struck everyone who had been within kilometers of the blast, though, eventually claimed its toll.

In one blow, the Middle Kingdom had crippled one of the Mexic Dominion's two major strongholds on Fire Star, all but eliminating any threat from those within Zijun. There remained, however, the question of the remainder of the Mexic forces, and particularly those in and around Ruosi.

☲
☶

Hexagram 56
The Wanderer
Below Mountain Above Fire

Above the Mountain, there is Fire. In the same way, the noble man uses punishments with enlightenment and care and does not protract cases at law.

By the time Double Thunder exploded, in the air above the Zijun colony, *Fair Winds for Escort* was already several kilometers to the west, traveling at several hundred kilometers per second. At its relatively high altitude, and at its increasing distance, the bomber was far enough from ground zero to escape the outrushing shockwave, but the light from the explosion overtook them almost immediately, spreading in an ever-expanding sphere of expelled photons.

Facing to the west, away from the explosion, Pilot Amonkar and Co-Pilot Seathl saw the conflagration only reflected in mirrors mounted outside the port and starboard viewports of the cockpit. To Amonkar, it was like a sun being born, their plane like a planet hurtling out from its fiery birth, a celestial wanderer cast out by a new-made star.

But it wasn't as bright as the sun, it was *brighter*.

The reactions of the other members of the crew varied, each following the dictates of their backgrounds and temperaments.

In her turret slung below the front of the plane, Nose Gunner Siagyo swiveled around to watch the blast behind them, folded her hands in prayer, solemnly reciting, "Namo-Amida-Butsu."

In the bomb-bay, peering back through the open bay doors, Bombardier Mehdi wept silently, not saying a word.

Navigator Geng was silent and motionless, her hands resting protectively on her belly.

And in the turret at the rear of the plane, Tail Gunner Lambert summed up her reaction in a single word: "Merde!"

Pilot Amonkar, for her part, stared unblinking into the reflection of the blast, its light dimmed by the tint of her helmet's visor, and solemnly intoned, "The splendor of thousands of suns..."

"What was that?" Seathl asked from the co-pilot seat at her side.

"Mmm?" Amonkar glanced over, musing.

"What did you say, skipper? Something about a thousand suns?"

Amonkar blinked, then nodded, remembering the line that had come unbidden to her lips. "It's from the Bhagavad Gita section of the Mahabharata." She paused, recalling the quote exactly. "It describes the god Vishnu, and his glory. 'If the splendor of thousands of suns were to blaze forth all at once in the sky, even that would not resemble the splendor of that exalted being.'"

Seathl nodded, glancing back at the mirror on the starboard side. "Sounds about right to me."

A chill fell over Amonkar, ice creeping down her spine, as she remembered another scene from the Bhagavad Gita.

"There's another story," she said, her voice sounding quiet and distant, as though it were coming from a long way off. "There was a prince, Arjuna, who was hesitant to order an attack on the enemy. To him, Vishnu says, 'I am death, the mighty destroyer of the world, out to destroy. Even without your participation all the warriors standing arrayed in the opposing armies shall cease to exist.'"

Seathl gave her a sidelong glance. "What does *that* mean?"

"It means that all men die, eventually, so what does it matter if a few enemies die? Vishnu tells Arjuna that he is only an instrument of death, nothing more, and that all of his enemies would have been destroyed eventually, even if he did nothing."

Seathl looked hard at the pilot, but said nothing.

"An instrument of death..." Amonkar repeated. Then, after a brief pause, she said in a choked voice, "Oh, what have I *done*?"

Seathl reached over and grabbed hold of Amonkar's arm, her fingers closing in a vice-tight grip. "What *we* have done is what we *had* to do, skipper."

Amonkar looked over and met the co-pilot's gaze.

"This was no arbitrary act, Arati," Seathl went on, "no senseless murder. This was an act of *war*, a swift, punitive action. Lives were lost, and at our hands. What of it? Through our actions, we've shortened the war, and spared the lives of all those soldiers who would have *died* trying to take Zijun by force. We prevented the needless deaths of Middle Kingdom soldiers, of our brothers and sisters. If that means becoming an 'instrument' of death, or becoming Death himself, then so be it!"

Amonkar licked her dry lips, her voice choked off in her throat. She nodded, unable to form any real reply. Seathl loosed her grip on the pilot's arm, and sat back in her seat.

"As for me," Seathl said, her own reaction finally bubbling to the surface, "I could use a *drink*."

☰

HEXAGRAM 57
COMPLIANCE
BELOW WIND ABOVE WIND

Wind following wind. In the same way, the noble man reiterates commands and has endeavors carried out.

It was as if a second sun had risen in the northwest.

The fighting between the Falcon's Claws and the Sikh Immortals on the one side, and the Shorn Ones on the other, had continued through a day, a night, and the early hours of a second day. To the north of them, the main body of the Middle Kingdom infantry was engaging with the Mexic defenders of the Ruosi crater colony. Niohuru knew that this could not be the last battle of the Second Mexic War, but he was hard pressed to imagine how the Middle Kingdom would have resources left for another.

Then, less than two hours after the sun rose in the east, bright white in the morning haze, another blinding light flared to the north and west, above the rim of Ruosi.

Niohuru had for a moment taken the light to be some explosion within the nearby crater, but shifting from side to side had shown that the parallax was all wrong for the source to be nearby. This was something more distant, a hundred kilometers away, perhaps even farther.

It was a short while later that the news came over the radio, apparently reaching the Middle Kingdom attackers and the Mexic defenders at about the same time. The explosion had actually been more than two hundred kilometers away, in the crater of Zijun.

The other stronghold of the Mexic Dominion on Fire Star, the Zijun crater colony, had been completely devastated by a single Middle Kingdom attack. It had been a nuclear fission bomb, in the eighty kiloton range, and it had obliterated the colony complex and all within it. Thousands of Mexic soldiers, an invaluable supply of arms and ammunition, stores of oxygen, water, and food supplies, all consumed in the burning heart of an atomic explosion.

Fighting continued in the Shorn Ones' compound, but it seemed that the news from Zijun had taken the heart out of the Mexic defenders.

An hour after the light had flared, a strong wind blew in from the northwest, kicking up clouds of red dust and rattling the broken shards of glass in the shot-out windows of the nearby habitats. The air was too thin for the gust to impede the movements of Niohuru and the others, but their vision was obscured momentarily by the swirling eddies of dust clouds, their radio transmissions peppered with static.

As the winds passed, Niohuru and the others who remained of the assault team readied to rush the final bastion of the Shorn Ones. Nearly a third of the Falcon's Claws and the Sikh Immortals had fallen in the course of the previous day and night, but the battle had taken an even heavier toll on the Mexic defenders, who had dwindled to a bare few holed up in the bombed-out remains of a habitat on the northern edge of the compound.

"Form up," Captain Hughes called over the radio, broadcasting on the frequency shared by the assault team. He had a grenade in either hand, his back resting against the burnt remains of a crawler, shielding him from the line-of-fire of those within the habitat.

Niohuru and the other surviving members of the Falcon's Claws, along with Ramdas Singh and the other Immortals, were strung out along a few dozen meters, in a wide arc centered on the habitat, all crouched behind whatever cover they could find. Niohuru tried not to think about the other members of his combat cell, Axum and Cong, both of whom had fallen to the enemy in the night, the Ethiop laid open from neck to groin by an obsidian-edged warclub, the Han's helmet and skull shattered by a barrage of Mexic weapons fire.

"I want every first and second man on the line to lay down suppressing fire," Hughes went on, "and the third man to rush the habitat with grenades primed. Grenades go in, the third man goes to ground, and once the grenades have popped, I want everyone up and running hell-for-leather for the hab. We'll take it in one last go, and put an end to this nonsense."

"Um, Falco?" came the voice of a bannerman from further up the line.

"What is it?"

"You might want to take a look at this, before you give the word."

Like Captain Hughes, Niohuru leaned to one side, peering around cover at the habitat.

It was a sight that Niohuru had never seen before. In fact, it was one rarely if ever glimpsed in all the days of the Second Mexic War.

"Eighteen hells..." Niohuru swore under his breath.

It was a line of Mexic soldiers, unarmed, with their hands over their heads, marching out of the habitat and into the open.

"They're *surrendering*!" Ramdas Sing said.

"I will be damned," said another bannerman.

"Hold your fire!" Hughes barked over the radio, clipping his grenades back onto his waist. "Hold your fire," he repeated, a little more softly. He pushed up onto his haunches, and slowly unfolded into a standing position. "I'll go…" He shrugged, chuckling. "Well, I guess I'll go *talk* to them."

It was the first time in the Second Mexic War that anyone had said *that*, as well, so far as Niohuru knew.

"It could be a trick," Ramdas Singh said, as Hughes slipped around the end of the burnt-out crawler, his rifle's barrel at the ground.

Niohuru shook his head. "I don't think so," he answered, peering around at the advancing Mexica.

The captain, broadcasting over known Mexic frequencies, commanded the Shorn Ones to lay down in the dirt, facedown, and spread-eagled. The Mexica exchanged glances for a brief moment, and then dutifully knelt, then spread out in the red dust.

"I don't think it's a trick," Niohuru repeated, rising to his feet and stepping out from behind cover. "I think maybe it's the *end*."

HEXAGRAM 58
JOY
BELOW LAKE ABOVE LAKE

Lake clinging to Lake. In the same way, the noble man engages in talk and study with friends. Clinging means "linked." No more flourishing application of Joy can be found than this.

"Corporal Carter! Looks like this lock's open."

Carter moved over to inspect the airlock the guardsman had located, last in a line of oversized locks. "Looks good to me, Bigfoot. Crank it open and we'll see what's inside." Leaving the Deutsch guardsman to deal with the manual crank, Carter motioned to the other members of First-Second, fanned out along the northern wall of the structure. "Form up, men. We're going in on points, leapfrogging, with safeties off and eyes open."

A ragged chorus of acknowledgements buzzed over Carter's helmet radio, as the men got into position. It had been a long day already, and a longer night before, and the fatigue was starting to show.

First-Second had been detailed to sweep the southernmost structures of the Ruosi complex. After that morning, when the Mexic stronghold at Zijun had been wiped out by an atomic blast, the Mexic forces at Ruosi had laid down their arms and surrendered. There were still a few holdouts here and there though, isolated pockets of fighting; but with the majority of the Mexic supplies, arms, and command structure destroyed in a single bombing run, the surviving members of the Mexic military had evidently chosen surrender over a protracted death in combat.

When Carter blinked, he could still see the greenish-pink after-image of the blast, seared into his vision hours before as he'd looked to the northwest. He couldn't image what it must have been like for those within the blast radius.

Many of the domes in the Ruosi complex had lost their pressure in the early morning hours, before the Mexic surrender, as the full force of the Middle Kingdom infantry fell on the crater colony like a hammer. But even the depressurized domes had to be checked, to make sure there were no Mexic holdouts in surface suits, waiting to make a final assault.

The structure that First-Second was now entering appeared from the outside to be a former habitat, one big enough to house a hundred families, at least. It was separated from the rest of the complex by an escarpment of white rock, a shelf several meters tall and a dozen meters wide. It was evidently this feature that had given the structure the name which appeared on the map of the colony that Carter had been issued by Lieutenant Seong: White Rock.

"Got her, corporal," Bigfoot said, giving a thumbs-up. The airlock door swung open, the carbines of half-a-dozen First-Second troops trained on the gap.

"Keep your suits sealed," Carter said, as the first pair of men slipped through the open lock. "Just in case we hit an unpressurized zone."

On the other side of the airlock, they found a deserted loading dock. From the tread-tracks in the dirt beneath the oversized locks outside, they figured that the locks had been designed for crawlers to back up and connect, loading and unloading goods without depressurizing the entire dock.

Carter hadn't the slightest clue what had originally come in or out of this dock, back when it had been a Middle Kingdom colony. All there was now was a smashed crate marked with Mexic glyphs, evidently dropped in haste, containing hundreds of small glass vials.

"Medicine?" Carter checked the air pressure with the sensors mounted on his forearm, and then risked opening his visor. He unstoppered one of the unbroken vials and sniffed the contents. It smelled cloyingly sweet, like flowers gone bad.

Carter dropped the vial to the ground, crushing it underfoot as he closed his visor.

"Move out," Carter broadcast at the lowest setting, motioning to the corridor leading away from the docking area.

The squad leapfrogged up the corridor in tight formation, watchful for any Mexic soldiers who might remain within.

They reached an open hatch. Inside was a collection of electronic equipment, radio transmitters, and receivers. It resembled the communications unit of a Middle Kingdom military post, but for one difference. Dominating the equipment was a raised platform, on which circuitry and ridges combined to form the image of a woman being cut to pieces by a warrior. The platform's surface appeared to be covered in rust, which on closer examination was revealed to be blood.

"Eighteen hells," one guardsman yelped, pulling his gloved hand back from the blood-stained altar.

"Jesus wept," Carter swore under his breath.

The platform's surface was a hemoglobin sensor. Like all Mexic technology, the communications equipment in the chamber would not function unless the altar's sensitive instrumentation detected the presence of human blood.

"Come on," Carter said, backing out of the chamber. "Nothing for us in here."

As they moved down the corridor, Carter couldn't help but think about the prisoners he helped rescue, back during the early days of Operation Great

Strength. If First-Second hadn't intercepted that transport, those innocent Middle Kingdom civilians might already have ended up here in this room, or another like it, bled over a Mexic ignition circuit in a ritual to vicious and blood-hungry gods.

They came to another hatchway. This one was bolted shut, but locked on the corridor side, not the inside. Not to keep anyone out, but to keep something in? From the footprints in the red sand that dusted the floor it appeared that Mexica had stood on either side of the door at length. Sentries, perhaps? Whatever their purpose, they had fled.

"Tejas?" Spitter was standing beside Carter. "Did you hear that?"

Carter exchanged a glance with the Rossiyan, then leaned forward and pressed his helmet against the metal surface of the hatch. He could hear the dim sound of voices from the other side, but couldn't make out what they were saying.

"Somebody's home," Carter said, swinging up his carbine, jaw set. "Crank her open, Spitter, and we'll drop in to say hello."

The Rossiyan opened the hatch, as Carter and the others took up position around the opening, minimizing their profile to any fire from within, while maximizing their cover of the doorway.

The precautions were completely unnecessary.

The chamber beyond the hatch might once have been an exercise yard of some kind, with bare walls and floors. It was about the size of the big indoor ringball courts in Brazon, where the Tejas regional champions were played two games at a time, side-by-side.

But even the capacity crowds at the regional ring-ball playoffs were dwarfed by the number of bodies crammed into the chamber Carter now faced.

There were thousands of them, some standing or shuffling, some sitting on the bare floor, some stretched out full length underfoot. Some of those who were lying still, Carter realized, weren't sleeping, but were staring sightlessly at the ceiling above, all life fled.

There were Han, Ethiops, Europans, Arabians, Persians, Athabascans... but virtually all ethnic distinction between them had been lost. With their sunken eyes, visible ribcages, and sallow skin, the living were like animated skeletons, starved and neglected, the dead too many to count.

Carter and the others stood at the open door, unsure what to say, what to do. They had expected perhaps to find a few Mexic troops refusing to surrender, not thousands of Middle Kingdom prisoners, dead and dying.

Seeing the guardsmen in Middle Kingdom armor, the prisoners began to shuffle forward like the undead in the ghost stories Carter's grandfather had told around campfires, skeletal hands reaching out, mouths working, able to do little more than moan.

"Tejas?" Spitter looked from the advancing prisoners to Carter, eyes wide. "Tejas?! What do we do?"

Carter shook his head, unsure.

One of the prisoners wrapped his bone-thin arms around Carter's abdomen, resting his skull-like head against his carapace. Another clung to his arm with a skeletal hand. They were all talking at once, their voices scarcely louder than whispers, and it was only after opening his helmet's visor that Carter could hear what they were saying.

They were thanking him, thanking the emperor, thanking whatever gods there were that help had finally come.

They would have wept, Carter realized, had they not been so dehydrated that tears would not come.

They clung to the men of First-Second in death's grips, not in fear, as they might have faced the Mexic warriors who came to fetch them for the sacrificial altars, one by one, but with joy.

HEXAGRAM 59
DISPERSION
BELOW WATER ABOVE WATER

The Wind moves atop the Water. In the same way, the former kings made offerings to the Divine Ruler and established ancestral temples.

Amonkar stood in the entrance of the hangar bay, the slight wind from the pressurized tunnel behind her pressing against her back, looking at the still and lifeless form of *Fair Winds for Escort*, a hulking shadow in the gloaming.

The unit's physicians had just given her a clean bill of health, and set her at liberty. Most of the rest of the crew of *Fair Winds* were still being looked over, to make sure there were no ill effects from the bombing. If the physicians hadn't shooed her out, she would still be there now, checking on the health of her crew, but since she had been ordered to vacate, she saw no reason not to return to the hangar to check with the remaining member of the crew. The most important member, as Amonkar often saw it, the plane itself.

If Amonkar and the others were suffering no ill-effects, the same could sadly not be said of *Fair Winds* herself. They had pushed her higher and faster than tolerances would allow, in the bombing run on Zijun, to get the bomb in place before the Mexica had a chance to shoot the bomber out of the sky, and then to get the bomber and her crew out of the range of the bomb before everything went to hell. This last run had taken a serious toll on the already beleaguered Deliverer-class bomber.

Which wasn't to say that previous runs hadn't taken their toll as well. But on those previous occasions, when they'd returned to base after a difficult run, ground crews had swarmed over *Fair Winds* from almost the moment they taxied back into the hangar.

But now? The bomber sat idly, in the shadows, with no ground crews milling around her.

It was an unfamiliar sight, and a surprisingly unsettling one. It seemed to Amonkar as though the plane had been left alone, abandoned, like a pet left tied up in the yard.

She crossed the grease-stained floor of the hangar, and reaching out patted a hand against the fuselage of the bomber, for all the world like a rider patting the neck of a horse at the end of a long run.

"Good girl," Amonkar said in a quiet voice. "Good girl."

"Do you and the plane need a little time alone?"

The voice from behind Amonkar startled her, but she smiled as her pulse crept back down again. She turned, to see Co-Pilot Seathl approaching, Navigator Geng following close behind.

"I mean, I know that you're a little hard up for it, skipper," Seathl said, leering, "but *really*... With a *plane*?"

Amonkar ignored the co-pilot, her attention on the navigator. "Geng, are you alright? What did the physicians say?"

Geng patted her belly, a slight smile on her lips. She wouldn't be showing for months to come, but Amonkar couldn't help but imagine the life growing within. "They didn't find anything worrying. Of course, even the ones who've studied gynecology haven't had a lot of experience with pregnancy, being stationed in a war zone all this time, but they're tracking down a colonist physician who delivered countless babies here in the colonies, who should be able to help." Her smile widened. "And if I'm lucky, Pak and I can catch the first transport back to Earth, and so long as I go full term and the trip doesn't take more than six months, we can welcome the birth of our baby back on Earth." She paused, sighing wistfully. "Back home."

Seathl turned and looked at the navigator, nodding slowly. "Home," she repeated, then shook her head in disbelief. She threw up her hands in frustration. "Is that even *possible*?!"

Amonkar knew what she meant. The merest idea of "home" had become nothing more than an abstract, long before. The thought of going *back* there was almost impossible to wrap her head around.

But it appeared to be happening, one way or another.

"This is it, then," Geng said, coming to stand beside Amonkar, resting her own hand on the hull of *Fair Winds*. "We'll all be dispersing, back to our homes, back to our lives."

As Seathl came over to stand beside them, Amonkar looked up at the curve of the bomber's nose, rising up above them, the ideograms marking out the plane's name just below the cockpit windows.

She reached out her hand once more to the fuselage, but stopped short, her fingers still centimeters away.

It finally hit home, for the first time.

"It's over," she said, her voice barely above a whisper. "*Over*. We won't be going up again, will we?"

Before the others could respond, before they could even properly process what she'd said, Amonkar could feel hot tears welling in her eyes, slipping down her cheeks.

"Skipper?" Seathl drew nearer, looking in her face with concern. "Are you alright?"

Amonkar shook her head. "No." She paused, then in a rush added, "I mean, yes. I mean..." She let out a ragged sigh, shoulder's slumped. "I don't know what I mean." And still the tears came, even faster now.

Geng put her arm around Amonkar's shoulder, drawing her close. "What is it, Arati? Tell us."

Amonkar took a deep breath, trying to collect her thoughts, and get her raw emotions under control. "I just... I just think it's that..." She looked from Geng to Seathl, then up to the plane before them. "I think I'd just accepted the likelihood that I wouldn't survive the war, is all. And now..."

After she'd trailed off, Seathl finished for her, "And now you have?"

In response, Amonkar dropped to her knees, head back and eyes closed.

"O Khandoba, sword-father, hear the prayer of this loyal Devadasi," Amonkar intoned, her voice cracked and strained. "O Khandoba, Siva incarnate and guardian of the country, hear the words of your faithful Murli."

Amonkar dropped her chin to her chest, eyes squeezed tight.

"Thank you for my life," she said, whisper-quiet.

Geng and Seathl knelt on either side of her, their hands on her shoulders, neither talking, but only providing support, lending her what strength they could spare.

"Please watch over all those brothers and sisters we've lost along the way."

Amonkar could picture the face of Tail Gunner Xiao as clearly as if he stood before her.

"And to all of those who I've killed, directly or indirectly, through action or inaction, both enemy and ally..." Amonkar opened her eyes, her jaw set. "Please forgive me..."

"God is great," Seathl said in her native tongue, eyes lidded.

"Namo-Amida-Butsu," Geng added, quietly.

The three women stayed in the shadows beneath the plane, leaning against one another, long into the night.

HEXAGRAM 60
CONTROL
BELOW LAKE ABOVE WATER

Above the Lake, there is Water. In the same way, the noble man establishes limits and evaluates moral conduct.

Niohuru Tie and the rest of the First Raider Company were gathered in a hangar at the heart of Fanchuan Garrison, deep in the Tianfei Valley, half a world away from the Tamkung Plain where the Falcon's Claws had fought and bled and died these long months. They were all in full dress uniform, presentation sabers at their sides. Above them hung a yellow banner, bordered in red, on which a dragon was emblazoned.

Over one hundred-thirty men stood in the ranks of the First Raider Company, with Captain Hughes Falco at their head, all that survived the final battle of the war. The fallen members of the company over the course of the Second Mexic War numbered nearly a thousand, the unit reinforced by new troops as the war progressed, but each of those deaths was bought at the price of dozens of enemy dead, at least, and as many as hundreds in some cases. No unit in the Middle Kingdom had made it through the war with a higher success rate, not even the fabled Akali Sena.

The Falcon's Claws stood to attention as an older man in an Eight Banners dress uniform entered the hangar, on the chest of his dark surcoat the lion insignia of a second-rank military officer. Niohuru had never seen him before, but knew him at a glance. This was the lieutenant general in command of the entire Bordered Yellow Banner, holding in his hands the lives of eight full divisions, more than 130,000 troops in all. The First Raider Company was just one of four companies that made up the Third Battalion of the Bordered Yellow Banner's Ninth Brigade. That the lieutenant general was appearing before them in a private ceremony was a signal honor.

"At your ease, men of the First Raider Company," the general said, standing before them. With a slight rustling sound, the one hundred-thirty men shifted to parade rest. "For those who do not know, should there be any among you, I am Lieutenant General Irgen Gioro, commander of the Bordered Yellow Banner."

Niohuru doubted that any among them didn't know who the general was. As for himself, Niohuru had known of the general's exploits when he was still a boy in Northern Capital, long before he enlisted in the Eight Banners.

He tried to imagine what the boy he had once been might think of standing so close to the famed General Irgen Gioro. A Manchu, and proud scion of one of the Eight Great Houses, Irgen Gioro wasn't just a decorated bannerman, but was a member of a clan distantly related to the imperial Aisin Gioro clan.

On the chest of Niohuru's own surcoat was embroidered the image of a rhinoceros, insignia of the seventh rank. The last time he'd worn a dress uniform, in the orbital city of Diamond Summit, his insignia had been that of the ninth rank, a sea horse. When they'd returned to Fanchuan Garrison, Niohuru was surprised to learn that Captain Hughes had put him in for a promotion, in recognition of his service. In any other unit, he would now be a lieutenant, placed in charge of an entire platoon of sixty four troops. In the First Raider Company under Hughes Falco though, he was still just another raider, another of the Falcon's Claws.

"If you decide to transfer to another unit, Tie," Hughes had explained, "at least this way you'll get the posting you deserve. But so long as you're serving under me, we're all just bannermen, right?"

Niohuru wondered what General Irgen Gioro, now deep into a speech about duty and honor, thought of the egalitarian anarchy of Hughes's raider company. The lieutenant general didn't seem the type to abandon protocols and etiquettes lightly.

"As you know, men," Irgen Gioro was saying, "we wage war to defeat our enemies, to guarantee the will of the emperor, and to protect the people. But let us not forget the glory of victory, while attending to our duties."

Niohuru couldn't help but remember Colonel Magiya, who had taught a younger Niohuru microgravity combat maneuvers, and been the first to inform Niohuru of his posting to the First Raider Company. Magiya had taken issue with the explanation of the purpose for war which Irgen Gioro had recited, the one which Niohuru himself had memorized from the pages of the bannerman's training manual. Magiya had suggested a different, even more profound reason to wage war.

Finishing his speech, General Irgen Gioro made his way down the line of men, greeting each of them individually, praising their service.

"Ah, Lieutenant Niohuru," the general said, reaching his place in the line. "I recall well the reports of your actions in Operation Great Strength." Irgen Gioro glanced over at Captain Hughes, standing at Niohuru's side. "And if the reports of your superior are to be believed, lieutenant, you are likewise to be commended for consistent bravery and quick thinking throughout the engagement." The general regarded Niohuru with an avuncular smile. "It swells the heart of his old Manchu soldier to see another of the Eight

Great Houses in imperial service. I know that your family must be proud of this honor you do their name, and the glory which their son has brought to their house."

The general paused, indicating an invitation for Niohuru to respond.

Niohuru swallowed, considering his answer. He thought of his brothers-in-arms Cong Ren and Axum Ouazebas. Had they fought, bled, and died just to bring pride to their families? "I don't fight for honor, begging your pardon, sir. Nor do I fight for glory."

The general raised an eyebrow, his smile fading. "Well then *why*, pray, do you?"

Niohuru took a deep breath, head held high. "I fight for peace, sir."

Irgen Gioro regarded him for a long moment. Then, without answering, he moved on down the line, greeting the other men in the company, citing their bravery, their quick thinking, their fast action in combat.

Steeling himself for rebuke, Niohuru glanced over at Captain Hughes. The captain though, merely smiled, nodding with approval.

HEXAGRAM 61
INNER TRUST
BELOW LAKE ABOVE WIND

Above the Lake, there is Wind. In the same way, the noble man evaluates criminal punishments and mitigates the death penalty.

Carter couldn't sleep, again, and so pulled back on his boots and went for a ramble around the perimeter of the hangar. Most of the refugees were sleeping, but those that were still awake were huddled around portable heating units here and there, their voices low in quiet conversation.

First-Second had been assigned to escort a group of colonists from the temporary shelters of refugee camps in the Great Yu Canyon to the newly rebuilt Shachuan Station, deep in Tianfei Valley. They had reached the last leg of their journey, a hangar just west of the station, and in the morning crawlers would arrive to carry them the rest of the way to their new homes.

And then, Carter's war would be over.

It felt strange to be out walking, with the slight breeze kissing his bare cheeks. Like the rest of First-Second, he was wearing only fatigues. He didn't even have a weapon on him, having left his carbine back by his pack at the bunk assigned to him. It wasn't as if they were expecting any trouble, after all. They weren't even really expected to provide any sort of protection. All they were really there for was to provide a sense of security for the refugees, to make them feel safe in their days' long trek across the red deserts.

Carter hadn't fired a shot in weeks, not since the retaking of Ruosi, and the liberation of the prisoners at White Rock. It had been weeks, and still his sleep was troubled. He was beginning to wonder whether he would ever sleep soundly again.

As he made his circuit of the hangar, Carter passed Spitter, walking in the other direction. The Rossiyan had pulled guard duty, and had a carbine slung over his shoulder. As they passed one another, the two briefly made eye contact, but neither spoke. Even so, Carter couldn't help but feel that he knew what thoughts lurked behind Spitter's furrowed brow. The guardsman still had that edgy look, as though he expected danger to leap out from the shadows at any moment. He'd had that look since Operation Great Strength, and what they'd encountered at White Rock hadn't improved matters at all.

Still, they had only a single night of duty left to fulfill, and then they would be heading home. Once the refugees were settled in, and First-Second's escort assignment completed, they would be heading back to Fanchuan, to catch the next transport back to Earth. Once Spitter was on his way home, Carter was sure he'd begin to relax.

Continuing his circuit around the inner wall of the hangar, he came to a large, reinforced window that looked out to the east towards the rest of Shachuan. This was the closest Carter had ever come to the colony, the first time he'd seen it. He'd heard about it, of course. Shachuan Station was the site of one of the worst losses faced by the Middle Kingdom in the course of the Second Mexic War, when countless civilians lost their lives to an attack by the Mexic Dominion.

Of course, once the final tallies were done of the prisoners, both civilians and captured military, who went under the black-glass blades of the Mexic executioners, it seemed likely that the massacre at Shachuan Station would quickly fade in comparison.

But even so, there was some poetic justice, perhaps, to the fact that this spot, which had been the site of such death and loss, would be a place for new beginnings and new life. Looking out over Shachuan, the last light of the setting sun touching only the tallest structures, the rest already swathed in shadow, Carter could see a skeletal steel frame rising in the midst of the colony. It was, he understood, to be a new community building, a place joined by tunnels to all of the habitats and hangars, where the people of Shachuan Station could gather. And though it was only a bare frame of girders so far, it already towered over the rest of the colony complex.

Carter was reminded of the abandoned steel skeleton that had shadowed the days of his youth, last evidence of his grandfather's follies. At least, until it had been torn down and donated to the war effort.

For all he knew, some of those same girders from Duncan might have ended up here, and used in the construction of this new community building.

Shachuan Station was the site of a great tragedy, a horrible massacre, but it was beginning again, rebuilding. The war was over, and the peace had finally begun.

Carter's reverie was broken by the sound of shots ringing out behind him. He turned on his heel and hurried back the way he'd come.

Had they missed some Mexic holdouts? Were there Jaguar Knights who refused to surrender, and who had lain in wait for unsuspecting civilians to chance by, and to revenge themselves at last?

What Carter found when he arrived at the scene of the shooting was no Mexic holdout, but something far worse.

"He wouldn't stand down," Spitter said, eyes wide, twitching. "I *told* him to stand down, and he wouldn't stand down..."

The Rossiyan was standing over a civilian, who lay lifeless on the floor in a pool of his own blood. Spitter still had his hand on the trigger of his carbine, the barrel pointed at the civilians already gathering around.

"Back off, all of you!" Spitter shouted, punctuating his word with thrusts of his rifle's barrel. "Stand back! Don't come any closer!"

Carter took a step forward, hand held out. "Oh, god, Spitter, what have you *done?*"

The Rossiyan looked up at the sound of Carter's voice, as if seeing him for the first time. "Tejas!" He looked from Carter to the body on the floor, and back again. "This rutting bastard wouldn't submit to a search. I *had* to shoot, I *had* to!"

Carter took another step forward, forcing himself to nod, trying to keep his features calm and his tone even. "I know, Spitter, it's alright. I'm here to relieve you. It's my turn for guard duty now."

Spitter's eyes flicked from side to side, and he licked his lips.

"At your ease, guardsman," Carter said, now within arm's reach. He held out his hand. "Give me the carbine and I'll take it from here."

Other members of the First-Second had arrived now, and looked with mute horror at what their brother-in-arms had done. Out of the corner of his eye, Carter could see Moonface muttering a prayer, and Bigfoot crossing himself in the ancient Europan fashion.

"Give me the carbine, Spitter," Carter repeated, carefully taking hold of the rifle's barrel and pushing it towards the ground. "It's your turn to rest, now."

Spitter nodded, absently, like someone coming out of a daze. "Alright, Tejas." He shut his eyes tight. "I'm just so *tired...*"

"I know, Spitter," Carter said, slipping the rifle from the Rossiyan's grasp. "We all are."

As soon as Spitter was disarmed, Carter motioned for Moonface and Bigfoot to take him into custody. They would have to turn him over to the military authorities, when they returned to Fanchuan, and Spitter would have to answer for what he'd done.

The war was over, Carter knew. But for some, perhaps, it seemed that the fighting might never stop.

HEXAGRAM 62
MINOR SUPERIORITY
BELOW MOUNTAIN ABOVE THUNDER

Above the Mountain, there is Thunder. In the same way, the noble man in his actions is superior in reverence, in his bereavement he is superior in grief, and in his expenditures he is superior in temperance.

From the pads outside Fanchuan Garrison, wave after wave of launch vehicles thundered up from the surface of Fire Star, their solid fuel rockets pushing them to escape velocity. In orbit above, massive troop carriers waited to carry them across the black void, back to Earth.

Some of the soldiers of the Eight Banners and the Green Standard, some airmen and sailors of the Interplanetary Fleet, would remain stationed on Fire Star, or in orbit above her, maintaining vigil in the event that the Mexic Dominion launched another attack. With so many Mexica in captivity on the planet though, and with the vacuum-craft of the Middle Kingdom embargoing the approaches from Earth, the odds of a recurrence of hostility were remote.

Some small number of the military forces, reaching the end of their service, had elected to stay on the red planet that they had fought and bled to protect, becoming colonists, making Fire Star their home. But for the rest of the men and women in service to the Dragon Throne, it was time to return to the world of their birth.

Some of the colonists, too, elected to return. Having survived the long years of the Second Mexic War, having seen so much of what they'd built in the colonies reduced to rubble and ash, they found they lacked the will to build again, and so returned, singly or with their families, to Earth, to return to the lives they'd once known. Some of the youngest, children born on Fire Star, were traveling to a world they knew only from stories and pictures.

As the launch craft thundered up from Fanchuan, carrying civilians and soldiers away from the planet-wide battleground where so much was lost, there was a strange commingling of grief, thankfulness, and sobriety. In terrestrial wars, when victory was won, celebrations would often rage for days, weeks at a time, both among the civilian populace back home, celebrating the victory won by their sons and daughters in the field, and among the soldiers, sailors, and airmen who survived the war. Not so on Fire Star. The end of the Second Mexic War was more temperate, moderated by a sense of grief that seemed to hang like a veil over the red planet.

The war had been won, and at long last. But the toll it had taken on civilian and soldier alike was a heavy one, and the wounds that persisted would take many long years to heal.

HEXAGRAM 63
FERRYING COMPLETE
BELOW FIRE ABOVE WATER

Water positioned above Fire. In the same way, the noble man ponders the threat of calamity and takes steps beforehand to prevent it.

The troop carrier was only one of hundreds, massive constructions of ceramic and steel, hurtling end-over-end through the void. Having left the gravity well of Fire Star, it spun opposite a counterweight, the rotations providing simulated gravity to those onboard. Throughout the six month journey, the rotations would accelerate, boosted by external thrusters, gradually increasing threefold, from the comparatively low gravitational attraction of Fire Star to which they'd all grown accustomed to the full gravitation pull of the Earth to which they would return.

Standing orders for all passengers onboard, guardsmen, airmen, and bannermen, called for regular rest, proper meals, and daily exercise, both to acclimatize them to the ever increasing gravity, and to keep them from descending into complete indolence in the course of the journey.

While orders called for exercise they were somewhat flexible on just what form that exercise might take. So while some lifted weights, and others sparred in boxing rings, others chose running, or simply brisk walks.

Amonkar and Seathl were of the walking persuasion, all things being equal.

"I wonder how Geng is doing," Seathl mused, as they made their way down the long corridor, which ran from one end of the ship to the other. There were others out for strolls or runs this evening, but the walls were far enough apart that traffic could pass in both directions, with only the occasional collision.

"I wonder how *big* she's gotten," Amonkar answered, wearing a sly grin. Their erstwhile navigator had left Fire Star nearly a full month before they did, and would now be more than halfway through her pregnancy.

Seathl chuckled ruefully. "I'll admit I regret a little not being able to ship out with her, if only because I miss the opportunity to mock her once she's as big as a house. Once we reach Earth, she'll be slim again, with a baby at her breast."

"If we ever see her again." Amonkar had said the words without thinking, and only after they'd been said did her hand fly to her mouth in shock. She turned to Seathl. "I mean, of *course* we'll see her again, but who knows when..."

Seathl held up a hand. "I know what you meant, skipper." She sighed, nodding. "We've all got places to go, lives to get started again. It's a big world, and who knows when we'll meet up again?"

Amonkar kept walking, dropping her gaze to the deck-plates beneath her strides. "I *suppose* I've got some place to go, but a life to get started...?" She shrugged.

Seathl patted her shoulder. "Look, you didn't marry the military, skipper, you just... *dated* it for a while. Now you're free to get on with it. You were telling me you hoped to become a civilian pilot?"

Amonkar nodded. There was need for pilots on civilian planes, at that. "I know, I know. It's just... Well, without you, and Geng, and the others... Without my *crew*, I'll just be flying... well, *alone*."

Seathl didn't have to point out that, of course, there would be crews on civilian aircraft. She knew what Amonkar meant. She draped an arm around Amonkar's shoulders. "Skipper, I think *that's* your problem."

"What?"

"Being alone."

Amonkar looked up, and Seathl indicated with a nod a man and woman walking the other way, arm in arm, lost in each other's gaze.

"*That* kind of alone," Seathl explained.

Amonkar blushed, and pulled out from under Seathl's arm.

"I know, it's just..." She shook her head in frustration. She'd so long denied the possibility of romance, of intimacy altogether, while there was still a war to be won, still a duty to be done. But with the war over...?

"'It's just' *nothing*, Arati," Seathl said, punching her lightly in the arm. "Look, orders are for exercise, right?" She smirked. "Well, *that* can be a kind of exercise, too, if you do it right?"

Amonkar's cheeks stung with embarrassment, and she averted her eyes. Coming in the other direction was a man stripped to the waist, chest and arms glistening with sweat as he jogged briskly along. As he passed the two heading the other direction, he caught Seathl's eye and grinned, hungrily.

"Now if you'll excuse me," Seathl said, patting Amonkar's shoulder, "I think I may have just found a new exercise partner." She turned and started after the shirtless runner, who even now was slowing his pace, glancing casually back over his shoulder. "I'll catch up with you later," Seathl called back to Amonkar, then sauntered over to introduce herself to the man.

Amonkar sighed, and then continued alone up the corridor.

As she walked, she thought about the war, all that she'd done, all that she'd been through. She thought about her decision to dedicate herself to service, and become a bride of Khandoba. It seemed a lifetime ago that she'd stood in her parents home in Bhopal, a storm rolling in, and announced her intention to join the Air Corps. Now her duty was done, and she was returning home, but to what?

She could find work, she had little doubt, but a life? That was another matter entirely. In her darker moments, Amonkar wasn't sure it was even possible for her to find love, as others did so easily.

Distracted in her reverie, she stepped around a slower moving couple in front of her without even noticing the guardsman jogging in the other direction down the corridor. They collided, head on, and Amonkar went toppling backwards onto her rump.

"Oh, I'm so *sorry*," the guardsman said in a Vinlander accent, reaching a hand down to help her up. "I wasn't even looking where I was going."

Amonkar blinked up at the fair-haired man, who sounded like a character from a gunslinger drama. "You look... familiar."

The guardsman smiled, and pulled Amonkar to her feet. "My name is ... My name is Carter. Carter Micah. Please, call me Micah."

Amonkar dusted off her backside.

The Vinlander studied her face for a moment. "Is... is your name Arati?"

Amonkar's eyes widened a bit, and she nodded. Then, smiling, she indicated the corridor ahead. "Well, Micah, I'm just out for a stroll. Care to join me?"

The guardsman paused for a moment, then nodded, his smile widening. "I think I'd like that."

Side by side, in no particular hurry, the two set off up the corridor. They weren't sure what the future held, but they'd find out soon enough.

HEXAGRAM 64
FERRYING INCOMPLETE
BELOW WATER ABOVE FIRE

Fire positioned above Water. In the same way, the noble man carefully distinguishes among things and situates them in their correct places.

Niohuru shifted his weight onto his back foot, blocking Hughes's punch, but having failed to compensate for the increased pull of gravity he found himself pushed off balance, and fell sprawling backwards onto the mat.

"Your speed is lagging a bit," Hughes said, taking Niohuru's hand and pulling him to his feet. "You need a break?"

Niohuru shook his head, thought better of it, then nodded. They'd been sparring for hours in the ring set up in the hold of the troop carrier, trying to keep their fighting edge honed, but Niohuru's energy was beginning to flag.

That Hughes didn't seem fazed in the slightest was humbling.

The captain fetched a towel from the side of the ring, and mopped his forehead. Niohuru retrieved a pair of bamboo vacuum flasks of water, and handed one to Hughes.

"A few more weeks and we'll be at a full standard gravity," Hughes said, taking a long pull from the flask. "A month or two of that and we'll be ready to stand on our own feet, back on Earth."

Niohuru nodded, taking a drink.

"So what are your plans for our return, Tie?"

Niohuru considered it for a moment. "I don't have any plans, Falco. I'll just go where the Eight Banners send me."

Hughes smiled slightly, nodding. "As will I." He took a deep breath, and sighed contentedly. "It's important that people learn their place, I've found. I learned long ago that I was a soldier, first and foremost, and that even if the battle is won or the war is over, I'll still be ready and waiting to serve in the emperor's name."

"With the Mexica defeated, though, where else is there service to be done?"

Hughes gave him a sidelong glance. "Tie, I'm surprised at you. Just because we beat the Dominion in one theater doesn't mean that they don't eye other venues. The latest reports from Earth are that the Mexica have been arming Maori insurrectionists in Queqiao. If I were a wagering man, I'd put my money on a posting for the First Raider Company there, as soon as we return." He cracked his knuckles. "A bit of counter-insurgency action to clear the palate."

"I've never been that far south, myself," Niohuru answered. Aside from the southern tip of Fusang, and a tiny outpost on the ice-bound continent of Bingshan, the Middle Kingdom colony of Queqiao was the southernmost inhabited spot on Earth. "That's a place I'd like to see."

"Well," Hughes said, "you may not get a chance, at that. There's also been some worrying signs on the border between Fusang and the Mexic Dominion, and talk of stationing a raider company there, in place and ready in the event hostilities break out."

Niohuru gave him a confused look. "But how can the Falcon's Claws be in both places at once?" He paused, a worried tone creeping into his voice. "Would you be dividing the force?"

Hughes smiled. "There's been discussion of founding a new unit, a Second Raider Company. With the successes we've achieved these past years on Fire Star, there's been a gradual shift in philosophy and attitude at the highest levels of the Eight Banners."

"But who would lead it?"

"Well, inarguably it needs to be someone who understands the principles and strategies we've hammered out in the Claws over the years. So the generals have asked me to make the final recommendation." He gave Niohuru a meaningful look.

"How about it, Tie? Have any interest in command?"

Niohuru was taken aback momentarily, but gradually a smile spread across his face. "I think... I think perhaps I have, at that."

Hughes grinned in return. "What was it they called you in training? 'Iron Wolf,' was it? Not a bad name for a raiding outfit."

Niohuru nodded. "The Iron Wolves," he repeated, admiringly. "Not a bad name, at that."

AUTHOR'S NOTES

I'm the kind of person who won't buy a DVD if the only "Special Features" are trailers for other movies, and who always feels a little cheated when the last words in a book are "The End." I always like a little extra material to dig into after I finish a story, a peak behind the scenes.

With that in mind, I offer the following notes.

On the Celestial Empire

The world in which *Three Unbroken* takes place is one in which I've set many stories and novels. Called the Celestial Empire, it is an alternate history in which China rose to world domination in the fifteenth century. In our own history, during the reign of Zhu Di, the Yongle Emperor, the Treasure Fleet under the command of admiral Zheng He, a Muslim eunuch, traveled as far as India and the east coast of Africa, and possibly even reached the west coast of South America. The Yongle Emperor's successor Zhu Gaozhi, also known as the Hongxi Emperor, ordered the Treasure Fleet destroyed and all seagoing vessels outlawed, under the advice of Confucian officials who felt that the previous emperor's expansionist policies had robbed them of influence and power. From that point onwards, China turned inward, and lost contact with its new-found trading partners across the seas.

The Celestial Empire diverges from our own history when the Yongle Emperor is instead succeeded by Zhu Zhanji, the Xuande Emperor, who not only continues to employ the Treasure Fleet, but expands its scope and mission. Before Christopher Columbus sets out to discover a new route to the east, dragon boats of the Treasure Fleet round the tip of Africa and arrive in Europe.

Three Unbroken begins some five centuries later, during the 52nd year of the Taikong Emperor, twenty-eight years after man first walked on the face of the red planet Fire Star.

On Sources

The list of sources used in fabricating the world of the Celestial Empire is always growing, but those titles which were instrumental in the writing of *Three Unbroken* were Pamela Kyle Crossley's *The Manchus* (Blackwell Publishing) and *Orphan Warriors: Three Manchu Generations and the End of the Qing World* (Princeton Paperbacks), Evelyn S. Rawski's *The Last Emperors: A Social History* of *Qing Imperial Institutions* (University of California Press), Stanley Wolpert's *A New History of India* (Oxford University Press), Anna L. Dallapiccola's *Dictionary of Hindu Lore and Legend* (Thames & Hudson), and Richard John Lynn's translation of the I Ching, *The Classic of Changes* (Columbia University Press). I am especially indebted to Stephen E. Ambrose's narrative histories of the Second World War, which provided a model for the present work, and in particular *The Wild Blue* (Touchstone), *Citizen Soldiers* (Simon & Schuster), and *Band of Brothers* (Touchstone), which collectively inspired many of the battles of the Second Mexic War.

On Celestial Empire Geography

Many of the Fire Star locales featured in this work, and in other Celestial Empire novels such as *The Dragon's Nine Sons* and *Iron Jaw and Hummingbird*, correspond to named locations on Mars in *our* history. The Tianfei Valley is the Valles Marineris, Bao Shan is Olympus Mons, the Three Purities are Elysium Mons, Hecates Tholus, and Albor Tholus, and so on. The two crater colonies that feature at the climax of the narrative have both been christened with the courtesy names of Chinese astronomers, Ruosi after that of Guo Shoujing and Zijun after that of Liu Xin.

As for locales on Earth in the Celestial Empire, anyone seeing parallels between the township of Duncan and the community of Duncanville in which the author spent his formative years is invited to draw their own conclusions...

On Acknowledgements

As in previous Celestial Empire books, I'd be remiss if I did not thank Lou Anders who commissioned the first Celestial Empire story, "O One" for his anthology *Live Without a Net*, and who inspired me to write more stories set in the world. I would also like to thank the various editors who have published stories in the sequence, helping me to map the world and its history in detail, including Andy Cox, Pete Crowther, Jetse de Vries, Gardner Dozois, Nick Gevers, George Mann, Sharyn November, Sheila Williams, and Bill Schafer. And, as always, I would like to gratefully acknowledge Solaris for the faith they've shown in the sequence by commissioning this second volume, and especially to George Mann, Christian Dunn, and Mark Newton for helping bring the project to fruition.

In closing, I should thank my wife Allison Baker, and point out that nothing I do would be possible without her love and support, and also thank my daughter Georgia Rose Roberson, who makes me laugh.

Chris Roberson
Austin, TX

ABOUT THE AUTHOR

Chris Roberson's novels include *The Dragon's Nine Sons* (Solaris, 2007) *Set the Seas on Fire* (Solaris, 2007), *Here, There & Everywhere* (Pyr, 2005), *The Voyage of Night Shining White* (PS Publishing, 2006), and *Paragaea: A Planetary Romance* (Pyr, 2006), and he is the editor of the anthology *Adventure Vol. 1* (MonkeyBrain Books, Nov 2005). Roberson has been a finalist for the World Fantasy Award for Short Fiction, twice for the John W. Campbell Award for Best New Writer, and three times for the Sidewise Award for Best Alternate History Short Form (winning in 2004 with his story "O One.") He runs the independent press MonkeyBrain books with his partner.